Rousing acclaim for Wayne Davis's
JOHN STONE AND THE CHOCTAW KID...

"TWISTS AND TURNS that make a reader want to keep turning the pages."
—ELMER KELTON

"GRIPS THE READER like a bench vise. It has country, cowboys and action steeped with mystery . . . A fine read."
—GARY McCARTHY,
author of *Rivers West* and *The Horseman*

"GRITTY REALISM . . . a rich and splendid story . . . there's magic here."
—RICHARD S. WHEELER

"FASCINATING . . . Davis is gratifyingly careful about historical details."
—*New Mexico Magazine*

"A WONDERFULLY ENTERTAINING AND OFFBEAT STORY."
—JOE R. LANSDALE

Berkley Books by Wayne Davis

JOHN STONE AND THE CHOCTAW KID
REKLAW
SILVERTHORNE

SILVERTHORNE

Wayne Davis

BERKLEY BOOKS, NEW YORK

SILVERTHORNE

A Berkley Book / published by arrangement with
the author

PRINTING HISTORY
Berkley edition / May 1997

The Putnam Berkley World Wide Web site address is
http://www.berkley.com

ISBN: 0-425-15764-4

BERKLEY®
Berkley Books are published by The Berkley Publishing Group,
200 Madison Avenue, New York, New York 10016.
BERKLEY and the "B" design
are trademarks belonging to Berkley Publishing Corporation.

PRINTED IN THE UNITED STATES OF AMERICA

10 9 8 7 6 5 4 3 2 1

This one's for Aunt Ginger

*She always welcomed the
big-eared kid to the Slash H Prod*

PART

I

LAMPKIN SPRINGS, TEXAS

ONE

TALIAFERRO LAFAYETTE SILVERTHORNE LAY STRETCHED out on his belly upon the rocky slope of a bleak New Mexico mountainside. The cold seeped from the rocks, penetrated his clothing and chilled his body. It would slow the flow of blood from the gunshot wound in his abdomen. Not that he wanted it to. He would still bleed to death, only slower. The curtain he'd ripped from a hotel window in Roswell to bind the wound would have the same effect. He didn't know why he bothered to postpone the inevitable. He supposed the survival instinct compelled him to do what he could, even when he knew it would be too little. And Silverthorne should know. He'd doctored a lot of gunshot wounds and he'd seen a lot of blood. Especially during the war.

People believe your whole life flashes before your eyes in an instant when you come face-to-face with death. Silverthorne reckoned his dying would be too slow for that. He'd have time for deliberate reflection. Time for regret. His greatest regret was Marylois. His mind traveled back to the first time he laid eyes on her. That was another bloody day.

The rising sun is a pink smear behind the early morning mists that shroud a killing field in northern Virginia. The lifting fog reveals the spectral forms of the dead of the previous day's battle, a helter-skelter scattering of twisted shapes that resemble rag dolls flung aside by fickle children who ran away to a new play pretty.

Upright forms materialize. They drift through the ghostly brume in pairs and bend to lift the stiff mannequins of death from the ground, carry them to waiting wagons, and hoist them aboard to be stacked like cordwood and hauled away to a common grave.

A solitary figure appears in the mists, clutching a woolen shawl against her nose to stifle the stench of blood and bowels. She accosts a pair of bearers, glances at the frozen face of agony on their grizzly burden, and moves on to intercept the next pair.

It is a sad memory, that vivid picture of his first sight of Marylois. The pity Silverthorne felt in his heart for her that dismal morning was an emotion that would haunt him many times over the years of their life together. He hadn't been able to provide the answer for which she searched on that day, and he would fail to resolve her problems in days and years to come. It was not for lack of trying.

At least on that first day he'd been able to convince her to desist her fruitless search for her brother's corpse among the fallen patriots in gray. He was not acquainted with Marylois's brother, but as Assistant to Chief of Surgery, Silverthorne was able to find out that her brother was not among the dead.

Silverthorne could not tell Marylois what had happened to her brother. Only that he was missing in action. He suspected her admired and beloved sibling had deserted, run away in the heat of battle. But Silverthorne would not tell her that, for he felt compelled to protect and comfort this sad-eyed, gentle daughter of a Meklenburg County planter. For some years to come he would do the best he could for her. But he could not save her.

It wasn't for lack of trying.

After Appomattox he courted Marylois whenever he could while he finished the schooling that the onset of war had interrupted. In a few years they were married, and he established a modest practice in Boydton, not far from the plantation where Marylois had been reared. Folks in Meklenburg County would say that Doc Silverthorne was a good doctor.

But Dr. Silverthorne could not save his own children.

In two years two babies were born and buried, and the sadness in Marylois's eyes cut him to the heart. She couldn't bear the thought of taking a chance on bringing another life into the world just to watch it flicker and fade. Silverthorne was patient, doing whatever he could to bring comfort and encouragement, knowing that sometimes only time can heal the broken spirit. He stayed on his side of the bed at night and immersed himself in his work during the day. Folks in Meklenburg County would say that Doc Silverthorne was a dedicated physician.

But Dr. Silverthorne could not help his own wife.

When the muscles of Marylois's lissome body slowly began to weaken and atrophy, Silverthorne was determined to procure the finest medical help that could be found, no matter the cost of the clinic, or how far they would have to travel to take her there. They traveled to Richmond, Washington, Baltimore, Boston, New York. . . .

Silverthorne's assets were exhausted. He could borrow no more. Marylois's father had managed to hold on to most of his land after the war, but now he was no better off than an ordinary dirt farmer. He could not help.

Silverthorne had read the glowing accounts of how men were making their fortunes on the western prairies by slaughtering the buffalo for their hides. Silverthorne was a dead shot with a rifle. He sold his property in Boydton and left Marylois in the clinic in Richmond under the care of a colleague, and the watchful eye of her mother, who arranged to move in with relatives in the capital city. Silverthorne went to Texas.

The slaughter grounds of the prairies were as repulsive to Silverthorne as the killing fields of the war had been. He hated what he was doing. But he was good at it. He made money, a lot more money than he could ever have made in medical practice in post-war Virginia. He transferred the profits East.

It didn't help. Nothing helped. The letters he received by way of Dodge City revealed that Marylois's condition continued to deteriorate.

Silverthorne knew the southern herds were bound to play out, just the same as the northern herds. It was difficult for some to believe that the great herds of buffalo could be killed off, but Silverthorne accepted the fact. There'd been a time when he'd thought Americans clad in blue and gray would slaughter each other until no one was left, so why could not the defenseless buffalo be eradicated?

Silverthorne was ready to pocket the last of his earnings and go back to Virginia to face the inevitable. Marylois was going to die and he could only sit by her bedside and helplessly observe.

But during his last visit to Hanrahan's Saloon at Adobe Walls, the night before he pulled out for Dodge City to catch the eastbound train, he heard the story about Lampkin Springs. The strong mineral waters cured all sorts of infirmities, it was said, both by bathing in them and drinking of them. The Comanche had made use of the healing waters for centuries. In more recent times, white settlers had discovered the story the Indians told was true, and they began to settle in the vicinity of the springs. During the summer months the population of the little town of Lampkin Springs doubled as campers came to partake of the soothing waters, and to load as many jugs as their wagons could carry back to their homes.

Silverthorne's medically trained mind rejected the idea at first. But he was desperate. None of the medical treatments they'd tried had helped Marylois. There was nowhere else to turn. Lampkin Springs was worth a try. Silverthorne returned to Virginia just long enough to collect Marylois and a few of their personal possessions, and came back to Texas. To Lampkin Springs, Texas.

Moses Lampkin was living near Georgetown in Williamson County when he heard the story the Comanche told about the healing springs near the headwaters of the north fork of the San Gabriel. Mrs. Lampkin had been ailing for many years, and the medical therapies of the 1850s had yielded no positive results, not even a satisfactory diagnosis. So Moses and his brother Nimrod loaded their families into their wagons and set out in search of the fabled fount in hopes that the mineral waters might restore the health of Mrs. Lampkin. They found a huge sulfur springhead where the legend said it should be. They settled in the little valley surrounding the spring run, sleeping in their wagons until they could build a small rock house, the first house built in what would become the town of Lampkin Springs. Mrs. Lampkin drank the water from the springs, and soon showed remarkable improvement. Eventually she completely regained her health.

This bit of history was part of the account that Silverthorne heard in Hanrahan's Saloon some twenty years after the fact. By the time he and Marylois arrived, the little town boasted a school, a church, several stores, and a gristmill. And there was Scotty's Saloon, on the west side of the square.

The community already had a doctor.

The Silverthornes had traveled by rail to the Texas-Pacific railhead at Dallas, where Silverthorne purchased a wagon and team for the remainder of the journey to central Texas. There was plenty of room among their meager possessions to arrange a comfortable pallet in the wagon bed upon which Marylois could rest.

As the journey progressed, Marylois spent less and less time in her bed. Silverthorne was encouraged to have her riding beside him on the wagon box, drinking in the changing scenery and talking about the fresh start they would have in Texas. She improved so en route that, even months after their arrival, Silverthorne could not be certain if her improvement was due to the waters of Lampkin Springs, the change of climate, or perhaps just a renewal of attitude. Whatever the reason, she rallied against the affliction that ravaged her body, and Silverthorne never had cause to regret the move to Texas. For even though he lost her, at least she died with hope in her heart.

TWO

Silverthorne eased his weight to one side and moved his hand down to reposition the blood-soaked curtain. It would've been better if the bullet had struck him in the heart and killed him instantly, as Marylois had been killed back in Lampkin Springs. He'd thought she would be the one to linger and gradually fade. If there was a good way to die, slowly bleeding to death wasn't it. Yet, he instinctively pressed the wad of cloth tighter against the wound and lay back down upon a rock he'd strategically positioned to hold the makeshift bandage in place. He rested his head on a forearm, closed his eyes, and thought back upon the events that resulted in Marylois's death and drove him to his own final resting place on this desolate New Mexico mountainside.

By the time Tal Silverthorne settled in Lampkin Springs, he'd left the War Between the States far behind. He'd long since resolved to let bygones be bygones. The "malice toward none—charity for all" approach advocated by the late president made sense to Silverthorne, whether Lincoln himself had actually believed in it or not. Those who agreed with the forgive-and-forget philosophy were scarce in Virginia, and Silverthorne found they were fewer yet in Texas.

Lampkin Springs's Doc Fowler was not among them.

When Percival Holloway engaged Dr. Silverthorne to be his family physician, Silverthorne did not know Major Holloway was the county's only veteran who'd come home wearing the hated Union blue. But old Doc Fowler certainly knew. Doc Fowler never refused treatment to anyone, but Percy Holloway recognized the aloof, methodical bedside manner the doctor displayed when dealing with the Holloways to be the same aversive attitude he assumed when obligated to administer to some smoky half-breed, or a sour-smelling field hand.

Horatio Fowler was a good doctor, but age and the aggravations of his own aches and pains had made him short-tempered and less sympathetic to the minor complaints of others. Every now and then a new patient would show up at Dr. Silverthorne's examination room in the front of the modest sandstone house he'd rented just off the square in Lampkin Springs. Doc Fowler's discontents did not make for a very substantial practice, and the Silverthornes were hard put to make ends meet.

Then Silverthorne saved Percy Holloway's prize stallion, and a whole new field of medical practice was opened for him.

In Europe in the nineteenth century many physicians doctored horses as well as humans. In fact, when that century's outbreak of the fatal rinderpest plague upon Europe's cattle herds resulted in a proliferation of veterinary colleges, many physicians were reluctant to relinquish the doctoring of animals to the newly educated practitioners of veterinary medicine. There was even greater resistance to the idea that the findings of animal researchers, such as the upstart Louis Pasteur, could be applied to the treatment and prevention of disease in humans.

Silverthorne was not opposed to new ideas. Among his library of medical books he'd transported from Virginia were several volumes dealing with medical findings based on the study and treatment of livestock. But it was his knowledge of anatomy and surgery that enabled him to save Holloway's big thoroughbred.

The mile-long racetrack at the edge of town was the focus of much activity and excitement during the summer months, when the population of Lampkin Springs swelled with the influx of health-seekers. Many of the visitors brought their own speedy steeds to race against the local horses in the Saturday races. None of them was as fast as Major Holloway's chestnut stallion. Calvin Howell's leggy bay came close every now and then, but the chestnut always managed to nose him out at the finish line. The permanent residents of Lampkin Springs and surrounds seethed at the continuing success of the damn Yankee's Kentucky purebred. Nobody else had the means to import a challenger of equal caliber.

Holloway's prosperity incited as much resentment as his victories on the racetrack. A double dose of Holloway salt galled the depths of the raw wound the late war had left upon the rebel pride of Lampkin Springs.

It was a noisy and boisterous crowd at the racetrack that Saturday, and a couple of skew-tailed and winking mares mingled in the parade of horseflesh. Holloway's stallion stomped his hooves, tossed his head, and nickered constantly as his handler held him alongside the rail, awaiting his turn to compete.

No one would admit to knowing exactly what spooked the high-strung thoroughbred, but Major Holloway swore it was a setup. For when the stallion bolted, jerking the handler to the ground and yanking the lead rope from his grasp, the only way the horse could run was right past where young Chadbourne Howell sat on

his big white gelding, and Chad already had his riata to
hand and a loop built.

Chad whipped the noose over the stallion's head as it
raced past, flipped the rope to the stallion's off side, took
a couple of dallies around the saddle horn, and turned
the big gelding away as he'd done many a time before
when busting a mossy-horned steer. When the thoroughbred hit the end of the rope in full gallop, the noose
snapped tight at the throatlatch with a *zing* and a *pop*
and the stud was jerked around by his head and snatched
off his feet and slammed to the turf on his side with a
resounding thud.

He didn't get up. He tried to lift his head a couple of
times and went limp.

Chadbourne Howell stared in disbelief for several
heartbeats, then nudged the big white horse forward to
give some slack and dismounted. He was making an
unsuccessful attempt to loosen the noose when Major
Holloway ran up and knocked him aside with an elbow,
at the same time jamming a hand in his pocket for his
knife. Before he could get it out, Dr. Silverthorne broke
through the gathering crowd, whipped a small scalpel
from his medical bag, severed the rope and cast it aside.
Silverthorne always brought his bag to the races in case
a rider was thrown or a handler was kicked, or some
such emergency.

Holloway watched as Silverthorne put his hand to the
chestnut's nose to check for breath, then quickly probed
the neck and throat with his fingers. Holloway turned
his glare upon Chadbourne. "You broke his neck, you
stupid young . . ."

"Get ahold of yourself, Major," interrupted Silverthorne, "and give me a hand! Hold the stallion's head
way back so that the throat is exposed, like this. Chad,
find a small stick, or a piece of wood, about two inches
long, and cut a notch in each end. Quickly! You can use
the major's pocketknife."

"I've got a small tatting shuttle in my handbag that's made like that," said a woman in the crowd.

"Excellent! Get ready to hand it to me." With his left thumb and forefinger, Silverthorne pulled the skin tight about five inches below the stallion's throat. Gripping the scalpel in his right hand, he quickly sliced through the skin lengthwise all the way to the windpipe.

Holloway slackened his grip on the stallion's head. "Don't cut his throat, Doc!"

"Hold steady, Major! The rope crushed the trachea—his windpipe. He's out of oxygen and can't get his breath. I've got to make an incision in the trachea so he can suck some air into his lungs."

"But he's bleeding, Doc!"

Silverthorne glanced at Chadbourne. "Chad, cut your bandanna into strips so I can pack them around the edges of the skin. Quickly, because when he gets some air he'll regain consciousness and begin to struggle."

Silverthorne sliced an opening between the trachea rings and reached for the tatting shuttle. He inserted it into the incision, positioning the notches so that it would hold the incision open. He snatched some scraps of cloth from Chad and packed them around the bleeding flesh, then put his ear to the hole to be sure the animal was drawing air into its lungs. He drew back quickly when the head jerked away from Major Holloway's grasp.

"Put your weight on his head, Major, so he doesn't struggle too much before he regains full consciousness." After a while, Silverthorne checked the stallion's eye, found it alert, and nodded for Holloway to release the stallion's head.

The crowd moved out of the way as the magnificent studhorse clambered to his feet. Some of the onlookers cheered. Silverthorne figured very few of the rejoicers were year-round residents of Lampkin Springs. By now Silverthorne knew the score.

Major Holloway looked toward Chadbourne Howell.

His father had pushed through the crowd and was standing next to him.

Silverthorne held on to the stallion's lead and watched as the two family heads leveled gazes at each other.

Holloway stood ramrod straight, a military man of average height with broad shoulders and a thick, muscular body. His dark eyes were matched by his beard, except that it was shot with a sprinkling of gray. It was always perfectly trimmed.

Calvin Howell was clean-shaven, at least whenever he came to town. He was taller than Holloway, but considerably more slender, and he stood with a thumbs-in-pocket easygoing stance that reminded you of the easy way he sat a saddle. His sandy hair was almost as light as his faded blue eyes, eyes that usually observed the goings-on of the world about him with an amused twinkle. Now they were hard and steady.

"The boy was only tryin' to lend a hand," he said.

The skin above Holloway's dark beard turned red. He took a deep breath and started to frame a reply. Abruptly he clamped his mouth shut and turned his back on the two Howells. "Galahad can't run races with a stick in his throat, Dr. Silverthorne."

Silverthorne cut his eyes toward the Howells with a slight nod of his head. They took the cue and turned on their heels. The rest of the crowd began to trail off after them. "The tatting shuttle is just an emergency procedure, Major. He could suck it into his windpipe and then we'd have another problem. I've got some small-necked medicine bottles at the office that have a wide lip on them. We need to cut one of the necks off and use it instead of the stick. I'll tie a string around it and around the animal's neck to hold it securely in position until he can recover to the point that he can breathe through the nose again."

"Then he *will* recover?"

"I want to keep him in town and keep a close eye on

him, but I don't believe his windpipe is permanently damaged. He'll be all right, but I wouldn't race him any more this year."

"Well, the Howells accomplished part of what they set out to do, anyway."

Silverthorne passed a hand across his dark hair and fixed his steady blue eyes on the major. "Major, I don't believe for a minute the Howells planned this thing."

"The hell they didn't."

Silverthorne breathed a sigh and handed the lead to the major. He and Percival Holloway disagreed on a lot of things, but at least they could disagree without being disagreeable.

"Bring Galahad on over to the office, real slow and easy. I'll trot on ahead and get to sawing one of those bottle necks off."

THREE

THEY COULD TELL FROM THE TRAIL OF BLOOD HE WAS *badly wounded. Would they send someone to make certain he did not survive? That possibility had compelled him to take a defensive position on his belly. He should get his .45 out and have it at the ready. He might get a chance to even the score, if he wasn't too weak when they came upon him. Silverthorne reached down and slid the Peacemaker from the silver-studded black holster, held it in front of him and admired its gleaming beauty one more time. He opened his fist and ran a thumb across the intricately carved eagles on the mother-of-pearl grips, then turned the long-barreled Colt this way and that, catching the reflection of the fading light upon the engraved, silver-plated metal. The flashy Peacemaker with its black-and-silver gunbelt had been Percival Holloway's gift to express his appreciation for the saving of his thoroughbred stallion. When he gave the set to Silverthorne, Holloway stated that a man who befriended a Yankee in Texas during those days of Reconstruction had best be well-heeled.*

Silverthorne had considered the expensive outfit a collector's item, something to be hung on the wall to be

*admired by visitors, except when he took it out to shoot
cans for sport. Otherwise, what need did a doctor have
for a six-shooter? Even a horse and cow doctor. Even
when a hapless beast had to be put down, it was cus-
tomary that the owner of the animal should perform the
execution. Major Holloway had strongly disputed Silverthorne's argument. But Silverthorne and Holloway
could disagree without being disagreeable.*

*Silverthorne chuckled at the thought, and remembered
another friendly argument.*

"I harbor no animosity toward the Rebs, Doc. Why, my
own two brothers who started this ranch with me gave
their lives for the Confederate cause. I honor and respect
their memory for what they did. But I don't understand
it.

"I can understand why you Virginians fought to keep
your darkies, but I can't fathom why these knot-headed,
cow-poor central Texans supported such a cause. Hardly
any of them owned a slave." Percival Holloway settled
a little deeper into the overstuffed chair in the parlor of
the rambling ranch house on the H3, pulled on his pipe,
and leveled his gaze at Silverthorne.

Silverthorne took a sip from his snifter of brandy and
set it carefully upon the crocheted doily on the end table
beside the satin divan where he sat. The Holloways had
chosen their furniture as carefully as they'd chosen their
racehorse. "Fewer than one in fifteen Southerners ever
owned a slave, Major. My family didn't have any. You
know damn well the South didn't secede because of the
issue of abolition. Lee, Jackson, and a lot of other influ-
ential Southerners felt that slavery was wrong. We all
knew it would have to be dealt with. But we didn't want
it forced on us. Surely we could have legislated some
method of gradually granting freedom that wouldn't

have wrecked the agricultural enterprise of the Southern states.''

Holloway blew smoke through his nose and removed the pipe from his mouth. '' 'Gradually' can take forever, Doctor. And you know as well as I do that a lot of wealthy plantation owners would've used all the political influence they could buy or coerce in order to drag it out forever.''

''It would've been a struggle, but it could've been accomplished. Anything would've been better for the country than the way it turned out.''

''At least it's still a country, one nation, like our founding fathers intended.''

''What our founding fathers *truly* intended brings us to the *real* issue, Major.''

Holloway rolled his eyes. ''Here we go with the Southern sermon about states' rights, and how the original thirteen joined the Union with the express understanding that they had the right to change their minds anytime they wanted to.''

''I wouldn't put it that frivolously, Major, but if you'll read Virginia's acceptance of the Constitution, the right to resume exclusive self-government is preserved by what was stated. Essentially the same thing is stated in New York's declaration. I believe all the state delegations viewed it like that. And the Bill of Rights of the Constitution itself grants any state the right to secede.''

''That's *your* interpretation, Doc. Besides, a lot of things had changed since 1787. It was imperative that the Union be preserved, *and* it was imperative that Lincoln should proclaim emancipation for all the slaves!'' Holloway gestured toward the ceiling with his pipe.

''*All* the slaves? Lincoln's proclamation didn't even mention Maryland, Kentucky, and Missouri! What's more, it specifically exempted West Virginia, thirteen parishes in Louisiana, and seven counties in Virginia, where Union armies were in control. The Emancipation

Proclamation abolished slavery only where Lincoln had no jurisdiction, and *protected* it where he did have the power to destroy it! I believe that proclamation was nothing more than a maneuver to shame the English out of recognizing the Confederate States of America!''

"Well, if it was, it was a damn smart maneuver," said Holloway, breaking into a chuckle.

"Don't let Percy badger you, Doc. He's awful good at that."

Silverthorne scrambled to his feet, realizing that Mrs. Holloway had entered the room unobserved as the two men bantered.

"Keep your seat, Doc . . . on second thought, y'all might as well come on into the dining room. Supper's about ready. I'm sorry Marylois didn't feel up to coming out with you today. Is she getting any better, Doc?''

"She thinks so. But I honestly can't say for sure, Alice. She's coping with her condition much better, but I can't swear that the disease is actually in remission. She does right well around the house where she can rest frequently, but she doesn't like to venture very far from home. Miz Huling stays with her whenever I'm gone for a night or two."

That particular visit was such a sojourn, for the Holloways planned to ''make some circles'' in their south pasture the next day. Silverthorne had discovered he very much enjoyed accompanying his ranching clients on their cow hunts. He'd missed his native Virginia when he first came to central Texas, but the high, rolling range country with its limestone-bottomed creeks winding through post oak and mesquite and its far, hilly horizons had captivated his soul. Riding horseback in the open country with the big sky above and a purpose for being there was exhilarating to him in spite of the tiresome work. When the day was done and he would sit down to a late supper with the family and helpful neighbors or hired hands, there was satisfaction in a job well done and contentment in the camaraderie of rough-country cow folk.

The Holloway family was short on manpower, what with the loss of Percival's brothers in the war. So Holloway had three hired hands: Alec Pabst, Fred Hunziker, and C. F. Andres, from down in Burnet County. "Those damn Germans that fought for the Yankees for thirteen dollars a month," they were called around Lampkin Springs, as if those thirteen dollars were the same as the thirty pieces of silver.

"Seems to me the H3 works its pastures a lot more frequently than any of the other outfits around here," Silverthorne commented as he and Alec Pabst rode out in the gray light of dawn, heading for the section of range they'd been assigned to work.

"And folks wonder why the major prospers," said Alec with a tone of irony in his voice. "We try to keep the H3 stock from wandering very far off our range. The cow thieves do not get so bold when the stock is not so far from the ranch. Still we lose cows to the thieves, but not so many as the other outfits, I think. And we save more from dying, too," said Alec with a pat on the saddlebag where he carried a can of screwworm dope.

Alec and Silverthorne worked the creeks, draws, and brush through the cool of morning and on into the heat of the day. They turned H3 cattle to the north and separated the pilgrims away to the south. That most of the otherwise-branded cattle bore the Rail H brand was to be expected, since the Howell range bordered the H3 on the south.

It was evident that the H3 cattle had been handled more than usual, for they were not quite as wild as those Silverthorne had worked on other outfits. Even so, mother cows are instinctively protective of their calves, and when Alec would rope a newborn to check its navel for worms, Silverthorne had to ride quick and smart to keep mama off his back. If Alec were working alone, it would be necessary to rope her and snub her to a tree before he could treat the calf.

When the sun was straight up, they dismounted in the shade of a big mesquite next to a granite island to eat the lunch Mrs. Holloway had packed for them to carry in their saddlebags. Silverthorne stood while he ate roast beef and corn dodgers, allowing the circulation to return to his backside. Alec sat down on a chunk of pink granite and gobbled his food as if he were afraid they would be interrupted before he could finish.

"We should be meeting up with the major very soon now," he said. "We may go over on the Rail H range to collect some strays, and he will want us to work closer together in case there is trouble."

"I don't think Calvin Howell would object to us sorting cattle in his pasture. It just saves him work at the next roundup."

"Major Holloway does not trust him, I think. But it saves us work later on, too. When we round up three thousand head of steers, we don't end up with two thousand that are not branded H3."

"I reckon it pays off in the long run."

"We are always among the first to go up the trail in the spring," said Alec, nodding his head and swallowing hard. "Like the time we got out ahead of the grasshopper plague in sixty-nine. For others who came along later there was no grass. The next year there was a corn surplus, and feeder beeves were selling very high. Again, we were among the first to market, and we had time to come back and gather another herd. Two drives in one year! Then in seventy-one, we got to Newton before the market was glutted and the price broke. The major consigned a few head to pool herds during the depression years and was ready to fill the demand when the market came back around."

"Besides you, Fred, and C. F., it appears nobody in these parts is interested in working for Major Holloway.

How can he raise a corrida to take a big herd to Kansas, Alec?''

"There are some men of color hereabouts who are desperate for the pay. They understand there is danger of reprisal, but they take the chance. They are very brave, and most of them are good hands.''

Alec finished eating, stood up, and eyed the top of the mound of granite. "I think I'll climb to the top to see what I can see.''

Silverthorne sat down on the vacated boulder and used the hooked blade of his pocketknife to open a small tin of peaches Mrs. Holloway had sent along in his pack. He used the longest blade to spear the slices of fruit and transfer them to his mouth, taking his time and savoring the sweetness. By the time he'd finished, Alec had climbed to the top of the rocky mound.

"Whatcha see from up there, Alec?''

"That last bunch of cows is still drifting north, just like we pointed them.''

"Good! We can go on and hunt us another bunch, then.''

"Huh! What's that?'' asked Alec, shading his eyes as he looked to the west.

"What do you see now?''

"Something on that ridge over yonder. Something bright yellow waving back and forth.''

"Yellow? Maybe somebody's trying to signal us with his slicker.''

"Yah! I think so! Must be the major. Maybe there is trouble. We better get over there quick as we can.''

"I expect you're right, Alec. He must have spotted you with that spyglass he carries.''

Silverthorne went to his mount and stuffed the empty tin in a saddlebag. By the time he'd tightened his girths and mounted, Alec had clambered down from his perch. When Alec was mounted he led the way toward the ridge where he'd seen the signal.

Major Holloway rode off the ridge to intercept them and motioned for them to follow him. "Figured you boys might take your dinner at that granite island. I knew Alec would climb up for a look-see if you did," he said when they rode up close enough to hear. "Got something to show you." He led the way along a twisting draw and out onto a flat where his son, Oliver, stood next to a hog-tied black calf that was lying on its left side.

"I wanted you to see this yearlin', Doc," said Holloway when they drew rein.

"A long yearlin', I'd say—else he's growthy."

"You got that right," said Holloway, dismounting and walking over to the calf. The calf's right eye showed white and it struggled against the pigging string. Holloway squatted down and lifted its head up so both ears were visible.

"Who does he belong to, Doc?"

"Double swallow fork on the left and an underbit on the right. That's your earmark, Major. . . . Are you testing me to see if I've learned anything since I've been doing day work, or what, Percy?"

Holloway let the calf's head drop and raised a hand. "Did you notice the double swallow fork isn't cut very far into the left ear and the underbit's not centered on the right ear? It would be pretty easy to change them to a crop left and double underbit right, wouldn't it?"

Silverthorne took a deep breath, recognizing Holloway's description of the Howell ranch earmark. Before he could speak, Holloway raised his outstretched palm higher and reached down to grab the calf's free leg and roll it over, exposing its left side. There was no brand.

"They whittled the ears before the calf was weaned, hoping we'd read the ears from a distance and assume we'd already burned it. They planned on coming back after the calf quit following mama around and change the earmarks and put their own brand on it."

Silverthorne released his breath and leveled his gaze at Holloway. "I understand the procedure, Major, but those ears could be recarved a lot of ways. The Howells have been neighbors for many years and you've never suspected them of stealing your cows before. Why would they start now?"

Holloway just returned his stare.

Silverthorne rolled his eyes. He knew what Holloway was thinking. "The war's over, Major. Didn't you ever hear of a place called Appomattox?"

"Ask that of your Texas rebels, Doc. *They* don't admit defeat! The only reason they came home was because everyone else quit fighting. Phil Sheridan himself made that statement and I know it for a fact! They got mad during the war and they'll stay mad for the rest of their lives! And when they're gone it still won't end, because the next generation has been raised up to fight Indians and hate the Yankees, and now, since Colonel Mackenzie's pushed the hostiles off to the west, they don't have any Indians to fight. So where does that leave us?"

"It still leaves us with the fact that we really don't know who's sleepering your calves, Percy." Silverthorne glanced at Alec Pabst, who just put his hands on his saddle horn and shrugged. Silverthorne got an affirmation from an unexpected source.

"He's right, Dad," said Oliver, looking at the ground to avoid his father's glare. "We've got no proof it was any of the Howells."

"Ollie, you're just saying that because you're sweet on Calvin's daughter," said Holloway. "I've seen you making calf eyes at Rachel when we see her at the racetrack," he added when Oliver gave him a startled look.

"Still got no proof," Ollie mumbled, turning his eyes away.

"It's proof enough for me," said Holloway, "and before I'm done I'll get enough proof to satisfy the sheriff.

That'll change things around here. Folks hate a cow thief as much as they hate a Yankee! Remember what you saw here, Tal Silverthorne, and I'd appreciate it if you'd keep your mouth shut and an eye peeled whenever you go out to the Rail H.''

"I'm not one to carry tales, Major. Neither will I be your spy. But I won't close my eyes should I see anything suspicious.''

"Fair enough, Doc.''

FOUR

SILVERTHORNE COULD LAUGH AT MANY OF THE DIS-
agreements he'd had with Percival Holloway. Much of
the time the major was just playing the devil's advocate
in order to stimulate thought-provoking conversation.
But he was dead serious when it came to his suspicions
about the Howell clan, and his determination to expose
Calvin Howell for a cow thief. There was no amusement
in the memory of that contention, or in the way Silverthorne had been caught in the middle of the Howell-
Holloway feud.

Silverthorne thought again of the confrontation the
day Chad Howell roped Holloway's racehorse. After
Calvin and Chad had walked away, some of the onlookers lingered long enough to overhear Silverthorne come
to the Howells' defense in response to Holloway's accusation. The incident was related to Calvin, and the
next time he was in town he came by the office to express his appreciation. And to see if the good doctor
would come out to the ranch and take a look at an ailing
colt.

"We've had foals with ruptured navels before, Doc,"
said Calvin as they walked into the Rail H stable. "Most
times they heal up by the time they come a yearling, so
generally I don't worry about it too much. But I've never
seen one that dribbles when the pony pees, like this'n."

"The urachus didn't close."

"The what?"

"Urachus. That's the tube in the umbilical cord that
connects to the bladder. It carried off urinary waste to
the outer water bag while the foal was in the mare's
uterus. It usually seals itself off when the umbilical cord
breaks."

Rachel Howell stepped out of a stall. She was a dark
silhouette against the sunlit square of the open door at
the opposite end of the barn, and she wore men's trousers as usual. But there was no mistaking the tiny-
waisted figure or the jaunty, hip-shot stance of the
nineteen-year-old beauty. By the time she spoke, Silverthorne was close enough to see her dark red curls and
green eyes.

"I put the foal in here, Doc, in case Papa talked you
into coming back out here with him."

"This'n belongs to Rachel, Doc. She's always wanted
a pumpkin skin," said Calvin.

Rachel stepped back into the stall and kneeled down
to steady the little palomino with an arm around the
neck. She petted the foal with her free hand and cooed
soothing words in its ear while Silverthorne squatted
down and gently probed the herniated navel.

"The doc already knows what's ailin' him," said Calvin. "Besides the rupture, he's got a tube from his pee
bag that didn't close up when the navel cord broke off."

"Can you fix it, Doc?" asked Rachel with a pleading
look.

"It's a simple procedure," said Silverthorne with a
reassuring smile. "And while I'm at it I'll fix this om-

phalocele, too . . . that's doctor talk for an umbilical hernia, or ruptured navel,'' he added when Rachel arched an eyebrow. "He'll be as good as new in no time at all.''

Rachel smiled and Silverthorne felt like a long drink of sweet red wine had just hit his brain.

He forced himself to look at Calvin while he instructed them how to restrain the colt for the operation, and he made sure to keep his eyes on his work during the procedure.

By the time the last suture was tied off, it was noon, so Silverthorne accepted Calvin's invitation to have a meal with the family. And quite a family it was.

There were actually two households on the Rail H, for unlike Major Holloway's brothers, Calvin's two younger brothers, Mart and Merrit, had survived the war. They were about twenty years younger than Calvin, the sons of his father's late-in-life second marriage. They'd fought the Indians with the Home Guard while Calvin went East with Ben McCulloch's recruits.

Evidently Calvin's wife had speculated that Dr. Silverthorne would be "taking dinner" at the ranch, for the bachelor brothers came over from their own house to have lunch and make the acquaintance of the new doctor who was just as good with horses as he was with folks. During the course of the mealtime discussion, Silverthorne learned that Calvin also had a sister, who was married to Mitch Warner. They ran cows on the range just west of the Rail H.

Calvin was quite a bit older than his siblings, and the only one who had children. He only had the two, Chad and Rachel.

Chad contributed little to the mealtime chatter, and Rachel nothing at all. Her eyes lingered upon Silverthorne every time he spoke, and frequently when the others were talking. He tried to act as if he didn't notice, but he could tell that she knew he did. Her green eyes

reflected the same amused observance he'd seen in her
father's, and a smile played at the corners of her mouth,
even while she ate.

Was she teasing him, trying to make him uncomfortable? Something in his expression must have given him
away when she smiled at him in the barn. The way he'd
avoided locking eyes with her ever since only served to
confirm it. This girl knew the effect she could have on
a man, no doubt about it!

FIVE

*SILVERTHORNE SLOWLY MOVED THE PEACEMAKER BACK
and forth, contemplating the reflected light upon the
long barrel and remembering the gleam in Rachel's
green eyes. Eyes that had lifted his soul like a spring
green-up after a hard winter.*

*Would he have felt the same if things had been dif-
ferent with Marylois? At times he'd tried to blame her.
But when all was said and done, he could only pity her.
The guilt was all his own. He let the pistol barrel slump
to the rocky turf.*

*If he'd never gone out to the Rail H, Marylois might
still be alive. If she had not been killed, he would not
have been swept along to this desolate New Mexico
mountainside, trying to find out who was responsible.
He had not gone to the Howell ranch expecting to find
anything more than a sick colt. But he found trouble all
wrapped up in an irresistible package. He should have
stayed away. But he didn't.*

"Doc, she's the best milker we've ever had. Part Jersey,
Pa says." Chad looked at Dr. Silverthorne with pleading

31

eyes that reminded him of Rachel's look when he'd examined her pumpkin-skinned colt. "I'll bet Pa will pay you double if you can save her!"

Marylois had ushered the young man into Silverthorne's study, and she lingered by the doorjamb between the study and the waiting room where very few ever waited. "Tal, you don't have any appointments today," she said, as if she had to remind him. "Why don't you go with him and I'll keep an eye on the office." The look she gave him also said, "Double fee! We sure could use the money!"

"It's like the old cow's turning inside out, Doc. Like her guts are coming out of her . . . you know."

"Vaginal prolapse," said Silverthorne. "I know longhorns are the toughest breed of cattle alive, but surely y'all have seen this problem before."

Chad glanced at Marylois and his cheeks turned red. "Most times the ol' cows are lying dead where they holed up in the brush by the time we find 'em," he said. "This here's our milch cow we're talking about, Doc. We depend on her for our milk and butter and cream and cheese . . . and like I said, we've never had one as good as her. What happened, Doc?"

"According to what I've been reading," said Silverthorne, putting a hand to one of his books on veterinary medicine, "the muscular structure that holds the cow's"—Silverthorne paused to make sure Marylois had shuffled away out of earshot so that Chad would not be embarrassed again—"the cow's vagina is inherently weak. If the area gets irritated, the cow will try to relieve the discomfort by straining, just like when she's calving. This can cause a prolapse, a distention of the inner lining."

"Sorta like the piles, huh?" said Chad.

"Sort of," said Silverthorne with a nod. "And if she keeps on straining, the uterus can come out, too. Then we've really got a problem. How large is the prolapse, Chad?''

" 'Bout the size of a three-gallon bucket, I'd say.''

"Well, it probably doesn't involve the uterus yet.''

"You'd best get on out there before it gets any worse,'' said Marylois from somewhere back in the house. She hadn't gone as far as Silverthorne had thought.

Silverthorne sighed, heaved himself out of his chair, and snatched his hat off the wall peg. "Bring your horse around back to the stable. I'll go out the back way and saddle up.''

Chad and Silverthorne took the nine miles to the Rail H at a fast trot. When they dismounted, Chad took charge of both horses to loosen the cinches and walk them out. Silverthorne took his valise and several large towels he'd brought and went straight to the milch pen.

Rachel was there with the Jersey, rubbing and cooing. She flashed her smile when he let himself in through the weathered cedar gate, and her eyes held his face with a probing fixity. "Took you long enough to come back to see me,'' she said in a sultry voice.

Silverthorne tried to slow his racing heartbeat and get wits enough to tell her the only thing he'd come to see was a sick cow. Finally Calvin Howell stepped through the gate behind him and broke the spell. Silverthorne set his valise by the fence and draped the towels over a top rail.

"You just tell us what to do, Doc, and we'll help you all we can,'' said Calvin. "Rachel's good with ailing stock, just like you are,'' he added, explaining why she was helping with the cow instead of Chad or one of Calvin's brothers.

Silverthorne gently inspected the prolapsed flesh. It was hanging almost to the animal's hocks. "The uterus is coming out, too,'' he said grimly.

"She shore swole up fast,'' said Calvin.

"Blood's not circulating good," explained Silver-thorne. "The problem's compounded because the swelling shuts off the elimination of urine." He gently lifted the fleshy mass and relieved a large amount of urine, which splashed on his boots and pant legs.

"That orter make her feel a sight better," Calvin said.

"She's trying to lie down!" Rachel warned, pulling up on the cow's halter.

"That's a natural reaction when the prolapse is handled. It makes her react like she's about to calve. Go ahead and let her down. I've got to keep the prolapse out of the way so she doesn't mash it. Calvin, you grab a couple of those towels and spread them underneath her rear end so we can keep it as clean as possible. Then fetch a couple buckets of water. We'll have to make sure it's good and clean before I push it back inside."

When the cow was down and the prolapse had been washed, Silverthorne wrapped it in a clean towel, raised it off the ground in order to let gravity help, and began hugging and squeezing it in order to reduce it. As it got smaller he wrapped the towel tighter and gradually worked the prolapse back into the cow's body, being very careful not to damage the walls of the uterus. He made sure everything was telescoped back the same way it had come out, in its normal position, straight, with no twists. Then he called for his valise.

"She might keep acting like she's in labor for a while, so I've got to sew the vulva up strong and evenly so the sutures will stand the pressure. We don't want a recurrence of the problem. . . . You can remove the sutures after three days."

"Aren't you coming back out to do it, Doc?" said Rachel in a hopeful voice.

"Anyone can pull stitches, Rachel," said Calvin. "You know that."

"Well, I just thought since this is so serious, he'd

want to be sure she's all right,'' Rachel muttered, stroking the milk cow's neck.

''I'll send Chad in to fetch him if there's any com-
plication,'' Calvin replied.

''All right, let's see if we can get her up now,'' said
Silverthorne as he tied off the last suture. ''I don't think
she'll be as likely to strain if she's standing.'' He
grabbed his valise and stood up. Rachel got the cow on
her feet without any help from the others.

Calvin looked at Silverthorne and started laughing.
''Great gobs, Doc. You couldn't have got any nastier if
you'd rolled in a hog waller!''

Silverthorne looked down at his clothes. They were
soaked with urine and smeared with bovine body fluid
from boots to collar, and the slimy mess was plastered
with dirt and debris from the ground of the milch pen.

''I'm sure glad it was just an ol' stool-and-bucket
cow,'' said Calvin between chortles. ''I'd purely hate to
see the muss a trotty ol' range cow would make of you.''

''A fellow could get in a storm, sure enough,'' Silverthorne chuckled. ''Next time I'm called on for this
procedure I'll take a change of clothes with me.''

''Between me and Mart and Merrit we can rustle up
some duds to fit you. Shore can't send you back to town
looking and smelling like you been rollin' in cow guts.
Mrs. Silverthorne wouldn't let you in the house!''

''By the way, how's Mrs. Silverthorne been doing,
Doc?'' asked Rachel. ''We hear she's kinda poorly.''

''I fear her illness is chronic, Miss Howell, but for
now she seems to be holding her own. Thank you for
inquiring.'' Silverthorne leveled his eyes at Rachel, but
she was looking at the cow. And smiling.

''Well, let's go to the house and get you cleaned up,
Doc. Rachel can keep an eye on Myrtle for a while.''

Calvin led the way out of the pen. ''You're shore
good with stock,'' he commented as he held the gate for

Silverthorne. "Course, I reckon if you can doctor people, animals are easy."

"Not really, Mr. Howell—"

"*Cal.* Cal's the handle, Doc."

"Well, you see, Cal," said Silverthorne as he stepped
through the gate, "animals can't tell you how they feel
or where they hurt."

"I never thought about that," said Calvin as he
latched the gate.

"Also, humans are all alike, but each species of animal is different. They're made differently and there are
afflictions that are peculiar to each species."

Calvin gravely nodded as they walked together toward
the house. "I can see as how doctorin' animals can be
downright complicated."

"It's quite a challenge. I've been doing a lot of studying since I became interested in veterinary medicine."

"Folks in these parts are more likely to call a doctor
for a good horse or a milk cow than they are for themselves." Calvin stepped up on the porch, opened the
door, and motioned Silverthorne inside. "And be
quicker to pay for it, too."

"Maybe I'll have better luck with livestock than I've
had with people," said Silverthorne, thinking about his
wife and their two babies.

Silverthorne was glad Rachel was occupied while he
was getting cleaned up and changed. No telling what
she'd do if she caught him with his pants down. No
telling what *he'd* do. He packed his soiled clothing in
an old flour sack Mrs. Howell had given him, gathered
it up along with his valise, collected his fee, and said
his good-byes before Rachel found an excuse to come
to the house. But as he jogged his red dun gelding back
to town, she was on his mind.

In these parts most girls were married before they
were twenty. Especially the best-looking ones. But you
could tell Rachel wasn't the type to get married just

because it was the traditional thing to do, or to accept the first proposal just because it seemed the best opportunity. She appeared to be ready to make her own opportunity.

Silverthorne wondered if she'd ever been asked. A lot of young men would be intimidated by Rachel. Most men expected a prospective bride to be at least a little bit coy, but demureness was not in Rachel's nature. She was one of the few women around Lampkin Springs who rode astraddle, and the only one he'd seen that preferred trousers to a divided riding skirt. He knew from the family conversation that she was always right in the thick of things whatever the chores the menfolk were doing. She could ride, rope, brand, and doctor right along with the rest of them. Unlike the men, she didn't wear a revolver, but he'd heard it said she could hit what she aimed at. She walked with a confident swagger and lowered her eyes before no one. What man in his right mind would want a woman like that?

"I must be going crazy," Silverthorne muttered to himself. He shook his head as if to clear his brain of the image of knowing eyes and smirky lips. He thought of the cozy, albeit platonic, relationship that existed at home, and the promise he'd made before God and witnesses several years ago.

"Come on, Rudy, let's get on to the house," he said, and clucked the gelding into a fast trot.

SIX

SILVERTHORNE REAFFIRMED HIS GRIP ON THE PEACE-maker and made a slight adjustment of his position on the rocky ground. He inspected the bloody pebbles his movement exposed and wondered if the internal bleeding was as bad, or worse. A large green fly buzzed down to alight upon the scarlet seep. It crept along on spindly legs, extending its proboscis here and there to test the sticky ooze. The fly was the first of many that would gather to the feast of fresh blood and raw flesh. Would he be conscious enough to feel it when they swarmed upon him? Silverthorne thought about the hordes of squirming screwworms he'd seen eating the living flesh from animals back in Texas.

It was a wet summer and a bad fly season. Already Major Holloway had his men working the south pasture again. Silverthorne showed up for day work. He brought his forceps and shears for removing worms and paring infested flesh. Holloway supplied the dope.

Silverthorne rode out from town late in the evening

and spent the night in the bunkhouse with Pabst, Hunziker, and Andres, and another hand Holloway had just hired. Guadalupe Proffit was one of the men of color who'd driven H3 beef up the trail to Kansas. He'd inherited the brawny physique of his black father and the smooth copper complexion of his Mexican mother. He shook hands with Silverthorne without smiling or getting up from his bunk, and lay down to sleep fully clothed with his right hand on the six-gun he wore butt-right on the front of his left hip. His elbow rested on the revolver he wore in conventional fashion on the right. Silverthorne took the next bunk and hoped the somber-eyed half-breed was not troubled by bad dreams.

When Silverthorne awoke to the feeble light of a single coal-oil lamp, Proffit was already sitting on the edge of his bunk, checking the cartridges in his converted Navy Colts. Silverthorne grabbed his hat and managed to get into his boots and leggings in time to follow the half-breed out to the cookshack.

"You men eat hearty," Major Holloway advised the crew. "This might be the only chance we get before sundown. There's jerky here you can put in a saddle pocket, or you can take leftover biscuit and bacon, if you think you can eat and ride at the same time."

Holloway chose Alec Pabst to ride with him and paired Hunziker and Andres to work together. That left the trio of Silverthorne, Proffit, and Oliver Holloway. Silverthorne knew he'd be the one to do most of the doctoring, since he was the least experienced roper of the three. The wet season meant softer hides and more cuts and scratches for the flies to blow, thus greater infestation of older stock. Ollie and Lupe would rope the cattle by the horns and the heels and stretch them out while Silverthorne administered to the wounds. An animal with a bad case of screwworms always found some place to lay out. Holloway sent the trio to the area with the most hiding places.

"I want you men to comb the draws and brush piles between Doubletree Creek and the southwest ridge," he said. "Ollie knows the country."

"I *knew* he'd send me to Doubletree," said Ollie when they were on their way. "He *always* gives me the worst of it."

"Probably just wants you to keep an eye on the new hands," said Silverthorne. "I don't know about Mr. Proffit, but I'd likely get lost over yonder in those cedar brakes."

"Mr. Proffit don't get lost anywhere," replied Ollie. "Do you, Lupe?"

Proffit just looked at him and smiled, the first pleasant expression Silverthorne had seen cross his face. Then he shifted his eyes to Silverthorne and uttered the first words Silverthorne had heard him speak.

"They call you Doc. Is you?"

"I'm afraid I'm a doctor with very few patients, Mr. Proffit."

"How come a doctor be punchin' cow? Don't pay much upside doctorin', I figger."

"It's better than nothing. Besides, I enjoy the work."

Proffit grunted, wagged his head, and kicked his pony into a trot. The .38s bounced along on his belt, which also held a scabbard with a huge bowie knife on his left hip just behind the cross-draw pistol. A Spencer repeater rode in a scabbard beneath his off stirrup leather. He was toting a lot of extra baggage for a cowboy. Yet, as the day wore on, Silverthorne could see Proffit was so used to the extra weapons that they slowed him down none at all.

Along about noon the three riders took a breather to rest their horses and take a pull on their canteens.

Ollie shoved his hat back with a forearm and wiped the sweat off his forehead with his shirtsleeve. "I reckon we could chew on some jerky or eat a biscuit or two."

Silverthorne untied his bandanna and used it to mop

his brow and neck. "I stay so thirsty I don't even think about eating. Can't imagine putting a dry biscuit in my mouth."

Proffit nodded and looked serious.

"Suit yerself," said Ollie, "but a piece of jerky might stir up a little spit." He turned to open the flap on his saddlebag.

Silverthorne removed his Stetson and wiped the sweat off the hatband. "Reckon it might, at that." He replaced his hat, retied his bandanna, and dug a strip of jerky out of a saddle pocket. He tore a piece of the dried beef off with his teeth and proffered the remainder to Proffit.

Proffit wagged his head. "I be hongry and thirsty so much it don't bother me none."

"I can chew while I ride," said Silverthorne.

"I'll catch up to y'all later on," said Ollie around a mouthful of biscuit. "I'm gonna check out a cedar thicket over south of here when I'm done eating, so I'll be awhile."

Proffit and Silverthorne continued to search for H3 cattle, pushing them north and doctoring any infected animals they found. About midafternoon, Silverthorne rode up to the edge of a brush-choked draw and drew rein. His nose detected the smell of screwworm-infested flesh before his eyes picked out the old bull that was laying up in a clear spot in the middle of the brush. He waved Proffit over and they found a way down into the ravine. Gradually they worked their way into the tangle of post oaks and persimmon brush. At the sound of their approach the old bull clambered to his feet and took a defensive stance upon shaky legs. He lowered his head and tried to paw the ground, but he almost fell.

Silverthorne nearly gagged when he caught sight of the ghastly wound between the dewlap and the shoulder bone. Several smaller wounds on his neck and sides also dripped with the bloody-looking drainage of the blowfly larvae.

"I reckon that old scaly-horn has fought his last battle," he said.

Proffit slid his carbine from the boot, jacked a shell into the chamber, and shot the old bull between the eyes.

"Better he be dead than sufferin'. I hates to see a critter suffer. Peoples, too. They be better off where they goin'. When you cain't do nothin' for 'em, it best you lets 'em go. *Help* 'em to go, if you can."

It was the nearest thing to a speech Silverthorne ever expected to hear from Proffit. He stared at the burly half-breed while he added another shell to the magazine of the Spencer and eased it back into the saddle boot.

"I reckon it all depends on *where* they're going," said Silverthorne, turning his mount to work his way out of the brush.

Proffit followed Silverthorne out of the thicket. "You ever hear a preacher-man preach anyone to go anyways but up?"

"He wouldn't get much of a collection if he did," chuckled Silverthorne.

When he regained the rim of the draw, Silverthorne held his horse until Proffit came up alongside. "I'm wondering what's happened to Oliver. He should've caught up to us by now. He can't be doctoring cows. He didn't even bring any dope."

"You can pack a sore with dry cow manure," said Proffit. "It shuts off the air to the screwworms and they die."

"Sometimes it works," said Silverthorne, "but I doubt Ollie's that resourceful. Besides, he's working by himself."

"Maybe he hear that shot and comes lookin' for us."

"He might. One of us better stay in this area in case he does. I'll ride west and see if I can cut his trail going south. I'll meet you at that big pecan tree on the creek in about two hours, three at the most."

Proffit nodded and Silverthorne reined away to the

west and slightly north, trying to ascertain where they'd parted company with Oliver Holloway. He'd hate to face the major if they dragged in at sundown without the boy. Silverthorne knew Proffit could probably read sign better than he could, but a trail as fresh as Ollie's shouldn't be difficult to spot.

It wasn't.

Silverthorne picked up Ollie's trail within four miles and started trailing the hoofprints south. It led Silverthorne to a dense stand of cedar on the slope of the southwest ridge that separated the Holloway and Howell ranges. This must be the motte young Ollie was intent on checking. Silverthorne reined in, looking to see if there was any sign that Ollie had already ridden back out. Suddenly he heard the sound of laughter. It sounded like a woman! Was he hearing things?

Silverthorne dismounted and tied the reins to a small post oak. He followed a narrow trail through the evergreen boughs and worked his way deeper into the cedar brake. The murmur of voices became clearer as he approached a small clearing deep within the stand of trees.

"No, Ollie. Now you just keep your hands to yourself. *Please. Don't*, Ollie. *Stop*."

Silverthorne heard what the words said, but Rachel's tone of voice said *Please don't stop*.

Silverthorne sneaked back to his horse and mounted up. This time he made as much noise as possible working his way back into the cedar across the rocky ground. Still they looked surprised when he rode into the clearing.

"What're you doing here, Doc?" said Ollie.

"I think you've lost track of the time, Ollie. We won't make it back to the home corral by dark if we don't get started."

Ollie glanced overhead, but he could not see the sun for the trees.

"Doc, are you gonna tell my paw?"

"Not if I can get you home on time. I'm glad to see a Holloway and a Howell on friendly terms for a change. Maybe something good will come of it."

"Not if the major finds out," said Ollie, grabbing his hat off the ground and heading for his horse. " 'Bye, Rachel, I'll get word to you somehow."

Ollie mounted up and nudged his mount down the narrow pathway. "Come on, Doc, let's get goin'."

"Miss Howell," said Silverthorne with a tug of his hat brim. He started to turn his horse away, but Rachel spoke first.

"Why, Dr. Silverthorne, I see you've been wrestling cows again," she said with a giggle.

Silverthorne glanced at the green smears of manure on his leggings and the specks of black medicine on his shirt, then looked squarely at Rachel. "Better button your shirt before you go home, Miss Howell."

"Perhaps you'd like to stay and help me with it," she said with a bat of her lashes and a pouting grin.

Silverthorne rolled his eyes and reined his horse around. He spurred headlong through the narrow outlet, as if to outrun the fire her invitation had kindled in his gut. When he burst out of the trees Ollie was waiting for him.

"What took you so long?" he said when Silverthorne pulled to a skidding stop. "How come your face is so red?"

"Must have got swiped by a cedar bough," Silverthorne lied, ignoring the other question. "How'd she know you'd be over here today?"

Ollie was not to be sidetracked. "Doc, how would you feel if somebody took your wife away from you?"

"What kind of a question is *that*?"

"Well, Rachel and me, we been sneaking around and meeting one another for quite a spell, and things were going good for us. But now she talks about you all the time, like you hung the moon or something. If I was to lose her I just don't know what I'd do.''

"Ollie, sometimes folks overreact to a doctor's successes, and tend to forget about all the patients he's lost. Rachel was probably overly impressed the time I operated on her colt, and when I saved the Howells' milch cow. It's just a girlish infatuation. She'll get over it.''

"No, Doc, you ain't knowing Rachel. She's not that way."

Silverthorne shrugged. "Well, she came over here to meet *you* today. Not me. How'd she know you'd be here, anyway?''

"She didn't know for certain sure I'd be able to sneak away. But Saturday at the racetrack I told her my father planned on working south today, and I figured he'd send me to Doubletree.''

"Speaking of Doubletree, Proffit's planning to meet us at the big pecan. We'd better get a move on.''

SEVEN

OLIVER HOLLOWAY. ANOTHER PITEOUS MEMORY THAT filled Silverthorne with remorse. A young man of less than average height and slight of build, with his mother's face and baby blue eyes, but having neither her mental toughness nor her emotional control. Always living in his father's shadow; never able to measure up, never able to please, no matter how desperate the need or how hard he tried. Oliver was obsessed with Rachel. But Rachel was only entertaining herself until someone more interesting should come along. Silverthorne could not help that he was the one. Could he have done more to resist her?

Whatever the answer to that question, no one could resist the feelings of bitterness and suspicion that crept over the ranch lands of central Texas as more and more stock began to disappear. Major Holloway's patrols of the H3 range had not stopped the theft of his cattle.

"It's like they know ahead of time where my crew is going to be," Holloway complained to Silverthorne. "While we're occupied with one sector of the range, they're driving off cattle from the sector farthest away. How do they know where we'll be? I've deliberately avoided a standard order of rotation. You're not telling Calvin Howell what we're doing, are you?''

''Major, I usually don't know where you're planning to send the crew until I get there. Besides, Cal's losing stock, too.''

''So he claims. Or maybe he's stealing more than he's losing.''

Silverthorne leaned back in his chair and laced his fingers behind his head. Suddenly he thought about Ollie's secret rendezvous with Rachel. How often did he reveal his father's plans to her? And why did she keep stringing him along?

Silverthorne blinked his eyes and wagged his head. The Howells wouldn't be involved in anything like that! He was letting Holloway's suspicious nature rub off on him.

''There have been a lot of strangers drifting through the country lately, Major. I'm sure Calvin Howell has nothing to do with the loss of your stock, or anyone else's.''

''Nobody else's, Doc. Just mine. I'm the blue belly. That justifies it, far as he's concerned. He wants to run me out of the county.''

Silverthorne leaned forward and rested his elbows on his desk. ''*All* of your neighbors are Southern sympathizers, Major. So why do you point the finger at Calvin? If you think he feels that strongly, don't the other ranchers feel the same way?''

Holloway shifted his position on his chair and looked away from Silverthorne for a minute or so before he answered. ''The Howells and Holloways were best of friends up until the secession issue came up, Doc. Calvin's sister was married to my eldest brother.''

''That's the woman who's now married to Mitch Warner?''

"Yeah, ol' Mitch is one of the clan now. He stands with the Howells on everything, just like he did back in sixty. Doc, I was one of less than half a dozen in the whole county who voted against seceding from the Union.''

"And if I know you, you didn't try to hide it, nor the color uniform you intended to wear.''

"Shouted it from the housetops, as they say, and tried to talk some sense into those stubborn secessionists!''

"I'm sure cool heads did *not* prevail.''

Holloway nodded. "I was bucking my *own brothers*, besides my brother-in-law and his clan. But Calvin's the one who issued the ultimatum.''

"Ultimatum?''

Holloway nodded, his brow deeply furrowed. "If I rode out of Texas to join the bluecoats, I was never to set foot in this county again. From the moment I 'turned my back on the land,' as he put it, they considered that I had voluntarily forfeited any right to any of the property I shared with my brothers.''

"That was just talk, Percy. Calvin had no legal say-so.''

"He'd talked my brothers into going along with it, Doc.'' Holloway's voice quavered and he turned his head away for a moment. "And he had his hand on his Walker when he said it. You've been in Texas long enough to hear about *that* law, Doc.''

"But you came back, Major, and it hasn't led to a shooting. So Calvin must have reconsidered what he said in the heat of patriotic fervor.''

"Calvin Howell means what he says. He doesn't let it show, but he's not one to forget a grudge. He's got several against me.''

"Several?''

Holloway focused on the framed diploma on the wall above Silverthorne's head. "Howell and my brothers were with Ben McCulloch's Texans at Pea Ridge. That's where my eldest brother was killed, the one that was Calvin's brother-in-law. He knew I was there, too, on the opposite side of the meadow, of course. In his judgment I share the blame for the death of my own brother.''

"How do you know he feels that way about it, Major?"

"He said as much when he sent word to his sister. She was staying with Alice and Oliver on the H3 at the time. She moved back to the Rail H after the news came.''

"It must have been difficult for Mrs. Holloway during the war.''

Holloway nodded. "There were a lot of Unionists around Austin, San Antonio, and Fredericksburg, but Alice was on her own up here. She endured threats and insults, in addition to the usual hardships. She stuck it out and maintained our claim on the land, never doubting that I would return.''

"She's an exceptional woman,'' said Silverthorne. "I can imagine how happy she was when you got home.''

"Yes, she was . . . until I went ahead and did something she begged me not to do.''

"Uh-oh. Something else that riled Calvin Howell, I'd guess.''

"That wasn't my intention,'' said Holloway, crossing his ankles and studying his boots. "I thought I should do something to help the postwar recovery, so I accepted an appointment as a justice of the peace under the Reconstruction government.''

Silverthorne whistled through his teeth and leaned back in his chair.

"Now don't jump to conclusions, Doc. I'm still a Texan first and foremost. I finally realized I couldn't go along with the methods the government proposed, so I resigned.''

"By then local resentment toward you had intensified."

Again, Holloway nodded. "There was one good thing about the Federal occupation. Everyone knew the military government and the state police would back my play, so I was able to reclaim my outfit. Now that local authority's been turned over to the disenfranchised Confederates, there's no telling what will happen."

"In other words, you think the Howells will try to drive you off your land."

"I think they're already working on the project."

"By mishandling your stock?"

"I think they've been doing that for a long while. Now they'll try something more desperate."

"Like what?"

"I don't know. Maybe they'll incite the mob against me."

"If the mob was after you they would have made their move when you were affiliated with the carpetbaggers. Anyway, I doubt Calvin Howell has anything to do with the vigilantes."

"Doc, you just never know who might be a member of the mob. Any member or ex-member who talks, dies. That's their code. I think most of the responsible citizens have pulled out, now that the state police force has been disbanded in favor of reorganizing the Rangers. Those who keep the mob alive are the ones who revel in having the power to decide who's fit to stay and live and who has to leave or die."

"Some don't even get the chance to leave, from what I've heard." Silverthorne stared out the window at the empty street that led to the town square, less than one block away.

Holloway rested his chin on his chest and contemplated the toe of his right boot. "Yeah, sometimes a man disappears and later his body's found out in the brush with a bullet hole in the head, or swinging by the neck from the limb of a big tree.''

''If the ranchers weren't so suspicious of one another they'd probably form their own vigilance committee. At least they could form an association so as to pool their resources and hire a stock detective to investigate the rustling problem. An ex-Ranger, or someone like that.''

''Good idea, Doc, but I'm way ahead of you,'' said Holloway, lifting his head with a smile.

Silverthorne stared at the empty street for a few more seconds, then swung his gaze to Holloway. ''Guadalupe Proffit?''

''He's no ordinary cowhand, Doc.''

''You're joking,'' said Silverthorne, furrowing his brow. ''I thought all cowhands slept with their hardware and rode around with deadly weapons sticking out of every nook and cranny of their outfit.''

''When you grow up in Texas as the son of a freed-man and a Mexican, you'd best be prepared to defend yourself,'' said Holloway, chuckling at Silverthorne's mock incredulity. ''Lupe's learned how to survive, which means he's learned how to fight and he's learned how to hide. In the process he's also gotten very good at finding out about folks who are trying to hide who they are and what they're doing.''

''You think Proffit's investigation will lead to Calvin Howell.''

Holloway's face turned solemn and he nodded slowly. ''I know he's not entirely responsible for the rustling. I expect we'll catch some strangers, too.''

''*I* expect *all* the evidence will implicate strangers, Major, the same strangers that are making off with the Howells' stock. And when it does, I hope you'll let me talk to Calvin about the situation between you two. Maybe I can find out how he really feels about it after all that's happened.''

Holloway straightened up in his chair and leaned toward Silverthorne. "I appreciate your concern, Doctor, but I *insist* you stay out of it. Everything I've said today is in strictest confidence. I don't want Howell to know I'm on the lookout for him."

"I just thought talking it out would be worth a try."

Holloway settled back in his chair with a dismissive wave of his hand. "He wouldn't reveal his true feelings. He holds his grudges deep inside and he never forgets. Sooner or later he'll try to get even. I've got to turn the tables on him before he makes his move."

Silverthorne returned his gaze to the window. "The street's as empty as my waiting room. Everyone must have gone down to the racetrack."

"Maybe your waiting room wouldn't be so empty if you weren't so friendly with a certain damn Yankee," said Holloway with a laugh.

"My choice of friends isn't based on the opinions of others or how they may react."

"So I've noticed," said Holloway, rising from his chair. "Let's go watch your *friend*, Calvin, win some more races with his long-legged bay."

Silverthorne stood up and headed for the bedroom. "Let me tell Marylois where I'm going and I'll be right with you."

"Don't forget your Gladstone bag," said Holloway as he made for the door. "Someone might have an accident, and old Doc Fowler quit going to the races when he realized no horse in Texas would ever outrun Galahad."

Silverthorne went out the back door of the house and got his red dun from the stable. He'd saddled Rudy earlier and had been getting ready to ride out to the track when Holloway stopped by to visit. He caught up to the major and his mount at the corner of the town square and they rode out to the track together.

"Looks like a fistfight!" said Silverthorne as they rode past the last building on the street and came in sight of the racecourse. "Everyone's running to the back side of the track."

"Good thing you put your Gladstone on the saddle. Fistfights usually degenerate to the use of knives or guns."

"Where's Henry Adkins when you need him?"

"Our town marshal is conveniently someplace else when there's real trouble. Usually at Jerry Scott's saloon. Except when there's a fight at the saloon. When he thinks serious trouble's brewing he runs over to the county seat to fetch the sheriff."

"At least he's good for something."

The two men eased their horses against the outside of the circle of yelling spectators and stood in the stirrups to see if they could recognize the combatants who rolled in the dirt, desperately clinging together while they slugged and kneed and gouged at each other however they could. One was decidedly smaller than the other, but he was a windmill of ferocity, and the larger man struggled to get into position to use his superior strength to shove him away. They rolled apart and scrambled to their feet, facing each other as they circled and watched for the advantage.

"You stay away from my sister, you son of a blue belly, or I'll kick your ass up between your ears every time I see you," said the bigger of the two.

"You've not done it the first time, you copperheaded cow thief!"

"*Cow thief*? Why, you—"

"Rachel don't know you and your paw and your uncles been mishandling your neighbor's stock, I bet. But we know it, and we've got proof!"

Silverthorne raised his brows and flashed a look at Major Holloway.

"Oh, hell," said Holloway. He slipped his horn string and shook loose his lariat as he nudged his black gelding forward and cleared a path through the mass of people.

Silverthorne reined the dun into his wake and followed him to the center of the crowd.

Oliver lunged at Chad, but the noose whipped around his shoulders and snapped tight as the major dallied his horn and backed his horse against the slack, stopping Oliver in his tracks. Chad was as surprised as Oliver and had already suspended his countermove when Silverthorne pushed his mount between the young men.

"Aw, Major! What'd you do that fer?" yelled someone in the crowd. "The boy was holdin' his own agin the big'n."

"Damn shore was," another one shouted. "I believe he'd of whupped the damned cow thief."

Chad's mouth fell open and he gave Silverthorne a wide-eyed stare. "They *believe* what Oliver said!"

"One does, maybe," said Silverthorne. "Folks say things they don't mean when they smell blood."

But Silverthorne knew how an idea, once sparked, could become a tide of opinion that spread across the countryside and swayed the sentiment of the majority of the populace the same way all at once. And the cattlemen were looking for something tangible to vent their frustration on.

He glanced at Holloway. The major held a smug expression on his face as he watched Oliver disentangle himself from the rope.

"Where's your father?" Silverthorne asked, returning his attention to Chadbourne.

"Him and the rest of 'em are out back of the stables warming Red Streak up for a race, I reckon. I seen that son of a scalawag loose-herdin' Rachel over by the springs and I been follerin' him around ever since till I got him cornered off to hisself."

"If Rachel was being loose-herded, as you say, it must not have been against her wishes. She's old enough to make her own decisions, Chad."

"The hell you say! Just wait till Pa hears about it!"

Silverthorne realized he could put to rest any suspicion that Rachel might be using Oliver to glean information for her father.

"Well, Chadbourne, you go tell Calvin what you saw if you've a mind to, but I think it's a sign that Howells and Holloways can get along with one another if they really want to."

"Not in a million years!" proclaimed Chad as he turned to follow the dispersing crowd.

Silverthorne dismounted and untied his medical case. "Let me put some carbolic in that cut on your cheekbone, Oliver."

" 'Tain't nothin', Doc. I'd of whupped him good if y'all hadn't busted in."

"Why do you insist on speaking like an ignorant trail hand, Oliver?" said Major Holloway, frowning at his son. "We don't use that kind of language at home."

"No call for me to be any more different than I have to, Daddy. It's bad enough being knowed as the blue belly's boy."

"*Known*, not knowed. And don't you get smart with me, young man, or I'll give you a worse beating than the Howell boy would have given you. It's a good thing we stepped in before you blabbered *all* my plans to the public."

Oliver returned his father's torrid glare. "You don't believe I could've licked him! You wouldn't even give me a chance to show you! Far as you're concerned, I can't do *nothin'* right!" Oliver turned on his heel and stalked away.

"*Anything!*" Holloway shouted after him.

Silverthorne sighed and turned away to secure his valise with the saddle strings. He mounted and followed the major back toward the center of town.

"If Marshal Adkins was on the job, that incident wouldn't have gone as far as it did," said Holloway when Silverthorne came abreast. "He should be down at the track patrolling the crowd. I know he can't always stop it when grown men start a ruckus, but he should be able to separate a couple of boys. I'm going over to Scotty's to give him a piece of my mind!"

"I understand Scotty's a close friend of the Howell boys."

"My business is not with Jerry Scott."

"Well, I'll bring my bag of instruments and disinfectants, ointments and anodynes, and trail along just in case he *makes* it his business."

"If he does, it would serve me better if you'd brought that fancy Colt I gave you. I've watched you target shoot, and you're good with it."

"That's a talent I'd just as soon have no need to exploit."

EIGHT

SILVERTHORNE SQUEEZED THE MOTHER-OF-PEARL GRIPS of the flashy .45 and angled the barrel to catch the gleam of sunlight on silver. That day he rode with Major Holloway from the racetrack to Scotty's Saloon was the last day he ever left home without it.

Silverthorne had a premonition of trouble when he and Major Holloway reined in at Scotty's and he saw the two Rail H cow ponies tied to the hitch rail. Silverthorne mentioned they looked like Mart and Merrit Howell's favorite mounts.

"Got no business with the Howells at the moment," said Holloway, swinging his leg over to dismount.

"At the moment, eh? That reminds me of what Oliver told Chad—that you have *proof* the Howells have been mishandling stock."

"I'm afraid Oliver jumped the gun," said Holloway as they tied their horses alongside the Howells', "but it's just a matter of time."

"Well, I think you're wrong about them, Major, and

I hope whatever evidence Lupe uncovers will convince
you of their innocence.''

Holloway pulled his slipknot snug on the hitch rail.
''I can understand how you've come to like them, Doc.
I did, too, once upon a time. Maybe you'd best wait out
here while I go in and talk to Henry Adkins.''

Silverthorne wagged his head and gestured toward the
door.

''All right, but I want to talk to Henry alone. Perhaps
you can take his place if he's drinking with the Howell
boys, and keep them occupied so they don't horn in on
our conversation.'' Holloway turned to cross the board-
walk and push through the door, with Silverthorne at his
boot heels.

Adkins was drinking alone at the bar and the Howell
boys were sitting at a table next to the wall on the right.
They were dark, lean men, not quite as tall as their older
brother. Mart and Merrit acknowledged the new arrivals
with curt nods of their hat brims and returned their attention to their beer mugs. The town marshal's bleary
eyes watched Holloway's approaching reflection in the
mirror back of the bar. Holloway came to the bar on
Adkins's left, away from the Howells. Silverthorne
paused just inside the door, thinking of what he should
say when he approached Mart and Merrit.

''Well, I declare. If it isn't Dr. Silverthorne.''

Silverthorne turned toward the sound of the greeting,
which came from behind him on the left. The man was
sitting in the corner just inside the door, idly dealing
playing cards onto the table in front of him. A tall man,
you could tell even while he was seated. His thick blond
hair was parted in the middle and hanging long and
wavy down the sides and behind. Long sideburns and a
full mustache, waxed and twisted on the ends. White
shirt, black string tie loose around the open collar. A
brace of butt-forward Smith and Wesson American .44s
graced the black gunbelt strapped on his waist. Silver-

thorne had heard a new gambler had set up shop at Scotty's, but he'd never seen him.

"How's the missus, Doctor?" Slender fingers continued to flick the cards, and the gambler did not look up. Something seemed vaguely familiar about him. Or was it just the accent?

"Mrs. Silverthorne is holding her own, thank you. . . . I'm sorry, sir. Have we met? Back in Virginia, perhaps?"

"There is an ample amount of Old Virginny in my manner of speech, I'm told. Only a hint of it in your voice, suh. . . . No, we've never met, but I've seen you about town and I made inquiry. One never knows when one may need the services of a capable physician." The gambler deposited his last card on the table, stood up and extended his hand. "Chance Rosser, at your service, suh."

"Rosser, I need a refill!" Adkins turned unsteadily from the bar, breaking off his quiet conversation with Major Holloway.

"Excuse me," said Rosser, releasing his grip on Silverthorne's hand. "Mr. Scott has left me to care for our infrequent race day patrons, with the promise that he will return before the evening crowd converges."

When Rosser moved behind the bar, Adkins turned back around and Holloway continued his low-voiced tirade.

Adkins took a long draught from his refill. "I don't get paid to play nursemaid to no whippersnappers," he yelled, slamming the mug down on the counter. He looked over his shoulder at Mart and Merrit. "The Howells ain't come around complainin' because Chad got in a scrap."

"What scrap?" said Mart. Both brothers straightened up in their chairs and eyed the town marshal.

"Aw, Major Holloway's whinin' about your nephew

pickin' on his little boy. Thinks I orter hang around the track and play babysitter."

"That's not the point and you know it, Adkins," said Holloway. "In fact, Oliver was winning the fight when I broke it up. All I'm saying is—"

" 'Tain't no way," said Mart. "Chad can lick that pint-sized whelp of your'n with one hand tied behind his back."

Holloway wore his revolver in front on the left with the grip right, a position favored by many who wore a side arm while working cattle on horseback. Adkins's body obscured the movement of his hand from the counter to the grip. The Howells' eyes opened wide when the six-gun suddenly appeared, accompanied by the clicking of the mechanism as Holloway thumbed the hammer back.

"Sir, you have just called me a liar and called my son an animal in the same breath. I demand an apology!"

Adkins turned around and pressed his back against the bar, sucking in his breath and lifting his hands to shoulder level as he stared at the weapon in Holloway's hand.

"Now hold on a minute," said Merrit, rising slowly from his chair and spreading his hands away from his sides. Suddenly he grabbed the edge of the table and upended it, but before he could dive for cover Holloway's .38 roared. Merrit fell back against the wall and slid to the floor, a dark stain spreading into his shirt just below the right clavicle.

A stain also spread upon Adkins's clothing, but it was on the crotch of his pants. His knees buckled and he sat down hard on the floor in front of the bar. His bugged-out eyes were still fixed on Holloway's revolver, which was now pointed at Mart Howell. Mart's dark eyes burned and his hand was on the butt of his pistol.

"Better leave it in the socket, Mart," yelled Holloway, "or there'll be one less cow thief!"

"You all are about even up on the insults, I'd say, so let's just call a truce."

Both men could see Rosser from the corner of their eyes, and the two Smith and Wessons, one leveled at each of them.

"Forgive me, gentlemen, but if any more blood is let upon Mr. Scott's floor during my stewardship, it is I who shall do the letting."

"It ain't finished," said Mart, taking his hand away from his six-gun.

Holloway started backing toward the door. "You stick your nose out that door before I'm well away from here and it will be finished for you."

Adkins scrambled around the bar on hands and knees, heading for the back door.

Rosser tilted his face toward Silverthorne while keeping his eyes on Mart and the major. "Dr. Silverthorne, I do believe Mr. Merrit Howell is in dire need of your services."

"I've got my bag on the saddle," said Silverthorne, moving out the door ahead of Holloway.

Silverthorne went to his horse and untied his valise from the saddle. Holloway followed him to the hitch rack and mounted, keeping an eye on the saloon door.

"Watch my back till I'm out of range, Doc. Mart might slip out the back and try to drill me from behind."

"I'll shout a warning if he does, but I've no way of stopping him—I've got no weapon."

"If that gambler wasn't armed, I would've had to kill Mart. You think about that next time you leave home without the Colt I gave you." Holloway wheeled his horse and galloped away.

When Silverthorne reentered the saloon, Mart and Rosser were hoisting Merrit onto the bar. Rosser got a stack of clean bar wipes and Mart peeled Merrit's blood-soaked shirt off his shoulder to expose the wound.

"Bring me a clean stein full of fresh water if you will,

please, Mr. Rosser,'' said Silverthorne as he began sponging the blood away from the bullet hole. Silverthorne held a wipe against the wound and lifted Merrit's shoulder off the counter with the other hand. Merrit winced and sucked in his breath.

''Sorry, Merrit. . . . Let me see. . . . The slug went all the way through. It exited high, missing the scapula— it's a good thing you stood up before you were shot. I don't think any bones are broken. Blood's coagulating now. You won't need to be shrived just yet,'' said Silverthorne with a reassuring smile.

''Well, since it ain't such an emergency, I reckon he'll be all right till I can fetch Doc Fowler,'' said Mart. ''He's been doctorin' us ever since we was born. He can do a damn sight better job on a human than a horse and cow doctor!''

Merrit raised his left hand. ''No need for that, Mart. Doc Silverthorne knows what he's doin'.''

''Just 'cause big brother trusts him don't mean I got to. You seen who he come in here with!'' Mart stormed out the door and they heard his horse galloping away down the street.

Silverthorne eased Merrit's shoulder back against the counter and gave him a questioning look.

''Go ahead, Doc. No tellin' how long it'll take him to find Fowler.''

Silverthorne spread his Gladstone bag open on the counter at Merrit's head, selected a vial of permanganate of potash, and deposited a few crystals in the stein of water Rosser had furnished. He finished cleaning the blood from Merrit's shoulder while the crystals dissolved. Then he dipped a clean wipe into the purple fluid and cleaned his hands. He'd just finished laving the area around the entry wound when Mart and Dr. Fowler came charging in the door.

''What are you doing to my patient, Silverthorne?''

said Fowler as he strode to the bar. "What's this purple stuff?"

"It's an antiseptic, Doctor. I'm sure you've read about Lister's theory of sepsis and antisepsis. It was published several years ago in *The Lancet*."

"To hell with theories. I'll stick with the facts."

"The theory has proven factual in my practice."

"What practice?" said Fowler with a sneer. "Now get your bag of magic tricks out of my way so I can go to work."

"Don't you think you should wash your hands first?" said Silverthorne as he gathered up his case.

Fowler clenched his jaw and his flabby jowls turned red around his thick white burnsides. "Young man, when you've practiced medicine as long as I have, you'll learn not to waste your time on foolish ritual."

Merrit put a hand on Silverthorne's arm as he was about to leave. "Thanks for what you done, Doc. And, by the way, Cal's been lookin' for you. We got a sick mare he wants you to take a look at."

"He can't do nothin' for that mare," said Mart. "I told Cal to put her down, but Rachel talked him out of it."

"I'll find Calvin and tell him about the difficulty up here," said Silverthorne, heading for the door.

"You do that," said Mart, "and when he gets here I'll tell him what *really* happened."

Silverthorne ignored the jibe and took his leave.

NINE

SILVERTHORNE RUBBED HIS THUMB ACROSS THE FRAME of the Peacemaker, feeling the swirls of engraving. How could an instrument of death be so beautiful? Yet it could also be used to prevent a killing.

Silverthorne remembered the desperate look of fury in Mart Howell's eyes. Mart figured Holloway would shoot him whether he went for his own weapon or not. He'd rather go down fighting, and he would have if not for Chance Rosser and his American .44s. Silverthorne had been helpless to do anything. He'd felt the same way when Major Holloway asked him to cover his getaway. That was the last day Tal Silverthorne had ever gone unarmed.

It was also the last day there was any veiling of the animosity between the Howells and the Holloways. From then on it was an out-in-the-open blood feud, and each family traveled together whenever they came to town, avoiding the other group, and always on guard. The three Dutchmen from Burnet County always came with the Holloways.

Silverthorne wagged his head in dismay at the thought of how he'd been caught in the middle, maintaining *friendly relationships with both Calvin and Percival, yet never able to moderate the hard feelings that each had for the other.*

Sunday noon after the Saturday confrontation at Scotty's Saloon found Dr. Silverthorne in the Rail H stable with his arm buried in the bowels of the white mare who'd dropped the palomino foal.

"I'm afraid Mart was right, Cal. There's nothing we can do for her. The intestine's twisted. That's why she's so bloated she looks like she's about to explode."

"I figured as much, but Rachel's partial to her, so I wanted to be certain before I put her down."

"Sorry, Rachel," said Silverthorne, casting a sympathetic look at Rachel, who was holding the mare's halter. "At least the colt's old enough to wean."

Silverthorne extracted his arm from the mare and followed Calvin to the hand pump outside the barn. Calvin pumped while Silverthorne rinsed, then handed him a flour sack towel he'd brought from the house.

"I'll go make sure Martha's set another plate on the dinner table," said Calvin, taking his leave. "Come on up to the house soon as you're ready."

Silverthorne finished drying off and went back to get his valise, which he'd left just outside the stall. Rachel was still standing by the mare, slowly stroking the animal's neck. Her back was toward Silverthorne and her head was bowed. Silverthorne hung the towel on a bridle peg next to the stall. He could not hear Rachel cry, but he noticed the tremor in her slender shoulders. The gate creaked as he entered the stall, but she did not look up.

"I'm sorry, Rachel," he repeated. "Doctors win a few battles, but we always lose the war." He placed a gentle hand on her trembling shoulder.

Suddenly she turned and flung her body against him, throwing her arms around his torso and burying her face in his chest. At first Silverthorne held his arms out in a gesture of helplessness, then he gradually clasped them against her back and held her gently while she had her cry. When her body finally ceased to shudder and her sobs subsided he released his grip and moved his hands to her shoulders, gently trying to extricate himself from her embrace.

"We'd best be going to the house now, Rachel. I think they're waiting dinner on us."

Rachel dug her fingernails into his back. "Just stay with me a little longer," she said, lifting her head and pressing her cheek against his.

"You've had your cry, Rachel; now it's time to move on."

"This part ain't about grief, Doc. This is about you and me."

Silverthorne felt her lips on his jaw and turned his head away before she could find his mouth. He tried not to be too rough as he broke her grip and pushed her away to arm's length.

"Don't tell me you don't feel nothin', Doc. I've seen it in your eyes. You got a hankerin', and it ain't gettin' took care of at home."

"I took a vow, Rachel, and when I give my word I take it very seriously. How about you?"

"What do you mean, how about me? I ain't beholden to nobody."

"What about Oliver Holloway?"

"I never promised him nothin'."

"Not in words, maybe. But you've done *something* to give him high hopes. Why, he's fought your brother and defied his own father for you."

Rachel took a moment to ponder what he'd said. "Makes no difference now," she said. "Not after what happened yesterday."

"I was hoping, since you and Ollie get along so well,

you could persuade the rest of the Howells and Holloways to get together and talk peace.''

''I doubt it. It's too late now, anyway. Colt and Winchester will be the only ones clearing their throats the
next time the Howells meet the Holloways.''

Silverthorne just stared at her. Was she actually looking forward to a confrontation with the Holloways? How
could a man figure a woman like Rachel Howell? Silverthorne turned away and let himself out of the horse
stall, gathered up his valise and the towel, and headed
for the house.

Calvin, Martha, and Chad were seated at the table,
waiting on Silverthorne. They figured Rachel was too
upset to eat, so they began without her. During the
course of the meal they heard her enter the house by
way of the front door, and a few moments later they
heard her go out.

A few minutes after she left, Calvin cocked his ear in
the direction of the stable. ''I think I hear hoofbeats,''
he said, and got up from his chair to peer out a window.
''What's that gal up to now? . . . I told her I'd take that
mare off and put her down. She come in the house to
fetch a Winchester.'' He returned to his plate wagging
his head, but there was a proud gleam in his eye.

''That girl!'' said Martha. ''I can't keep her in the
house long enough to be of any help with the household
chores, but she's always ready to do any kind of man's
work. I don't see how she can shoot that mare, though,
seein's how she set so much store by it.''

''That's why she figures it's her responsibility,'' said
Calvin.

''She'll do it, all right,'' said Chad. ''She can do anything once she sets her mind to it.''

Silverthorne eyed the bruises Oliver Holloway's fists
had left on Chad Howell's face. Looking at Chad made
him think how so often sons take after their mother's
side of the family. Oliver was another example. And

Rachel was so much like her father, except for the green eyes and dark red hair. Then he thought about the differences between Calvin and his half brothers. They were also tall and lean, but dark-featured, not fair-haired and blue-eyed like Calvin.

''Have you gotten a report on Merrit's condition today?'' Silverthorne asked.

''Mart come by this mornin','' said Martha. ''He said Merrit's kept his arm in the sling like the doctor told him. His shoulder's real stiff and sore, and Doc Fowler says he'll have some stiffness even after the bullet wound heals up.''

''It's a good thing Merrit's left-handed,'' said Calvin. ''We can't afford to be short a gun hand, the way things are shapin' up.''

Silverthorne took a deep breath and let it out slowly. ''Cal, do things *have* to shape up for a gun feud? The Howells and Holloways were friendly before the war; can't you and Percival talk things out and reach some kind of peaceful solution to your differences?''

Calvin put his fork down and wiped his mouth with his napkin. ''This trouble's been brewin' a long time, Doc—ever since Holloway turned agin his family and his country and fought with the very army that killed his own brother, who was also my brother-in-law. And now Percival Holloway's spilt Howell blood and branded us cow thieves. Any one of them things has got to be avenged, not to mention all of them together. The only way he can escape the vengeance of the Howells is to quit this part of the country. And them that stands with him will leave with him or be buried with him, includin' them pro-Union Dutchmen, and *anybody else*.''

Silverthorne would have liked to say more, to discuss the details of Holloway's complaint against the Howells, but the major had sworn him to silence. The meal was finished in an uncomfortable atmosphere and Silverthorne was glad to be on his way. He knew "anybody else" was aimed at him.

Calvin did not know about Guadalupe Proffit.

Lupe Proffit rode his personal horse that he'd broke and trained himself, a dark brown with no markings. *Trigueño*, Lupe's mother had called horses of that color, so Lupe called him Tree. Tree blended with the shadows during the day and reflected no moonlight at night.

The brown man on the brown horse ghosted along the arroyos and across the flats and rolling hills of the H3 range, probing the brush and the juniper thickets for signs of rustler activity. Here and there Lupe found small heaps of ashes and partially burned limbs that had served to heat some long-liner's cinch ring or running iron. There were tracks where cows, singly and in small bunches, had been driven by one or two men on horseback. A lot of those tracks tended to the south.

On the third day he came upon a fresh set of prints, dismounted, and squatted down for a closer look. There were two sets of cow tracks overmarked by one set of horseshoes. Lupe put a forefinger in a depression where an overturned rock had been. The morning sun had not yet sucked the moisture from the dirt in the dent. The thief was not far ahead of him. Lupe remounted and eased the brown horse along, following the tracks of the two cows and one horse away to the south.

Lupe reined the brown to a halt when the trail led him onto Rail H range. He pulled his battered black hat off and tugged his bandanna loose to wipe the sweatband, his neck and forehead. He replaced the hat, and as he retied the neckerchief his black eyes surveyed the terrain ahead and to either side. Whether the major's suspicion about the Howells was correct or not, the evidence he hoped to uncover would implicate someone, and they would do whatever was necessary to prevent him from spying on them, or from delivering his report should they discover him after he'd found them out.

Lupe smiled. He'd taken a few unbranded calves himself in times past. He'd done it when his family was hungry and he had no other way of feeding them. The men Lupe sought were stealing cattle to sell, and altering the marks on branded cattle.

The Texas Stock Law of 1873 made the selling of cattle by men not owning them punishable by not less than five years in the penitentiary. The on-the-spot punishment meted out by the owners of said stock if they themselves should catch the thieves red-handed would likely be far worse than five years in the pen, even worse than life behind bars.

Rustling was risky business, yet from his own experience Lupe could see how a man could slide into it. A man might think he would take just one calf for food, as Lupe had done. Then he gets to thinking how easy it was and he decides to take just one more. But he doesn't stop with the second one, either. Soon he gets caught up in the excitement of harvesting where he hasn't put in a crop and the adventure of risking the consequences of discovery. To Lupe the thrill was like catching a big catfish and playing high-stakes poker with four kings while looking for an ace, all rolled into one. He might have become a rope-and-ring man himself, had Major Holloway not given him the opportunity to earn an honest wage trailing cattle to Kansas.

Proffit checked the loads in the Navies before he moved on. The major was trusting in his abilities to read sign, travel quiet, and keep out of sight. But desperadoes survive by the same cautions, and Lupe was acutely aware of the likelihood of gunplay.

The trail of the man and the stolen stock wound through the rocky, juniper-studded hills of the Rail H range, angling westward toward the brakes of the Colorado, a tangled land of clear creeks and crooked canyons, briery brush and twisted trees. *Terreno quebrado—*

broken land, Lupe's mother would have called it. A land
that secluded bears and mountain lions from hunters
could also hide desperate men with their ill-gotten booty.
Guadalupe Proffit would follow no matter where the trail
should lead.

Lupe tugged the brown pony to a halt and eyed a tuft
of switchgrass that had been bent over. It was just beginning to straighten up. His quarry was not far ahead.
A southwesterly breeze gusted for a moment and he
turned an ear to it. He was sure he heard the lowing of
cattle in the distance. No doubt the rustlers were holding
their gather short of the deep canyons while they accu-
mulated a herd.

Proffit studied the terrain, mapping out a course
through the stunted trees and brush in the lowest levels
that would conceal his approach to the long, low ridge
less than a mile ahead. The outline of a higher ridge
could be seen just beyond. Probably there was a creek-
bottom valley between the ridges where the rustlers had
built a brush-fence trap to hold the stolen stock. There
would be grass and water, and seclusion for the illegal
work of burning brands and whittling ears.

There was a stand of four or five close-growing ju-
nipers in a saddle in the low ridge, and Lupe decided it
was the best place to scout the setup in the creek bottom
without being seen. He ground-hitched his pony in the
shade of a trio of post oaks near the bottom of the slope,
took his Spencer and the field glasses Major Holloway
had loaned him, and carefully made his way to the saddle. He went under the juniper boughs on hands and
knees, bellied down on the rocky ridge and squirmed
forward until he could peer into the little valley below.

Lupe counted thirty-four head in the holdup, mostly
market-age steers, with a few head of younger and older
stuff of both sexes mixed in to make the herd easier to
handle. Two men were conversing outside the gate. The
one on horseback had to be the one Lupe had been track-

ing, and the other had no doubt opened the gate to accept the two animals the rider had driven in. On the opposite side of the bottom under a fringe of stunted live oaks, Lupe could see a canvas lean-to shelter. With the field glasses he could make out three bedrolls, a saddle, and several items of camping equipment. Four horses were hobbled on the grass between the cow pen and the camp.

Two men, two saddles, counting the one the rider was sitting on, and three bedrolls. One horse under saddle and four on their heads. Each rustler probably had two mounts. One horse and one saddle out of camp, then, along with the man who owned the third bedroll. *Where was he?*

An explosion of sand and gravel in front of Lupe's face followed by the sound of a rifle shot from the far ridge answered the question. Lupe dropped the glasses and rolled over behind the trunk of a juniper, jacking a shell into the chamber of the Spencer as he rolled. *Got to cut the odds, pronto!* he thought as he came up on his knees alongside the tree. He threw his torso against the trunk and rested his rifle barrel on a low-growing limb. The man afoot was sprinting for the lean-to, and the man ahorse was galloping toward the cover of a tangle of trees and brush on the near slope. The man ahorse would only get closer, but the one afoot was getting farther away and going for his rifle, so Lupe drew a bead on the spot where his galluses crossed in back and squeezed the trigger.

Lupe knew he'd scored without watching the man fall. He slammed another shell into the chamber, ignored the zinging lead and flying twigs, and pivoted the Spencer on the juniper limb until the sights zeroed on the left shirt pocket of the oncoming rider. He pulled the trigger and dropped to his belly on the ridge, again knowing he didn't have to watch to be sure.

Lupe stretched his arm and retrieved the field glasses. The flash of the setting sun on the lens had given away his presence, he suspected, but he put the glass to his eyes long enough to see the puff of smoke when the rustler on the ridge let go another shot. Proffit sent his remaining five shots across the chasm as fast as he could work the lever, aim, and fire. At that distance it would be blind luck if he hit anything with the Spencer. He grabbed the glasses and scooted out of harm's way behind the ridge.

"Got to git me a Winchester when the major pays me," he muttered to himself as he reloaded. This time he put a cartridge in the chamber in addition to the seven in the magazine.

Lupe scurried along the ridge for about ten yards, staying far enough down the hillside not to be skylined, then turned uphill behind a clump of buckthorn. He removed his hat and crawled alongside on his belly to peek over the rim. The two rustlers he'd shot lay still, right where they'd fallen. *Where was number three?*

The third man must have been on lookout duty. He had a horse up there with him, and although he'd surely shifted positions after Lupe's five-shot volley, it was doubtful he'd stray very far from his mount. Lupe began to study the trees and brush on the hillsides and in the bottom to see how he could best approach the outlaw's position. Suddenly from the far hillside came the sound of rattling stones and crackling brush. Lupe glimpsed a horse scrambling up the ridge. He sent one last shot to speed the rustler on his way and discourage any thought of coming back.

Lupe got to his feet and made his way down to his horse. He stowed the field glasses and the carbine on the saddle, mounted, and rode over the ridge to the creek. After he'd watered the brown he led him into the trap, closed the gate, and remounted to ride slowly around and through the grazing cattle. Six head were branded H3, including the two most recently captured.

All the rest had been H3 cattle, but their brands were reworked into a Ladder 8 configuration.

Lupe side-passed Tree through the gate, opening and closing it without dismounting. A quick survey of the hobbled horses revealed a Rail H cow pony among the four. The horse he'd tracked had sought the company of the others after losing its rider. It also bore the Howell brand. Lupe dismounted and caught it up and stripped the saddle and bridle before turning it loose.

When Lupe pulled the saddle he saw that the dead rider had been equipped with a new Winchester '73. It was personalized with a diamond-shaped brass plate on the stock that was engraved with the initials G. P.

"The Lord must have meant me to have it," said Lupe with a shrug. He untied the scabbard and put it under the near stirrup leathers of his own saddle.

"Maybe I can git a dollar or two for that old Spencer," he said, and mounted up to go report to Major Holloway. He would ride till pitch-dark, rest until moonrise, and get to the ranch in time for a couple hours' sleep before leading the major and the H3 crew back to the cow trap.

TEN

"POOR LUPE," SILVERTHORNE SAID ALOUD, REMEMBER-ing the somber half-breed. "I know you felt beholden to the major. But you did not owe him the ultimate sacri-fice, and he had no right to let it go that far."

Silverthorne had begun to realize just how far Hol-loway was willing to go to implicate the Howells the day he rode with the H3 crew to the cow trap.

"Are you sure the cow trap's on Howell range?" said Silverthorne, gazing around at the creek bottom and up at the ridges.

"If it's not, it's close enough," said Major Holloway. He bent over the dead rider and rummaged through his pockets. "Fellow's name was George Parker," he said, looking at one of the papers he'd found. He stuffed it into his shirt pocket and put the others back on the corpse. "Anybody recognize him?"

Andres, Pabst, and Hunziker nudged their reluctant horses close enough to glance at the pale face and wagged their heads. Lupe had seen him the day before. Oliver didn't even bother to look.

79

"How about Mr. Suspenders over there?" Holloway walked over and rolled the body over on its back. Silverthorne and the three Dutchmen followed and rode by single file to take a look. Andres was last in line.

"Yah, I see him," he said. "One time in Bluffton, it was, over on the Colorado. He was clerking in the grocery store over there. I do not know his name."

Holloway made a quick search of the body and found no identification.

"I guess selling stolen beef pays better than selling groceries," he said.

"It ought to, considering the risk," said Silverthorne.

"When you take cards in a game you better know what you're laying on the table, eh, Lupe?" said Holloway with a wink at Proffit.

"If the Lord in His mercy grants them the upward callin', then I done them a favor, I reckon," answered Lupe in a subdued tone.

"Cow thieves in heaven? I doubt it," said the major. "Anyhow, we'll put the earthly remains in that ravine over there at the foot of the slope and cover them with rocks. It's a wonder the varmints didn't get to 'em last night."

The dead rider's horse had stayed with the hobbled horses after Lupe turned him loose. Major Holloway left the burying to the crew and hunted up a pair of hobbles in the rustler camp. He roped the loose horse and hobbled it. They would take all five horses back to the H3 corrals along with the cattle, but Holloway was especially concerned with the two that bore the Howell brand.

It was almost dark by the time the bodies were covered. The H3 riders staked their horses on the grass, made supper from the provisions the rustlers had stowed in their camp, then settled down to await the dawn.

"It's a good thing you were on hand when Lupe rode in with the news of his discovery, Doc," said Holloway, tossing a twig onto the embers of the campfire.

"I just came out for a few days' work. Didn't figure on being a material witness to criminal activity," said Silverthorne, knowing what Holloway was thinking.

"Like it or not, you're known to be friendly with the Howells as well as the Holloways."

"I'll testify to what I've seen, Major. But I *am* impartial about your so-called evidence against the Howells."

"Those Ladder 8 brands haven't peeled off and healed yet, Doc. You can still feel the ridges of the old brand and trace out the H3. We'll slaughter a steer and skin it out if we need more proof. The original brand will be on the inside of the hide."

"It's your brand that's been altered, Major; there's no doubt about that. But the Ladder 8 brand doesn't belong to the Howells."

"Of course not. It hasn't been recorded by any outfit in these parts, as far as I know. They're just using it like a road brand to get those steers out of the country and sell them to a cattle buyer—probably some unscrupulous trader that clerk from Bluffton knew about."

"And those Rail H ponies really don't prove anything either," Silverthorne continued. "They could be stolen, or the late Mr. George Parker could have bought them from the Howells."

"If Calvin had lost some horses, we would've heard about it. He'll claim he sold them. Anyway, we'll see what the sheriff thinks about my evidence. Doc, when you get back to town you better tell that excuse for a town marshal that if he doesn't want to get caught in the middle of a 'ruption like he did that day in Scotty's, he'd best get some backup from the county seat over to Lampkin Springs next race day."

Silverthorne stared at the dying embers. He visualized the burner-branded cattle being driven through Lampkin Springs and into one of the corrals at the racetrack, along with the two Rail H cow horses. What a crowd would be attracted! It would be like the day Oliver and Chad were fighting out behind the racecourse, only a herd of cattle with worked brands would attract even more attention.

"You're going to make a public display, aren't you, Major? It doesn't matter what the sheriff thinks of your evidence, does it? You know the effect it will have on the crowd. You saw how they reacted when Oliver called Chad a cow thief the day of the fight. You're trying to isolate the Howells from the rest of the locals by casting suspicion on them!"

"It's about time *they* know how it feels." The major flung another stick on the coals and looked away from Silverthorne.

"Major, there's got to be another way to handle this."

"Why are you taking up for the Howells, Doc?" said Oliver. He was the only other one still sitting by the fire. The rest of the crew had spread their blankets beneath the live oaks and gone to sleep. "Is it because of Rachel?"

"Oliver!" said Major Holloway. "What a thing to say! Just because you've got Rachel Howell's scent up your nose doesn't mean everybody's in rut for her. Dr. Silverthorne is a married man!"

"Married to a terminally ill cripple, folks say."

"Oliver!"

"Rachel's been horsin' for the doc ever since he come to town. Why do you think he's all the time going out to the Rail H?"

"That's enough, young man! If you think you're too big for me to take a limb to your backsides, you're about to find out different! Now you apologize to Dr. Silverthorne, and then you go to your bedroll."

The stick Major Holloway had tossed on the coals caught fire and the flare-up was reflected in the moisture in Oliver's eyes. He stared at Silverthorne for a moment.

"You just don't know how it feels to lose your woman," he said, and got up and went to join the other men beneath the live oaks.

"I'm sorry, Doc," said Holloway, wagging his head. "That little tease has got the boy's head spinning and he can't do anything about it the way things are. I reckon his imagination runs away with him when he thinks about you being over there around her."

In spite of what Holloway said, Silverthorne could see the suspicion in his eyes. Oliver's speculation had infused his mind with a picture of Dr. Silverthorne and Rachel Howell together. It was an image Silverthorne constantly fought to expunge from his own brain.

The arrival of the strange-branded cattle in Lampkin Springs did not immediately attract as much attention as Silverthorne had anticipated, for the H3 crew drove them in on Friday before the Saturday race day, penning them in one of the corrals at the track along with the two Rail H horses. The little herd was a curiosity nevertheless, and the wonderings of the locals as well as the summertime health-seeking visitors sparked a buzz of speculative talk among the populace. The fact that two Rail H horses and six head of H3 steers had been driven in along with the Ladder 8 cattle did not go unnoticed.

Sheriff Al Sweet rode into town at sunset. He heard the gossip at the livery stable and then he knew why Major Holloway had sent word to Marshal Adkins to get a bona fide officer of the law to Lampkin Springs by race day.

Sweet expected to find Holloway at the hotel, but he was disappointed. The desk clerk said he'd been told a half-breed Negro was riding with the H3 men, and knowing the Negro would not be welcome in a reputable hotel, he assumed the H3 group had decided to spend the night in a camp somewhere outside of town.

Sweet expected to find Marshal Adkins at Jerry

Scott's saloon and he was not disappointed. He *was* disappointed that Adkins had not been brave enough to question the major when he'd come to town with the cattle and horses, and therefore knew no more about the situation than the guessing gossipers.

Two facts were plain—the Ladder 8 brand was a forgery of the H3 original, and the presence of the Rail H horses suggested the Howells were in some way implicated. No doubt Holloway would be at the racetrack corrals in the morning, and Sweet decided then would be soon enough to find out the details. He had a drink and went back to the hotel to turn in.

Sweet arose early. He ate a leisurely breakfast and lingered with the refills of his coffee cup, thinking there was plenty of time to talk to Major Holloway before the Howells arrived with their racehorse. The nine-mile ride to town was a good warm-up for the big bay, if they took it slow.

On this Saturday, Calvin Howell arose even earlier than Sheriff Sweet, ate a quick breakfast, and rode fast to town ahead of the rest of the family, as he needed to get the blacksmith to repair a bent ring on the special snaffle his stallion was used to running with. He did not expect the H3 crew to be in town when he got there.

Sheriff Sweet did not expect Calvin Howell to show up at the corral while he was conferring with Major Holloway, but he did. The smith told Calvin about the cows and the horses the H3 crew had corralled at the track, and about the talk that was circulating. Calvin did not wait for the snaffle to be repaired, nor did he wait for the rest of the Howell clansmen to arrive in Lampkin Springs.

Sheriff Sweet had barely gotten the particulars from Major Holloway when he caught sight of Calvin Howell approaching the corral. A large crowd of curious townspeople had already gathered, and when word of How-

ell's arrival spread among them they all turned to see
what he would have to say for himself.

Howell rode easy and loose as usual, but his right
hand was not far from his revolver and his blue eyes
were hard and watchful beneath the brim of his sand-
colored Stetson. He eased his dun gelding through the
parting crowd and up to the fence. He sat very still and
scanned the H3 riders inside the corral. The three Dutchmen and Oliver, as usual. There was the Negro the smith
had mentioned. Doc Silverthorne was standing off to the
side, separate from the crowd but not with the H3 crew
either. Sheriff Sweet was standing in the corral next to
Holloway's horse. Howell looked directly at Major Holloway for a moment, then at the sheriff.

Sweet cleared his throat. "Ah . . . Calvin, these here
cows was found in a brush trap on your range, Major
Holloway claims. A few of 'em is still branded H3, but
most of them's been worked over to a Ladder 8 brand.
Holloway's men shot and killed two of the rustlers. One
of 'em was riding a Rail H pony. There was another
Rail H horse in the rustler's remuda."

"I see the horses," said Howell. "And I see the stock
of George Parker's carbine sticking out of that nigger's
scabbard. I sold those broncs to Parker. I've got a copy
of the bill of sale at the ranch."

"We didn't find a bill of sale on Parker's person or
in his possibles," said Holloway, looking at Sweet instead of Howell. "The man with the horses is the one
needs to have proof he bought them. A description
doesn't require the buyer's signature. It would be easy
to forge a copy."

Silverthorne thought about the paper Holloway
slipped into his pocket when he was searching Parker's
body for identification. Why was Holloway compelled
to keep that one paper?

Calvin Howell sat quiet, his eyes cold and steady on
the sheriff while he waited to see how Sweet would re-

spond to Holloway's accusation. Sweet looked away
from Calvin's gaze and pulled on his goatee as he pondered the situation.

Silverthorne was glad Holloway hadn't told Sheriff
Sweet the precise truth about how Parker and the clerk
from Bluffton were killed. A ranch crew that executed
a couple of rustlers while reclaiming stolen stock was
one thing. A Mexican-and-Negro half-breed who shot
two white men was quite another, no matter what the
circumstances, as far as the white citizens of postwar
Texas were concerned. Silverthorne regretted Lupe had
seen fit to take Parker's Winchester, for it called attention to the fact that he was present at the killings and
might even educe the assumption that he was the very
one who'd shot Parker.

Finally Al Sweet let go his goatee. He wagged his
head as he began to speak. "Holloway, you've got nothing that could persuade a grand jury to indict. Anybody
could of worked them brands. Just because there was
Rail H hosses at the rustler camp don't necessarily mean
any of the Howells was ever there. And when rustlers
build a cow trap they've got to put it on somebody's
range. Just because they built it on Howell land don't
mean Calvin had anything to do with it. I can't take
Howell into custody on evidence that circumstantial."

Holloway faked a disbelieving look at Sweet, then
shifted it to the crowd, shrugging his shoulders and gesturing at the captured animals. The crowd began to murmur, and someone said, "Ought to hang the damned
cow thief!" Several shouts of agreement were heard,
some of them spiced with expletives.

Calvin Howell backed his dun away from the corral.
"If anybody wants to hang me today, I'll be waiting for
you at Jerry Scott's," he shouted. He yanked the dun
around and a touch of the spur sent him galloping away
toward town.

Sheriff Sweet went to his horse and followed Howell.

Holloway edged his horse over to the fence near Silverthorne. "Thanks for making sure Adkins got the message to the sheriff, Doc."

"Looks like you've got 'em on your side now," said Silverthorne with a glance at the dispersing crowd.

"Not so, Doc. They'll never forget where I was during the war. They're just seeing Calvin Howell for what he really is."

"For what you think he is, Major."

"They saw the evidence and made up their own minds, Doc, just like a trial by jury."

"What if they'd seen the paper you took off George Parker's body? Would they still have been convinced?"

Holloway quickly looked around to see if anyone was close enough to hear. "We'll talk about that in private, Doc. You come out to the ranch first chance you get." With that he wheeled his mount to join his men as they exited the corral.

Silverthorne went home to his wife. For the last time.

ELEVEN

Silverthorne thought about all the times he'd left Marylois alone. He'd felt justified at the time, for animal patients don't usually come to the office, and the meager wages he'd earned doing day work on the ranches were sorely needed. Should he have stayed home and put more effort into his regular medical practice? Did he choose the way of veterinary medicine and ranch work just because he liked it better? Did he prefer it because it provided escape from Marylois—freedom from feeling the stress and pain of her suffering and the helplessness of his inadequacy? He'd pondered those questions many times since the day he held her for the last time in the street near Scotty's Saloon.

Jerry Scott was not the only faithful friend Calvin Howell had. Another friend intercepted the rest of the Howell clan just before they reached Lampkin Springs and advised them of the situation. Mart sent the womenfolk back to the ranch with the stallion. Mart, Merrit, their brother-in-law Mitch Warner, and Chad rode cautiously through the back streets of the little town until they reached the alleyway door of Scotty's Saloon. They'd just taken their chairs around the table where Calvin and Jerry were seated when Rachel burst into the barroom from the back entrance, brandishing the carbine she'd been carrying on her saddle since the day Holloway shot Merrit.

"Rachel, what are you doing here?" said Mart. "Put that rifle down! Nobody's here but us and our friends."

"*He's* no friend of mine," said Rachel, wrinkling her nose at Marshal Henry Adkins, who was leaning against the bar. "And I don't even know him," she added with an appraising glance at Chance Rosser, who sat with his back to the wall at his usual corner table practice-dealing cards.

"Chance Rosser, at your service, ma'am," said the gambler, rising from his seat for a moment.

"Rosser works for Jerry," said Mart, "so he's on our side. Adkins is just here, as usual. He don't count for spit one way or t'other. You know that."

"Mart, you got no call to talk about me like that to the girl," said Adkins, turning from his drink to face the Howells. "I'm the marshal of this here town, and—"

"You're no marshal, Adkins, and you won't have that badge no more come November. Now put your lip back on the rim of that stein and shut up."

Adkins glared at Mart for a moment, glanced at Rachel's smirky sneer, and returned to his hunched-over position against the bar.

Calvin Howell sat quietly until he was sure Mart was finished. "Rachel, I believe Uncle Mart sent you back to the ranch with Mother and Aunt Millie."

"Mart's not my boss!"

"He is when I'm not around. Now *I'm* telling you. Go home, Rachel."

"Daddy, you know I'm a good shot. Please let me stay with you."

"Rachel, I've let you ride and rope and do most every

kind of work the menfolk do, but this is where I draw the line. A saloon's no place for a young lady, and besides, I don't want you to get caught in the middle of a 'ruption. Not that there will be any more trouble today. We're going to stay here till the Holloways leave town, just so folks know we're not backin' down and we're not admittin' to guilt. I expect we'll be on home by dark or soon after. Now you go tell your ma what I said.''

At that moment the man who'd met the Howells outside town pushed through the batwings. ''Cal, Holloway's movin' that bunch of critters back to the H3. He's left your horses at the track.''

''They're not my horses no more, Ramey,'' said Calvin. ''Well, Rachel, you can tell your ma we'll be home by suppertime.''

''The H3's fixin' to drive them cows right through town, just like they brung 'em in, Calvin,'' said Ramey.

''Like hell they will,'' said Mart. He stood up and kicked his chair away as he drew his six-shooter. ''I'll scatter that herd to hell and breakfast.''

''Now just hold on a minute, Mart,'' said Calvin and Merrit simultaneously, coming to their feet along with Scott and Warner.

Rachel gripped her rifle and smiled. ''Let's go get 'em, Uncle Mart,'' she said, giving Adkins a contemptuous glance.

Adkins saw her in the mirror. He hung his head for a second, then shoved himself away from the bar and turned around. ''You just stay where you are, Mart Howell. You go stampeding them cows all over town and somebody's likely to get hurt. It's my job to protect the citizens of Lampkin Springs and I'm ordering you to—''

''You're the one's gonna get hurt, Henry,'' said Mart. ''Now you just crawl on out the back door before you piss on yourself again.''

Adkins glanced at Rachel, saw her laugh, and reached

for his revolver. "No, I ain't kowtowin' to you no more,
Mart Howell."

Mart couldn't believe his eyes. He almost didn't lift
his pistol in time.

"You put that smoke pole away, Mart Howell, or I'm
gonna . . ."

Just before Adkins's gun came level, Mart jerked his
.44 up and pulled the trigger.

". . . arrest you."

Henry got the words out just as Mart's pistol exploded. He slumped against the bar and looked down at
the crimson circle that quickly spread out to engulf the
stains of spilled beer on the front of his shirt. "Oh,
no–o–o . . ." he said, looking at the ceiling. His eyes
rolled back and he slid down the front of the bar, jamming the barrel of his unfired pistol into a brass spittoon
as he sat on the floor and toppled over on his side.

Nobody said anything. The only sound was Rosser's
incessant shuffling and dealing of cards.

"Go home, Rachel. *Now!*" said Calvin, breaking the
silence.

Rachel stalked out the back.

The sound of Mart Howell's shot reached the ears of the
H3 crew just as they were about to push their little herd
of oddly branded cattle into the town square. They were
on edge, knowing the Howell clan was holed up in
Scotty's Saloon.

"Somebody in the saloon has took a shot at us, Major!" yelled Alec Pabst.

Major Holloway reined his horse around, looking for
his son. "Oliver! I want you to circle around the square.
Take the back streets and stay out of sight. You can
rejoin us on the other side of town."

"*Pa!* I'm not afraid," said Oliver, pulling his revolver. "I want to fight!"

"Your mother would never forgive me if any harm

should come to you, Oliver. *Now do as you're told!*"

Oliver hung his head, holstered his pistol, and reined his horse aside, heading for the nearest alleyway.

Holloway turned his attention to the rest of his crew. "You men take your weapons to hand. Push these critters hard all the way through and throw some lead at the saloon to keep those jaybirds ducking instead of shooting. Now let's go!"

Silverthorne was standing in the doorway of his office when he heard the first shot. He ducked back in the room and grabbed his medical kit. Marylois shuddered at the sound of the gunshot. She watched him pick up his valise and thumb the keeper from the hammer of his shiny Colt.

"Tal! Don't go! It's none of your affair. You'll just get yourself killed trying to help those bloodthirsty Texans!"

"They're all my friends, Marylois. Maybe I can talk some sense into them."

"Tal, they're determined to kill each other. There's nothing you can do."

"At least I can try to keep them from bleeding to death when it's over. Then maybe they'll sober up and find a better way to settle their differences."

"I've got a bad feeling about this, Tal," she said, extending her arms as she shuffled toward him.

He was out the door before she could touch him. She struggled outside and into the street in time to see him round the corner at the town square. A few moments after he disappeared from view a volley of shots rang out.

"*Ta–a–al,*" she screamed.

By the time Silverthorne reached the corner, the H3 crew was driving the herd hard and fast across the open square, attempting to cross diagonally in front of

Scotty's Saloon, which was the third building from the corner, in order to reach the road west at the end of the block. Silverthorne flattened himself against the second storefront when the H3 riders started shooting. He could see puffs of pulverized stone, shattered glass, and splintered wood exploding from the wall, window, and woodwork of the front of the saloon, and then there was fire and smoke belching from gun barrels poking out the door and window.

"Tal! Come back!"

Silverthorne spun around. Marylois was at the corner, grabbing a wooden awning pole for support. She pushed some strands of damp hair back from her sweaty forehead with her other hand. *"Please!"*

"Marylois, get back around the corner! I'm coming."

Hot lead whined over Silverthorne's head and he looked back and saw that the H3 riders had reached the corner down the block where the road exited the square. They were trading shots with two of the Howells, who'd darted out of the saloon and taken cover behind a barrel and a parked wagon. Others were still shooting at the riders from the window and the doorway. Silverthorne scrambled for the corner, looking over his shoulder at the battle going on behind him. He heard the *whop* of more stray bullets and faced forward to concentrate on his running.

Marylois was still holding on to the awning post, with both hands now. Silverthorne grabbed her around the waist with his free arm as he sped by and carried her around the corner. She slumped against him and he thought she'd fainted. When they were safe behind the wall of the building he set his valise down, gently lowered Marylois to the ground, and pulled his hat off to fan her face. He stopped in the middle of the first wave. Her eyes were open and staring. Her mouth was agape, as if uttering a silent scream. Then he saw the blood on her dress, just under the left breast. He laid a finger on her jugular just to be sure, then put two fingers to her eyelids and gently closed them. He sat on the ground next to the body and hung his head between his knees and wept. That's how Sheriff Sweet found him when he came running up the street from the hotel.

"Oh, my God!" said Sweet. "Who shot Miz Silverthorne?"

"My fault," said Silverthorne with a sob. "When I heard the first shot I went to see if I could moderate the situation. She was afraid for me. She came after me. She was hit by a stray bullet."

"Howells and Holloways, I reckon. Well, the shootin's stopped. I better go see if anybody's still livin'. Ah . . . I know it's a bad time for you, Doc, but I see you've got your medical kit. . . ."

"If anyone needs attention you may send for me," said Silverthorne with a nod. "I'll wait here for a few minutes before I take Marylois home."

Silverthorne was still sitting by his wife's body when Sheriff Sweet came back around the corner.

"Didn't figure you'd still be here, Doc. Thought somebody would've come along to help carry Miz Silverthorne home by now."

"Don't need any help, Sweet. She doesn't weigh . . ." Silverthorne took a deep breath. "Anyhow, everyone's out at the track. I guess they didn't hear the shots, what with all the yelling and cheering out there.

"I assume no one's in need of my services at the saloon, or you'd have sent for me."

"No. Merrit got a little bullet burn on the arm. Nothin' serious. Found a little blood on the ground down at the corner, so at least one of the H3 boys was hit, but they all got away."

"I'll go out and check on them soon as I can."

"Henry Adkins is dead."

"Henry? How? He's got no stake in the Howell-

Holloway fracas. I'd expect him to be hiding behind the bar.''

"Not this time. 'Pears Mart had been makin' fun of him, and he tried to arrest Mart to keep him from startin' trouble with the Holloways, and Mart shot him.''

"Henry must have been some agitated. I never thought he had it in him to stand up to anybody.''

"Neither did Mart. Took him by surprise and he just reacted when Adkins pulled his shooter.''

"And they admitted Adkins was trying to make an arrest?''

"I'm sure the Howells didn't aim to. That fellar Ramey let it slip while I was questioning him. He's pretty rattled by the whole thing.''

"I'm glad you're smart enough not to try what Adkins did.''

"It'll take a company of Rangers to put Mart Howell under arrest. That's what it'll come to after I file my report. You can't go and shoot a duly appointed officer who's in the line of duty and just ride away from it. At the same time, Texas courts are very lenient when it comes to a case of two armed men in a shoot-out.''

Silverthorne nodded, for he'd taken notice of the fact. "Under normal circumstances, Mart could give himself up to stand trial with a high expectation of being acquitted. But not now, with public sentiment running so strong against the Howells. Mart won't take a chance on getting a change of venue.''

"Onliest thing Mart will take a chance on is that hog leg he totes on his hip,'' said Sweet, looking up to watch the Howells ride out of the alley and turn south toward the Rail H.

Calvin Howell pulled out of the bunch long enough to speak to Silverthorne. "Sheriff Sweet told us about your wife, Doc. All I can say is, I'm sorry, and you know what direction that slug come from.''

"No one's to blame but me, Calvin. She came after

me. It was an accident. But I know where the bullet came from.''

A short while later Silverthorne wasn't so sure.

Chance Rosser walked down from the saloon to express his condolences. He insisted on helping Silverthorne carry Marylois home. They laid her out on the operating table in Silverthorne's little clinic. Rosser looked at her for a long moment, and Silverthorne was surprised to see strong emotion pulling at his features. The gambler left with tears in his eyes.

When Rosser was gone, Silverthorne undressed Marylois to examine the gunshot wound. The back of her dress was bloody as well as the front. The slug had passed all the way through her body. The hole in her back was the smaller of the two.

She was shot in the back! He'd thought she was facing west all the while she was standing at the corner. Could it be that while he was looking behind him she'd turned to run, been shot all the way through her body from behind, and turned back around, all the while holding on to the awning post? It seemed impossible, but that was the only explanation. Unless one of the Howell supporters had joined the fight from one of the buildings on the east side of the square. If so, he was so close to Marylois that a wayward shot was inexcusable. Hadn't Silverthorne heard a shot from that direction? He couldn't remember for sure, there had been so much noise and confusion.

Silverthorne washed the blood away and dressed Marylois in her favorite blue dress for her burial.

TWELVE

*THE LAST DAY WITH MARYLOIS HAD ALWAYS
haunted Silverthorne. He wished he hadn't walked away
from her when she reached for him. He'd never forgive
himself for that. Perhaps it was justice that he was lying
here bleeding to death from a gunshot wound similar to
the one that had taken her life, but different enough that
he would have plenty of time for final remorse.*

Silverthorne buried Marylois early the morning after she
was killed. He didn't want a lot of people around. Just
himself and the undertaker and his crew. Chance Rosser
was there, too. He must have seen them carrying her out
to the cemetery. He was awake mighty early for a gambler.

After the coffin was lowered, Silverthorne read some
of Marylois's favorite passages of scripture, said a few
words of farewell, and walked away. Rosser walked with
him back to the house, where Silverthorne shook his
hand and thanked him for his concern.

"Doctor, perhaps this is an inappropriate time to

speak of it,'' said Rosser, ''but I want you to know that, should you seek vengeance against those responsible for Mrs. Silverthorne's death, I shall be honored to back your play.''

Silverthorne looked Rosser in the eye, puzzled that the man was willing to risk his life over the death of the wife of a man he hardly knew.

''I'm much obliged, Mr. Rosser,'' said Silverthorne, ''but I'm afraid you're looking at the responsible party. If I'd stayed home as she wanted, she wouldn't have come into harm's way. I don't blame the H3. In fact, I'm not even sure it was one of their strays that hit her.''

Rosser raised his yellow brows.

''She was shot in the back,'' Silverthorne explained, ''and I think she was facing the action when it happened. But I was looking over my shoulder, so I can't say for certain. Whatever the case, I'll say this again: It was my fault she was there and I don't hold the H3 responsible. In fact, I'm about to saddle up and go out there to see if anyone needs a doctor.''

''You're riding out to the Holloways'? Doctor, you're going to have to choose one side or the other, real soon!'' Rosser turned on his heel and stalked away.

Silverthorne was greeted by the Holloways with heartfelt expressions of regret that their clash with the Howells had occasioned the death of his wife. Sheriff Sweet had ridden by the H3 the previous day to see if they'd suffered any casualties and told them about it. Again Silverthorne expressed his judgment of the matter, emphasizing for their sakes that she was shot from behind and he didn't think she'd ever turned her back to the fracas.

''Maybe all the Howell sympathizers weren't at the saloon,'' said Holloway, wanting very much to believe it was not one of the H3's bullets that had struck Marylois. ''Oliver, did you see anyone suspicious when you circled the square through the backstreets?''

"Aw, Pa, don't be telling everybody you didn't let me fight," said Oliver, shamefaced.

"Well, what did you see?"

Oliver's eyes remained downcast and he waited a moment before he answered, as if he were collecting his thoughts. "Didn't see nothin', Pa. Everybody was down at the racetrack, I reckon."

"*Anything*. Didn't see anything."

"That's what I said, Pa."

"No, you said—oh, never mind," said Holloway with a sigh. "Doc, I see you brought your Gladstone. Fred Hunziker caught a slug in the thigh. I wish you'd have a look at it."

"Sheriff Sweet said he found blood on your trail, so I rode out here soon as I could."

As Holloway led the way to the bunkhouse he told Silverthorne he'd managed to get the bullet out of Hunziker's thigh after they got home with the herd.

Hunziker's injury was a nasty sight, but at least it was just a flesh wound. Alice Holloway had cleaned and dressed the wound, but Silverthorne laved it again with carbolic and rebandaged the thigh. He took Hunziker's temperature—103 degrees. He would try to lower the fever with cold compresses and give the cowhand a few drops of laudanum to ease the pain.

Hunziker's fever had not broken by sundown, so Silverthorne decided to stay the night in the H3 bunkhouse. Andres usually had the bunk next to Hunziker, but he moved to another so the doctor would have a place to stretch out that was close to the patient. Silverthorne had a knack for waking himself up at regular intervals during overnight vigils at bedside, although he doubted he would sleep very much anyway. The ache in his heart had allowed him little rest the night before, and he did not expect this night to be any better. He was glad to have something to do.

Silverthorne was dozing when the hooded riders came. They began to walk their horses slowly before they came within earshot of the H3 bunkhouse. There was a whinny from the horse trap but the riders picked up on their reins and kept their mounts from answering. They oozed single file out of the darkness into the meager light coming through the bunkhouse window from the lamp Silverthorne kept burning on a bedside table, and lined up in front of the building. Ten of them there, and ten more rode on past to surround the ranch house. One of the riders in front of the bunkhouse held an extra horse on lead by the bridle reins.

Silverthorne came half-awake at the sound of careful footsteps, but he didn't open his eyes, thinking one of the hands was going out to the privy. At the sound of five carbines being cocked in unison he bolted upright in the bed. Andres and Pabst reacted as Silverthorne had; Hunziker, too, but slowly due to the effect of the laudanum. Lupe had been sleeping with his hand on his front-side revolver, as usual, and he sprang off his bunk with pistol in hand and firing. The vigilante right in front of him doubled over and crumpled to the floor, but the one on the right crashed his rifle barrel hard against Lupe's cranium and laid him out on the floor next to the wounded man. The other three held their rifles on the cowhands. The one who'd struck Lupe quickly covered Silverthorne.

Another hooded figure stepped through the door. "What happened?" he said in a hoarse voice.

The vigilante covering Silverthorne answered, also disguising his voice. "The nigger sleeps with his six-gun, I reckon. He woke up shootin'. We've got a man down."

"Ain't too bad," said the man who'd been shot, struggling to his feet. "Just help me to my hoss. I can ride."

"Better bring the doc along just in case," said the

man who'd entered last. He helped the wounded vigilante outside and sent two more men to haul Lupe out. They relieved him of his second revolver and his bowie knife before they piled him on the extra horse and tied his hands to the pommel.

Silverthorne did not sleep with his revolver, but they checked him over before they put him up behind Lupe. Lupe was regaining consciousness, but Silverthorne had to help him stay in the saddle as the mob and their captives swept out of the yard and rode off into the darkness. When they were out of rifle range, the vigilantes slowed their pace and plodded on through the darkness. A man was assigned to ride a distance back from the main body to listen for pursuing riders. There were none.

The leader of the vigilantes asked the man Lupe shot if he wanted to stop so they could build a fire and have the doctor examine his injury.

"Naw, I don't think it's too bad," Silverthorne heard him say. "First let's do what we come to do."

Silverthorne doubted he could do much for him anyway. They had forgotten to bring his medical kit.

When Silverthorne was sure that Lupe was wide-awake he spoke quietly in his ear. "I thought Major Holloway and his men would have caught up to us by now."

"Ain't comin'," said Lupe. "Not tonight, anyways. It's just him and Alec and C. F., and they's at least twenty men in this gang. Major can't be messin' with the mob, nohow. He's just glad it weren't him they come for."

"They want you because of those rustlers you shot for Holloway, I assume."

"The mob don't care nothin' about them rustlers. They mad 'cause a colored man kilt some white men."

"I know that, Lupe. Yet Holloway never revealed which of his men did the shooting."

"The rustler that got away, he knows it weren't but one man done the killin'."

"Ah," said Silverthorne, "and you showed up with that monogrammed Winchester."

"Yeah, and they know it ain't likely the major would have them Dutchy boys doin' that kind of work."

"So the escaped rustler got word to the mob some- how."

"Could be he's a member hisself. They protects one another no matter what any of them does. They's all afeared one of them will squeal on the rest. Whatever you do, Doc, don't let on you recognizes none of them."

"I don't," said Silverthorne. He put his hands to Lupe's wrists and began to untie the rope.

"Ain't no use, Doc. No way you can get me away from them. My time has come, and when it comes your time you just gotta go on and go. I ain't afeared. But, Doc, I wants you to take care of Tree, my *Trigueño*. He's a good pony and he's yours now."

A vigilante reined in close and tapped Silverthorne's shoulder with his pistol to get his attention. Then he touched the barrel to the mouthhole of his hood. Silver- thorne stopped talking, but when the vigilante pulled away he finished untying Lupe's hands.

"Lupe, reach up and slip the bridle," Silverthorne whispered.

"Better not, Doc. They determined to hang me, but they won't do nothin' to you if you don't make 'em mad."

"Just do it!"

Lupe heaved a sigh and leaned forward as if he were still groggy. He ran a hand up the horse's neck beneath the mane, found the throatlatch, unbuckled it, and shoved the headstall over the horse's ears. When the horse felt the slack he opened his mouth and dropped the bit. Silverthorne heard the bit rattle across the inci- sors as the bridle fell. He kicked the horse viciously in the flanks. The startled beast leaped ahead and burst through the riders in the font of the pack. Silverthorne clung to Lupe's torso to keep from falling and kept on kicking.

The vigilantes preferred to see Lupe swing, but some of them pulled their revolvers and fired when they realized he was making a break. A bullet stung the fleeing horse on the hip and it lunged ahead even faster.

"I'm jumping, Lupe. Run like hell!" shouted Silverthorne. He let go of Lupe and pushed hard against the cantle, propelling himself away from the flying hooves. The ground came up quick and slammed against his body, driving the breath from his lungs. Silverthorne ignored the pain in his chest, scrambled to his feet, and charged into the brush before he collapsed. Just in time! Twenty horses galloped across the spot where he'd landed.

When he was finally able to breathe normally, Silverthorne got to his feet and stumbled after the mob, following the trail of torn-up sod in the dim moonlight. He had to find out whether or not Lupe had escaped.

Two hours passed and he was feeling the aching effects of the fall from the running horse. The hoofprints were not as plain, indicating the horsemen had slowed their pace. Silverthorne had to walk stooped over and concentrate on the ground to keep from losing them.

Silverthorne froze in his tracks. What was that creaking sound? Then he knew. He'd found what he was dreading. He lifted his eyes. Just ahead, a tall elm tree was silhouetted against the lightening eastern sky. A body was swinging in the breeze by a rope that hung from a big limb about fifteen feet off the ground.

"Oh, Lupe," said Silverthorne, dropping to his knees. "I failed to save my babies, I failed to save my wife, and now I've failed to save you." He took a deep breath. "And how many in between?"

Silverthorne got up and approached the tree. The

hangman's noose had been tossed over the limb and the
other end of the rope was tied to the tree trunk in the
usual fashion. Silverthorne fished his pocketknife out,
supported the body upon his shoulder and walked it
close to the trunk and cut the rope. As soon as the hemp
was severed he quickly caught the torso and eased the
body to the ground.

The mob intended their victims to hang for a spell, as
a grisly warning to any who might be inclined to defy
their rule. If Major Holloway was reluctant to fetch
Lupe's body home for proper burial, Silverthorne would
do it himself, and to hell with the consequences.

Silverthorne rested until full daylight and started his
trek back to the H3. He was glad he was wearing his
low-heeled boots. He had a pair with heels more than
twice as high, but he only wore them when he was cow-
boying. Still, his feet were burning by the time he got
back on H3 range. The sun was high and his shirt was
soaked through with perspiration. He breathed a sigh of
relief when he reached Doubletree Creek, but he still had
a long way to go.

After he drank of the cool, clear water, Silverthorne
decided to soak his weary feet for a few minutes. He
was sitting on the bank drying his feet when he heard
the sounds of splashing water and horseshoes on rock
from upstream. Quickly he pulled his socks and boots
on and ran to higher ground so he could see. Oliver
Holloway had crossed the stream and was about to ride
out of sight behind a tangle of brush.

"Ollie!" yelled Silverthorne. He ran to the brush
where he'd last seen him, yelling his name all the way.
But Oliver had ridden on.

"That boy must be deaf as a post," muttered Silverthorne, looking off in the direction Oliver had taken.
Where was he going, anyway? He shouldn't be riding
off by himself, conditions being what they were. Especially not toward the Rail H boundary.

Silverthorne's eyes narrowed. Could it be . . . ? How would she know to meet him? Maybe they had a regular meeting day arranged from before the outbreak of hostilities. If Oliver and Rachel were still talking, maybe there was hope for their families. Perhaps he should follow and see if he could get them to help him arrange a powwow. Silverthorne struck out on Oliver's trail.

He'd walked about a mile when he realized he was dreading seeing Rachel with Oliver again. Why? Was he jealous? Was that the real reason he was following Oliver? His wife one day in her grave and he's worrying about a relationship with another woman? He hadn't been able to get Rachel off his mind for the last couple of months Marylois was alive, so why should he feel so guilty now? But he did.

Yet he kept on walking toward the cedar copse where he'd found Rachel with Oliver the time before.

When Silverthorne finally topped the last rise before the cedar thicket he was surprised to see Oliver sitting his horse about eighty rods ahead. His first impulse was to hurry and catch up to Oliver. He took three steps and halted in his tracks. Oliver should be anxious to see Rachel, yet he'd ridden very slowly, and now he seemed reluctant to enter the cedar brake. Something was wrong. Was Oliver being torn by conflicting loyalties? Why else would he be holding back?

Silverthorne carefully worked his way through the brush and approached Oliver's position as close as he could without giving away his presence. When Oliver rode into the cedars, Silverthorne followed. He crept up to the clearing, expecting to hear Rachel's voice any second.

"You didn't tell us about that nigger gunman your pappy hired."

That wasn't Rachel's voice! It was masculine, but it wasn't Oliver's.

Oliver's was the next voice Silverthorne heard.

"I didn't know Pa hired him to hunt rustlers. Honest, Briley. Besides, with all the rustling goin' on in these parts, what were the chances you all would be the ones he'd catch?"

" 'Twas a good chance, I'd say, seein's how we was specializing in your pappy's beef."

When the reality of what he was overhearing hit Silverthorne's brain, he closed his eyes and bowed his head. Major Holloway had said it was as if the rustlers knew ahead of time where the H3 crew would be working on a given day. And they did! They'd been warned by his own son!

"Can't you get a couple more men and get started again?" said Oliver. "I promise I'll let you know if Pa hires another detective."

"I don't know. We'd have to find another hideaway and build another holdup. I'll see about it. Meet me out behind the bathhouse at Lampkin Springs next race day, about two o'clock. And don't keep me waiting like you done today."

"It was a wonder I was able to come at all today. Pa wanted to take me with him and C. F. and Alec to hunt for Lupe Proffit and Dr. Silverthorne, but Ma talked him out of it."

"Mama's still wet-nursin' you, is she?"

Oliver didn't reply.

"Well," said Briley with a sarcastic laugh, "if we get our little deal workin' again you can take your cut and fly the nest."

So Briley was the rustler who fled the scene when Lupe killed his partners. He clearly knew about Lupe's demise, else he'd have been inquisitive when Oliver promised to warn him if Holloway hired *another* range detective, and when Oliver mentioned his father was out looking for Proffit and Silverthorne. Silverthorne hoped the significance of the rustler's unconcern did not penetrate Oliver's thinking. But it did.

"Ain't you curious about what happened to Lupe?" said Oliver.

"Lupe?" said Briley, realizing his mistake. "Oh, you mean the nigger detective."

"Yeah. But you didn't say nothin' when I said—you already know about it, don't you? How—"

Oliver's eyes got big and his mouth dropped open. Briley had drawn his pistol before Oliver could finish sorting things out in his mind.

Silverthorne knew Briley would shoot. He had to. He couldn't let Oliver ride away knowing he'd been under one of those hoods last night.

Silverthorne bolted from his hiding place. *"No,"* he bellowed, trying to distract Briley's aim. Too late! Briley's revolver roared and Oliver catapulted backward over a knee-high boulder, vainly trying to get his own pistol up but dropping it as he fell. Silverthorne dove at Oliver's .45, scooped it up, and rolled over beside him behind the boulder. Briley had gotten off two shots at Silverthorne after he drilled Oliver, but failed to hit the moving target. He was desperate. He could leave no witness to the conversation. He rushed the boulder. Silverthorne anticipated the rush. He rolled over to the side of the rock and shot from the ground. The bullet struck Briley in the neck and blew the back of his skull away.

Silverthorne lay on his back, his chest heaving. He felt sick. It wasn't because of what the bullet had done to Briley's head. Silverthorne had seen so much blood and guts during the war that mayhem no longer affected him that way. It was the thought that a doctor was supposed to save lives, and he'd been forced to take one.

He heard Oliver gasp. Silverthorne scrambled to his side, wishing he had his medical kit. He took one look at the hole in Ollie's chest and he knew instruments and medicine wouldn't make any difference.

Oliver's eyes fluttered open and he looked at Silverthorne. "You again," he said in a whisper. "Eavesdropping.'' Oliver sucked a ragged breath into his lungs. ''Please don't tell my folks.''

Silverthorne wagged his head. ''I won't. It would break their hearts. But *why*, Ollie?''

''For money. So me and Rachel could run off together.''

Oliver gritted his teeth and a trickle of blood ran down his jaw from the corner of his mouth. ''It hurts, Doc,'' he said, closing his eyes.

''I know, Ollie, I know how it hurts,'' said Silverthorne, patting his shoulder and wishing he had an anodyne to give him.

''No, you don't,'' said Oliver. ''You ain't never been shot.'' He forced a small laugh and looked Silverthorne in the eye. ''But now you know how it hurts to lose your woman, don't you? Sheriff Sweet said you cried like a baby.''

Silverthorne glared at Oliver. His father had sent him down the alley to circle the town, just before Marylois was killed. He had a grievance—he thought Silverthorne was trying to take Rachel away from him. But Oliver wouldn't . . . *Ask him! Before it's too late!*

''Oliver, did you shoot Marylois?''

''Oh, no, Doc. I wouldn't do nothin' like that! 'Twasn't none of our side done it.''

''Oliver, who did you see? Oliver!''

Silverthorne shook his shoulder. Oliver's eyes stared at Silverthorne, but they did not see him. Oliver Holloway would never answer another question.

THIRTEEN

OLIVER WAS RIGHT. SILVERTHORNE REALLY HADN'T known what it felt like to be shot. But he did now. He wasn't shot in the chest, so the pain probably wasn't as severe as Oliver's had been, but the end result would be the same. Except that there would be no one to take Silverthorne's body from this mountainside, no better place to take it, and no grieving loved ones to shed tears over him.

Silverthorne stopped to water the horses when he reached Doubletree Creek. He rode Briley's bay and led Oliver's gray with the bodies tied to the saddle, one across the seat and the other across the horse's loin, just behind the cantle.

When he left the stream and topped out of the draw he saw Holloway and his two healthy hands coming along the track Silverthorne's boots had left earlier in the day. Pabst was leading an extra horse with Lupe's body on it.

Holloway's face was ashen. He stared at Oliver's

horse and the two limp forms upon its back. Finally he looked at Silverthorne.

"Oliver found the other rustler," Silverthorne explained. "There was a confrontation and neither survived."

"You saw it?"

Silverthorne nodded. "I saw Ollie ride by the creek when I stopped to drink and rest my feet. He was out of earshot so I followed him, hoping he'd stop so I could catch up and ride double with him back to the house. I got close enough to hear the man admit who he was, and I tried to help, but I didn't get there in time and I had no weapon."

"You'd just have gotten yourself killed too, no doubt." Holloway rode close and took the lead rope from Silverthorne. "The Howells will pay dearly for this," he said as he turned toward home.

"From what I heard him say, that rustler was an independent," said Silverthorne. "He had no connection with the Howells."

Holloway gave no indication that he'd heard.

Silverthorne spent another night in the H3 bunkhouse to make sure Hunziker was mending properly. In the morning he returned to his empty house in Lampkin Springs, riding Rudy and leading Tree. At least he thought the house was empty. The first clue that such was not the case was the Rail H cow pony in the extra stall of the little stable out back. Silverthorne put *Trigueño* in Rudy's stall and hitched Rudy to a post.

Somehow he wasn't surprised to find Rachel waiting in a chair in the reception room.

"The door wasn't locked," she said.

"Nobody locks their doors in Lampkin Springs, except places of business. You know that, Rachel."

"Well, this is a place of business, isn't it?"

"Supposed to be, I reckon, but I don't think of it like

that. . . . What's wrong, Rachel? Is someone out at the ranch sick or injured?'' Silverthorne didn't really think she'd come to fetch medical help to the ranch.

Rachel answered with a wag of her head. She got up and walked toward him. ''Where you been, Tal? I've been waitin' all day.'' It was the first time she'd ever called him anything but ''Doc.''

''I've been out at the H3 treating a bullet wound.''

''Who was shot?''

''Hunziker. He'll be all right. But . . . Rachel, I've got some bad news. You better sit down.''

His direct look and serious expression stopped her short of reaching out to touch him.

''What is it, Doc? Go ahead and spit it out.''

''Oliver's been killed, Rachel.''

Rachel stepped back and eased into the chair. ''But they said he wasn't there.''

''Not in the skirmish on Saturday, Rachel. Yesterday. He confronted a cow thief out in the south pasture. Both of them were killed.''

''He was the only boy my age who ever took a shine to me. I never expected to ever see him again, but I never thought he'd go and get hisself killed. Poor li'l Ollie. . . .'' Rachel stared at the floor. Her eyes were misty but she didn't cry.

''You never expected to see him again? Why?''

Rachel leaned back in her chair, took a deep breath, and looked at the ceiling. ''Because of what happened night before last,'' she said as she exhaled.

At first Silverthorne thought she was referring to the mob's raid on the H3, but she couldn't know about that. He waited for Rachel to continue.

''Sheriff Sweet and half a dozen of his minutemen surrounded Mart and Merrit's house and walked in on them about daybreak, while they were sleeping. They arrested Uncle Mart for killin' Marshal Adkins and took him off to Georgetown and locked him up.''

"I thought Sweet was going to let the Rangers take care of Mart."

"That's what he told Mart Saturday. Uncle Mart was gonna hide out before Sweet had time to get the governor to send the Rangers. But I reckon Sweet had him figured for that, so he come in unexpected before Uncle Mart could get away."

"It's best that Mart stands trial, Rachel. He'll be acquitted and he won't have to hide out."

"He won't be acquitted in this county."

"He'll get a change of venue."

"No he won't. And no bail. Daddy and Uncle Mitch went to Georgetown yesterday and the talk is that Judge Blackburn's already said he'll not allow either. You see, Uncle Mart's got a reputation for a heller. He's been before Blackburn's court for several shootin' scrapes and he's always got off. Blackburn figures it's time he paid the piper."

Silverthorne was silent for a moment, absorbing what she'd said. "Mart's in a pickle, all right. But what's all this got to do with you not seeing Oliver again?"

"We're changin' our range, Doc. There'll be no peace for the Howells in Texas anymore. We've already commenced gathering all our cows we can find. We're gonna sell them to Cooksey and Clayton over in Coleman County on our way west, except for three or four hundred head of young breeders we'll drive to New Mexico for seed stock. Doc, they say there's grama grass tall as a horse's belly out west of the Pecos!" Rachel paused to let her announcement sink in.

Silverthorne wasn't surprised. He'd heard Calvin Howell talk about New Mexico before, and how crowded central Texas had become since the war. But Calvin would not leave without Mart. That meant they were planning a jailbreak, which would make their departure imperative, and force Calvin to abandon his vendetta against Percival Holloway.

They'd have to enlist the help of all their loyal friends to pull off the jailbreak, and those men would probably go west with the Howells. When Oliver said the man who shot Marylois wasn't on the Holloways' side of the fight, Silverthorne took him to mean the killer was a Howell partisan. No doubt he'd ride with them to free Mart, and he'd probably go to New Mexico with them. The man should be called to account for his carelessness.

"Tal, come with us!" said Rachel, breaking in on his thoughts. "There's nothin' here for you no more, except bad memories."

"Is that what you came to see me about?"

"Yes, and to see if I could bring some comfort to you. We're all real sorry about Miz Silverthorne."

Silverthorne wondered what kind of comfort she had in mind.

"Will you come with us to New Mexico, Tal?" she said, rising from her chair.

"I'll talk to your father about it," said Silverthorne. "I've got to get some rest now, but I'll ride out this evening."

Rachel beamed, and for a moment she was poised to fling herself against him, but she decided not to press her luck. She turned and snatched her Stetson off the hat rack.

"Come out in time for supper, Tal. I'll fix you somethin' special."

Silverthorne raised his brows.

"Oh, I know Ma's always complainin' that I don't help her around the house enough, but I'm a good cook when I want to be. You'll see!"

Silverthorne walked her to the stable.

"Where'd you get the brown?" she wondered as she led her horse out.

"Guadalupe Proffit bequeathed him to me, just before the mob hanged him."

Rachel's eyes got big. "The mob? Don't tell me

they're stirrin' things up again. That could mean trouble
for us if they believe the rumors Major Holloway started.
How did they—''

"I'll tell all of you about it tonight, Rachel. I've got
to get some shut-eye if I'm gonna make it in time for
supper."

Rachel flashed her smile again and bounded into the
saddle. "*Hasta la vista,* Tal," she said.

When she was gone, Silverthorne moved Tree into the
stall she'd vacated and unsaddled Rudy and put him in
his regular place. He took a manure fork from the tool
rack and picked up a pile of horse apples Rachel's mount
had deposited. He walked into the backyard and dumped
them on a pile he kept for fertilizer for Marylois's little
vegetable garden.

Silverthorne gazed at her collection of tomato, cucum-
ber, and pepper plants. The squash vines had withered
and dried up. He felt like his heart had done the same,
and left a hollow in his chest. He stood the manure fork
against the stable wall and stumbled into the empty
house.

After a few hours' respite in the deep sleep of exhaustion, Silverthorne awoke to the same feeling of empty
spirit and empty home. He was glad for the opportunity
to get away from the house and he looked forward to
being in the company of other people. Except Rachel.
He knew what she had on her mind and it was too soon.

Did Calvin and Martha know about their daughter's
interest in the human, horse, and cow doctor and part-
time cowboy from Virginia? Probably. Rachel wasn't
one to hide her feelings. And what really were her feelings for the cowboy Dr. Silverthorne? There was a
strong physical attraction between them, that much was
certain. Could there ever be a deep and loving friend-
ship, such as he'd shared with Marylois? Would he ever
feel that he could trust Rachel to be true to her vow?

Only time would tell, and he must keep the situation under control until he knew the answers.

Mealtime at the Howells' was more pleasant than the last time, despite the problems that oppressed the family. They were excited about their plans to seek a fresh start in New Mexico, and gratified that Silverthorne was joining them. By his presence the Howells at least gained a moral victory over the Holloways.

Silverthorne brought them up to date on the events of the past two days and how what he'd seen and heard proved that Major Holloway's charges against the Howells were unjustified.

"For a while there I was thinking you was like them baseball players back East, Doc," said Calvin.

"How's that, Cal?"

"An article I read in the *Austin Statesman* said a lot of the best players are quitting their hometown teams to play for opposing teams for money."

"They're gettin' paid to play a game?" Merrit exclaimed. "Imagine that!"

"What's the world coming to?" said Martha.

"I wish somebody would pay me to rope steers for fun," said Chad.

Rachel just looked at Silverthorne and smiled.

"Holloway did pay me, Cal," said Silverthorne. "He paid the same for day work as the other ranchers. I reckon a lot of folks thought me disloyal to 'the home team,' as you put it, when I befriended a Unionist, but for me the war was over a long time ago."

"Not in Texas, it ain't," said Merrit.

"Well, let's hope it is in New Mexico," Silverthorne replied.

"If you'll help us gather the rest of our cows and Mitch Warner's, we'll be on our way that much sooner," said Calvin. "Ramey's comin' out tomorrow and Jimmy Grizell and Allen Whitecraft will be here the next day. They're all goin' west with us, plus Scott and Rosser.''

Grizell and Whitecraft. Two of Calvin's close friends who were in town Saturday, but not at the saloon. Silverthorne would bet his bottom dollar one of them was the Howell partisan Oliver saw in the alley.

"Will you lend us a hand, Doc?" said Calvin.

"Huh? Oh . . . sure, Calvin. But I'll have to get my stuff together first. I hope you don't mind hauling some medical supplies and my library in one of your wagons.''

"You help us push them breeders to New Mexico and we won't even charge you no freight," said Calvin with a chuckle.

The next day Silverthorne rode back to Lampkin Springs for the last time.

It was a sad and lonely chore, disposing of Marylois's personal effects and most of the things they'd brought with them from Virginia. Some things he was able to sell and the rest he left with Mrs. Huling to be distributed by her group of charity workers as they saw fit. After two heart-wrenching days, on the morning of the third he packed his indispensables on Rudy and led him out behind Tree upon the road to the Rail H.

It occurred to Silverthorne that he should ride by the Holloways' to bid them farewell, although his decision to go west with the Howells would be tantamount to taking their side of the issue as far as the major was concerned. If Holloway still blamed the Howells for Oliver's death and he learned about their plans to leave he might try to get even before they could get away. And if he knew about Mart's capture he would guess that Calvin would lead a raid on the Georgetown jail before he left. It would be best for Silverthorne to leave without saying good-bye.

Within five days of Silverthorne's return to the Rail H the gather was completed and the wagons loaded. It was time to fetch Mart Howell from the Georgetown jail. Calvin left Chad, Rachel, Silverthorne, and Charlie Ramey to hold the herd and rode away with Merrit, Mitch Warner, Jim Grizell, and Allen Whitecraft. They were joined in Lampkin Springs by Jerry Scott and Chance Rosser. The seven heavily armed men expected to reach Georgetown after dark, hoped to be back to the Rail H by sunrise, and out of the county by nightfall.

If their mission was successful, Mart would flee Sheriff Al Sweet's jurisdiction as fast as a fresh young horse could carry him to the Rail H and another could carry him across Burnet County to the Tanyard Crossing of the Colorado. It was planned that he should wait at the tanyard for the herd to catch up so as to join the drive northwest to Coleman County, where most of the cattle were to be sold.

Silverthorne was riding night herd with Ramey and wondering what had happened in Georgetown when he saw the fire. It was just a glow on the horizon, but he knew what it meant. He was less than two miles from the ranch house and his first thought was for Rachel, Chad, and Martha. He shouted at Ramey to stay with the herd and rode hard for the house, unlimbering his Peacemaker on the way. When he was close enough he could see it was the barn, not the house, that was burning. The raging flames lit up the area around the barn and it appeared he was the only one on the scene. The screams of the terrified animals in the barn would soon penetrate the sleep of someone in the house. Silverthorne holstered his revolver and rode for the horse corral next to the barn. The Rail H cow pony he was riding rolled its eyes, fought the bit, and shied away from the inferno, but Silverthorne yanked him around and spurred viciously, forcing him up against the corral gate so as to pull the bar and spring the gate. Rudy and Tree were among the first horses to bolt through the gap and gallop away to safety.

There was nothing Silverthorne could do for the animals inside the barn.

Rachel's scream pierced the roaring of the blazes like a bullet cuts the wind. Silverthorne yanked his bronc around. There she was! Clad only in a nightshirt, she was fending the heat from her eyes with a forearm and searching for a way into the burning barn! "No, Rachel!" he yelled as he raked the spurs and drove his wild-eyed mount as if to run her down. He leaned to the right from the saddle and reached to snatch her off her feet, but at the last second the terrified horse bolted left and dumped him on top of her, knocking her to the ground. Silverthorne scrambled to his feet, grabbed Rachel around the waist, and dragged her away from the flames.

"Let me go! Let me go!" she pleaded, tears rolling down her cheeks. "Pumpkin's in there!"

"Rachel!" yelled Silverthorne, "you can't save the colt! It's too late!"

Her wiry strength took Silverthorne by surprise. She wrenched her body downward and slipped out of his grasp. He grabbed her by the wrist just before she could pull away and run back to the barn. As he spun her back around she kicked him on the shin, but she was barefoot and he hardly felt the blow through the tall top of his riding boot. She doubled up the fist of her free hand and made a looping swing at his face. Silverthorne ducked the swing and when she drew back for another try he slapped her face hard with the flat of his hand. Rachel went to her knees, stunned. Silverthorne knelt beside her and grabbed her with all his might, but she had ceased to struggle.

"Rachel, I'm so sorry. I didn't want to hit you, but I had to keep you away from the barn. There's nothing you can do for the colt and you would have been killed if you'd tried to save him. I'm sorry about the colt and I'm sorry for striking you, but I couldn't let you get away from me."

Silverthorne felt her body shudder. Once again he
held her while she cried, trying not to think about the
supple young body under the flimsy cotton beneath his
hands.

"What started the fire, Doc?"

Silverthorne looked up to see Chad and Martha approaching out of the darkness. Silverthorne slowly got
to his feet, lifting Rachel up alongside, and gently passed
her over to her mother's embrace.

"I don't know, Chad. I'll take a look around before
the flames burn out. You'd better go help Ramey keep
watch on the herd. My horse is around here somewhere.
He won't go far before he steps on a rein."

"I seen him over yonder back of the house. I'll catch
him up and be on my way in two shakes of a churndash
tail."

Chad went to catch the horse, and Martha took Rachel
to the house.

Silverthorne began to study the ground around the dis-
integrating barn by the light of the flames. It was un-
likely he'd be able to determine a strange footprint or
hoofprint in the frequently trodden, hard-packed ground.
He found nothing unusual. If the fire had been set, the
arsonist either took his coal oil container with him or
tossed it inside the barn. By the time the ruins were cool
enough to permit further investigation the Howells and
their friends would be well on their way to New Mexico.
Silverthorne supposed it really didn't matter how the fire
was started, since they were leaving anyway, but he
couldn't help but wonder.

A breeze stirred the blazes and Silverthorne looked
around to see what outbuilding might be in danger if the
wind got up. That's when he saw the hood. The white
cloth contrasted with the shadow of darkness at the edge
of the firelight. Silverthorne didn't know what it was
until he walked over and picked it up and saw the mouth

and eye holes. A corner of the mask was badly scorched, as if the wearer had gotten too close to the flames he was starting. He must have panicked and jerked the hood off and cast it aside as he ran from the scene.

Had the mob been here? Cold chills ran up his spine and Silverthorne gazed off in the direction by which they most likely took their leave. They probably rode away just before he came in sight of the barn!

What was that? Silverthorne's eyes narrowed, and he slipped the thong on his Peacemaker. He was sure he'd seen something move in the darkness.

Silverthorne hastened to get out of the illumination of the fire and crouched in the shadows, all his senses on edge. Away from the crackling flames, he could hear the light footfalls of slowly departing horses. The raiders had been sitting their horses in the dark, watching! Gloating over their handiwork!

Silverthorne thought about the colt he'd saved, only for it to die a horrible death along with the other animals helplessly trapped in the burning barn. The terrified screams of burning animals echoed in his brain and mingled with the heart-wrenching sobs of Rachel's grief. He couldn't let the raiders just turn their backs on their terrible deed and fade away into the night. He jerked the Peacemaker from the holster and jogged after them.

What would he do if he caught up to them? Before he could think of a sapient answer, he drew close enought to see there were only three riders. Where were the rest of the vigilantes? Why had only three tarried to watch the barn burn? The answer to those questions became apparent when he tripped over a root, crashed into a bush, and ended up sitting on his fanny in the middle of the trail. Silverthorne looked up at the silhouette of the last rider in time to see him twist around to take a look behind. There was something very familiar about the torso delineated by the star-bright sky, and the way the man swung his shoulders when he turned to look back.

"*Major?*"

All three riders swung their mounts and rode back to Silverthorne as he got himself to his feet. He was still clinging to the burned hood with his left fist and the Peacemaker with his right. He leveled the Colt at Major Holloway.

"I'm surprised, Major. I didn't think you'd stoop to burning barns." Silverthorne raised his left hand and waved the hood. "And trying to lay the blame on others, besides."

"What are you doing at the Rail H, Doc? Have you taken up with the Howell girl already?"

Silverthorne just glared at him and continued waving the white mask slowly back and forth.

Holloway heaved a sigh and rested his hands on the saddle horn. "Silverthorne, I'll do whatever it takes to hold on to what's mine. I'm not leaving my range. As far as Calvin Howell's concerned, one of us has got to go or one of us has got to die."

"So you figured if he interpreted the raid on his barn as a warning from the mob, maybe he'd leave." Silverthorne holstered the revolver and stuffed the hood in his waistband. "Well, that's not as bad as what I thought you'd do. Hell of a way for good stock to die, though."

"I'm sorry for that, Doc. I didn't expect the barn to burn so fast. I thought sure some of the menfolk would get out there in time to turn the stock out. Where are Calvin and the boys? You and Chad are the only men we saw."

"The others rode in to see Jerry Scott."

"Hanging out in the saloon while their barn burns." Holloway turned his head and spat. "Serves them right. By the way, what did you think I was going to do that's worse than burning a barn and blaming it on the mob?"

"You held the Howells accountable for the death of your son. I expected blood for blood."

"I know you think I'm hardheaded, Silverthorne, and maybe I am. But I studied on what you said about Briley and the other rustlers having no connection with the Howells. I know you wouldn't lie about it."

"And I won't lie to Calvin Howell, either. I'm going to show him this hoodoo hood and tell him how I found it. But that's all I'll tell him. You may be surprised at how fast he clears out, Major." Silverthorne turned to go.

"Silverthorne."

Silverthorne stopped and looked over his shoulder.

"That's the way you did with me, too, isn't it? Told me the truth about Oliver, but not all of it. *Isn't that right?*"

Silverthorne turned slowly back to face him. "Forget it, Major; you really don't want to know."

"I think I already know, Doc. Like I said, I pondered what you told me about Ollie's confrontation with Briley, and it's just too damn simple to add up. I also recall that Oliver didn't object when Alice refused to let him go with me and Alec and C. F. to look for you and Lupe. There was more to his meeting up with Briley than happenstance, wasn't there? He'd been telling the rustlers where we were going to be on the works, hadn't he?"

"It was his dying request that I should keep that secret, Major. Alice doesn't know, does she?"

"No, she still thinks he died a hero defending the ranch."

"In the end he did, when he found out Briley had been with the mob. That's what is most important. Always cherish that thought, Major."

"Thank you, Silverthorne, I shall."

"So long, Major."

Silverthorne never expected to see Percival Holloway again.

Soon after Silverthorne had made his way back to the ranch, Mart Howell showed up on a lathered horse. Mart briefly told how Calvin and his men had surrounded the Georgetown jail in the pitch-dark of early evening and how the brawny Jimmy Grizell had beat the door in with a sledgehammer ''borrowed'' from a blacksmith's shed. Once the door was broken the night deputy surrendered in the face of overwhelming odds and unlocked Mart's cell for them. A few shots were fired at them as they fled the scene, but it was a clean getaway.

Mart took Ramey's night horse and a sack of provisions and lit out for Burnet County. He wouldn't stop riding until he reached the Colorado.

Dawn was breaking by the time the rest of the men rode in from Georgetown. Martha greeted them with the vigilante hood in hand and quickly explained the glowing embers where the barn had stood. She told them Silverthorne had taken one of the two remaining night horses and ridden out to jingle the remuda, and they rode on to help recapture the fresh horses.

The sun was not far above the eastern horizon when the riders were freshly mounted, the last of the supplies loaded on the wagons, and the extra horses and the cattle bunched and ready to move.

The Howell brothers and their friends composed a formidable unit of fighting men. All were well-armed and all were crack shots, with the exception of the near-sighted Jimmy Grizell. Calvin regretted the entire crew had not been at home when the raiders came to burn the barn. His confidence in his men was such that he'd told the Georgetown deputy to inform Sheriff Sweet and his minutemen that the Rail H would be exiting the county by way of Russel Gap, in case he wanted to try to stop them.

He didn't.

So Silverthorne and the Howell clan rode west for New Mexico, away from the turmoils of central Texas.

And into more trouble than they'd ever known.

PART
II

SEVEN RIVERS, NEW MEXICO

"Whoop-a-la-ya, go along ye little dogies,
You're bound for a land you never have known;
Whooping and yelling and shoving the dogies,
We're bound for New Mex for to find us a home."

FOURTEEN

THE RAIL H GROUP CROSSED THE COLORADO ON THE second day out, the San Saba on the fourth, and three days later forded the Colorado again as the hard-riding crew took the huge herd of cattle into Coleman County. At the holding pens of Cooksey and Clayton they separated about three hundred head, mostly heifers, with some cows and bulls. They threw a few head of steers in with the breeders, hoping to make them easier to handle, for a mixed herd is less troublesome than a strictly breeder herd.

Calvin collected his gold for the surplus cattle and the little herd was pushed back across the Colorado and up the Lower Concho to the junction of the north, south, and middle prongs of the river. They selected a grassy flat and put the cattle on their heads. They would take a day to rest before continuing their quest to the west along the Middle Concho.

Silverthorne knew that Calvin would have no dealings with the military if it could be avoided, so he volunteered to ride to nearby Fort Concho to inquire about conditions along the trail to the Pecos. Chance Rosser offered to accompany him.

"Wal, did you smooth-talkin' Virginny boys get them blue bellies to admit to any information?" asked Calvin when Silverthorne and Rosser rode back to camp shortly after noon.

"We were advised to stay out of that dirty little village across the river from the fort if we don't want trouble," said Rosser. "But should I go over there tonight for a game of chance, I'm confident some blue-clad gentlemen would donate their Yankee pay to our cause."

"Better save your luck for the Pecos trail," said Calvin. "What did they say about grass, water, and Indians?"

"Lots of beeves been down the Goodnight-Loving cow path this year," said Silverthorne. "Not much grass left. It's about seventy miles from the headwaters of the Middle Concho to the Pecos."

"That's a five-or six-day drive," said Calvin, "maybe seven. And according to my tell, they's not many water holes between the Concho and the Pecos."

Rosser nodded. "The soldiers mentioned Mustang Holes and Flat Rock Ponds, but at last report they were about dried up."

"And there's a place called Wild China Pond about a dozen miles east of Castle Mountain," said Silverthorne, "but it's most likely dry this late in the year, too. There's another twelve miles of desert west of the mountain to Horsehead Crossing on the Pecos."

"Ain't there no water holes in the mountain?"

"Yes, but most of them are alkaline, not fit to drink. There's a good seep spring at that ruins of the old Butterfield stage station at the west end of the gap in the mountain. From what the soldiers told us, I doubt it's adequate for watering the herd, but we might be able to water the horses there. They said by the time we get that far, if the wind is right the cattle will smell the Pecos and stampede to the river."

"I've heard some snaky stories about pileups at

Horsehead," said Rosser, "cattle drowning, getting bogged down in quicksand, or just drinking themselves to death. Lots of cows die of thirst before they ever get to the Pecos."

"I know," said Calvin. "Cooksey told me one of John Chisum's drives left Coleman County with eleven hundred steers and got to Fort Stanton, New Mexico, with six of 'em. But he's had some successful drives, too. Goodnight and Loving took a couple thousand head through to Fort Sumner in sixty-six with eighteen hands. Course they lost a lot of stock along the way, but we've got less than four hundred head and eleven drovers. Chad, Rosser, and the doc are takin' turns riding herd on the remuda and I'll be scoutin' ahead, so that leaves nine men with the herd: two point men, two swing riders, two flankers, and three to ride drag."

"Let's see," said Silverthorne, holding up a fist and extending a finger as he named off each man, "besides Rosser and me there's Ramey, Whitecraft, Grizell, and Scott; that's six. Then you and Chad and Mart and Merrit; Mitch Warner, too. That's five in the family, plus six—yep, eleven hands."

"Don't forget me," said Rachel. She'd been lounging nearby against one of the wagons, listening to the conversation.

"I was gonna get you to scout for Injuns, Rachel," said Calvin with a grin. "Them Comanches and Kiowas might get restless and stray off the reservation."

Rachel laughed at her father's joke. She'd be right there with the menfolk when it came time to "pound 'em on the back" as they pushed the cow brutes across the desert to the Pecos. Her mother and her Aunt Millie Warner could drive the mules pulling the spring wagon and the bump wagon most of the time. There would be little concern about Indians until they approached Apache territory at the Pecos.

"What did them soldier boys say about the

Apaches?'' asked Calvin. ''Are the soldiers at Fort Stanton keepin' them on the reservation?''

''The whole tribe jumped the reservation in January, but they think they got most of 'em back. The rest went to Mexico. There's always a few who never come in. At the moment the Indians are getting their beef issue on schedule, but they're still not getting everything they were promised, and the bootleggers and squatters on the reservation keep them stirred up, as well as gangs of horse thieves. The military believes some of the raids on homesteads and immigrant trains and trail herds that are blamed on the Mescaleros are actually the work of outlaw gangs, both white and Mexican.''

''Anybody that challenges the Rail H better come cocked and primed, whether they're red, white, or brown,'' said Calvin. ''Sweet and his minutemen knowed better, and them vigilantes should be thankful we had business elsewhere when they come to burn the barn. Sticks in my craw for folks to think the mob run the Howells out of the county.''

''They don't,'' said Silverthorne. ''By now everyone knows you left because of Mart and the jailbreak, and they know you already had your stock gathered up for the drive before the raid on the barn.''

''Yeah, I guess you're right. The only thing I left undone was settling the score with Percival Holloway. But someday . . .'' Calvin's eyes narrowed and he gazed off to the east as if conjuring up a vision of a future day of retribution back at Lampkin Springs.

After a moment he returned his attention to Silverthorne and Rosser. ''We'll loose-herd the cows up the Middle Concho, letting 'em graze all the way. Then we'll rest 'em a day or so at the headwaters. By then the moon will be waxin' bright and we can push 'em hard day and night till we find water. We should make the Pecos in three days if we don't have no extra trouble.

We'll lose a few head of the weakest cows along the way, but everybody loses some.''

Some lost a lot. The farther the Rail H progressed beyond the Concho the more carcasses they saw along the trail. The mesquite trees, which had grown to twenty feet at the beginning of their journey, gradually decreased to mere bushes. The scrubby mesquite was interspersed with clumps of creosote bush and other species of thorny brush, and the ever present prickly pear shared the gravelly sand flats and rocky hillsides with cholla, yucca, bear grass, sotol, and other varieties of cacti and agave.

The hands were too busy and too tired to pay much attention to the changing scenery, and the dust was too thick to see very much. They goaded the cattle mercilessly across the arid terrain day and night, never allowing them to rest. When a cow dropped a calf, Calvin cut its throat and left it to rot. Later they would carry the newborns along in one of the possum bellies, the cowhides suspended beneath the wagons for the collection of firewood and buffalo chips to be used for cooking fires, until they were strong enough to keep up. But there was no time for them now, and no opportunity to turn them out with their mammies at night, because the herd moved constantly, racing the limit of time the cattle could travel without dying from thirst.

The water at Wild China Pond was sufficient only for the horses and mules, and the water holes in Castle Gap were already full of dead cattle. The narrow rocky walls of the canyon cast a refreshing shadow upon the hardworking drovers and their little herd of thirsty cattle. The early morning coolness of the canyon depths and the stench of rotting flesh imparted an eerie atmosphere, and the overhanging walls of the chasm reminded the riders of stories about outlaws and Indians who fired from the bluffs upon hapless travelers.

On this day Martha Howell and Millie Warner drove

the wagons in the wake of the herd, remembering that
the cattle might stampede at the western mouth of the
gap if they scented water. The men would run with the
cattle while the women pulled in to fill the water casks
from the seep spring at the old stage stand. They figured
springwater would be more potable than river water, and
they didn't plan to cross the wagons at Horsehead.
They'd been advised at Fort Conchos to proceed up the
east side of the river until they reached Pope's Crossing
near the New Mexico line in order to minimize the
chances of a raid by stray Apaches.

Rachel was unhappy when her father instructed her to
assist Martha and Millie with the water casks, but she
was too tired to argue.

The cattle stumbled out of the gap into a strong wind
and quickened their pace. The riders knew they'd
scented moisture on the breeze. They made the wild dash
to the river with the cattle, plunged down the steep
banks, pushed the leaders on across to make room for
the rest, then allowed them to turn back to the water.
They strung the herd out as much as they could and kept
watch for any that got bogged down in quicksand. Finally they drove the herd out of the river channel and
upstream along the east bank to let the cattle rest in a
bend of the river near another abandoned stage station.
At last livestock and humans would get some much-
needed recuperation.

The men took turns standing guard in pairs at two-
hour intervals throughout the night and for much of the
next day, except for Calvin. He took his rest in snatches
and arose at every changing of the guard to ride out and
inspect the herd.

When Silverthorne and Rosser went on lookout about
midmorning, Rachel rode out with her father. When he
returned to the wagons she remained and rode along
with Silverthorne as he circled the herd. They had not
been alone together since the drive began.

"I don't know what Daddy's so worried about," she said. "After what these cow brutes have been through, they'll be content to rest and graze and water for a couple of days. As long as we don't get a sky-fire thunderstorm they won't go anywhere unless they're pushed."

"He's mostly worried about Apaches, Mexican *bandidos*, and outlaw gangs, I expect. He told us to keep a sharp eye for dust clouds." Silverthorne reined in and scanned the horizon. Nothing moved upon the sunscorched land of rocky sand and scrubby clumps of thorny vegetation.

Rachel dismounted and kicked at a tuft of dry bunchgrass. "I sure hope there's better grass west of the Pecos."

"A lot of herds have rested at the crossing this year, on both sides," said Silverthorne, still looking across the river. "But it will be different in New Mexico." He gave her a reassuring smile.

"Why don't you step down for a spell, Tal," said Rachel, with a come-hither look. "Mr. Rosser won't be able to see us from across the herd."

"Mr. Rosser's riding around the herd to join us," said Silverthorne, shifting his gaze to the east.

"Dammit! Why don't he stay put?" Rachel stepped into her stirrup and remounted.

"Maybe he's afraid you'll hamper my vigilance," said Silverthorne with a grin.

"No, that's not it. I caught him staring at me a couple of times lately."

"Can't blame him for that," said Silverthorne as she turned her horse away.

Silverthorne watched as she rode past Rosser on her way back to the wagons. He tipped his hat to her and her response was anything but unfriendly.

A man would be crazy to get mixed up with a woman like that, Silverthorne told himself for the umpteenth time.

When Rosser rode up to Silverthorne he looked over his shoulder and watched Rachel ride up to the wagons and dismount. "Is that why the good doctor left Lampkin Springs with a trail herd?" he asked when he turned his eyes to Silverthorne. "She's had her eye on you ever since we left the ranch, I've noticed."

"Which means you've had *your* eye on *her*, I presume."

Rosser grinned, and the tips of his waxed mustache moved against his clean-shaven jaw. "The possibility of shooting you out of the saddle has occurred to me," he admitted. "She's a fine figure of a woman, even if she is just a tad on the lanky side. She's tough as whang leather, stong enough to stand by a man through thick and thin."

Silverthorne ran his fingers across the dark stubble on his own jaw. "Strong body, strong mind, and a strong will," he agreed. "If I'm tall hog at the trough it's strictly her choice. It's too soon for me to be making plans."

"The social proprieties of Virginia do not apply in Texas, Doctor, much less in New Mexico, where white women are few and far between, I'm told."

"I'm not concerned about proprieties, Rosser. But before I look to the future I feel I must put the past to rest. There's a matter I'm compelled to settle, in my mind at least, before I can do that."

"Concerning the death of Mrs. Silverthorne," stated Rosser with a knowing look. "You see, I myself have contemplated the mysterious circumstances of that occasion. Considering the velocity of the bullet was such that it passed all the way through her body, it isn't likely it came from the Holloway faction across the square. She was undoubtedly shot from closer range. From behind, as you suspected. You must have reason to believe it was someone who was backing the Howells—someone who's traveling with us."

Silverthorne gave Rosser a steady look, but said nothing.

"Whitecraft and Grizell are the only men who weren't already in the saloon. Which one is the killer?" Rosser returned Silverthorne's steady gaze for a moment. "You don't know, do you?"

"I don't know anything for sure, Rosser. I still accept the responsibility myself for Marylois even being there, but no man should be so careless with a firearm as to shoot an innocent bystander at close range. I figure some word or action will give him away sooner or later. I don't know what I'll do when I discover who it was, but I've got to know how it happened."

Rosser cocked an eyebrow and nodded his understanding.

"And what about you, Rosser? Why would a professional card slick with your skills settle in a backwater village like Lampkin Springs? New Orleans, Galveston, even San Antonio would seem more appropriate."

"Now, now, Doctor. You know personal questions are against the code out here."

"You opened the ball, Chance. I'm just taking my fair turn."

"Perhaps I'm just working my way to San Francisco."

"You can get to California without getting calluses on your fingers riding herd on someone else's beeves."

"You'd be surprised how close my motive is to your own, Silverthorne." With that, Rosser wheeled his mount and trotted away to resume his vigil on the other side of the herd.

FIFTEEN

RACHEL HOWELL SAT HER HORSE RAMROD STRAIGHT, steeling herself against a nippy northwesterly wind. She set her jaw to stop her teeth from chattering and willed her slender shoulders to stop shivering. Sometimes the wind blew strong in central Texas, but never like this. Here there were no trees to break its force. The sea of black grama that covered the vast country west of the Pecos undulated like waves of the ocean beneath the thrust of its chilling gusts. It wouldn't be as piercing if she hadn't gotten so wet pushing the cattle across the Pecos. If only she could change into dry clothes. None of the men had left the herd to change clothes, but none of them had gotten as wet as she had when she'd spurred her horse splashing into the middle of the river to head up that stupid heifer who'd started to swim with the current.

Rachel nudged her pony to the top of a rocky hill to see how far ahead of the herd the wagons were traveling. A sudden blast almost dislodged her Stetson. She reined in to snug her hat and tighten the stampede string, ducking her head to the left to block the wind with her hat brim. Her eye caught the gray silhouette of a mountain range dimly visible against the dark sky of the western horizon. It must be the Guadalupe Mountains, the last stronghold for those Mescaleros who eschewed the government handouts to live wild and free and make their own living by hunting and gathering—and raiding. Rachel shuddered; this time it wasn't from the cold.

She'd lived with the sensation of constant watchfulness most of her life, always listening, always looking, never allowing her mind or her mount to wander and bring her to an unguarded moment. One never knew where the Indians might be or when they might attack. The full of the moon was the worst. They'd drift into central Texas on foot in squads of a half-dozen or more and hide out in the cedar brakes and the hills until they could sneak up to a settlement or a farm or a ranch and locate a bunch of horses to steal. Many a hapless individual had stumbled upon one of their hiding places during the daylight hours. They'd become more openly aggressive while the majority of the menfolk were away fighting the Yankees. The very old and the very young men of the Home Guard were an inadequate defense against the depredations. There were stories of women and children who were slain in their own homes and fields. Children were stolen and never seen again.

At long last her father and the other survivors of the war had come home. Then the Yankee soldiers came to fight the Indians, even Negro soldiers. Finally the Comanche, the Kiowa, the Lipan, and the Kickapoo were pushed out of central Texas, and Rachel could ride and roam without the constant vigilance.

So what do the Howells decide to do? Drive a herd of cattle into Apache country. She laughed out loud at the irony of it.

"Your good humor defies the gale, Miss Rachel."

"*What*? Oh! Mr. Rosser! It's been a long time since I've let anyone sneak up on me."

"I beg your pardon if I startled you, Miss Rachel. I

should have realized the wind would muffle the sounds of my approach, and it was obvious you were lost in your thoughts. Good thoughts, judging by the jovial outburst. Why, Miss Rachel! You are soaked to the skin. You should dash ahead to the wagons and change into dry clothes.''

The wind gusted again and a chill seized Rachel's torso.

''Why, you're shivering, Miss Rachel. Perhaps you should ride in one of the wagons for a while, until the day becomes a mite warmer. I shall be happy to take your place on the flank. Mr. Whitecraft and Mr. Grizell can handle the drag without me.''

''Anything beats riding drag, don't it?'' said Rachel with a grin. ''Even Doc Silverthorne's got it better today,'' she added with a glance at the remuda, ''and the wrangler's supposed to be the lowest man on the totem pole. Thanks, Mr. Rosser, but I reckon the wind's bound to dry me out sooner or later. Reckon I'd best get back to my position before someone else volunteers to take my job.''

Rosser smiled, touched a finger to his hat brim, and pulled his bandanna over his nose as they reined their horses and went back to their respective assignments.

Such a bright smile, thought Rachel. And a handsome face, even beneath a coat of trail dust. Always the charming Southern gentleman, that Chance Rosser.

Rachel again cast her eyes in the direction of the remuda. She was sure Silverthorne had been watching her parley with Rosser. She hoped he was jealous! Rosser had taken advantage of every opportunity to speak to her during the drive from Horsehead to Pope's Crossing. Silverthorne had spoken with her whenever there was an occasion, but he never went out of his way to do so.

She knew he needed some time to put his wife's death behind him, yet he'd been strongly attracted to her even when his wife was alive. The only thing that had kept them apart was his sense of duty to his sick, slowly dying wife. By now she was nearly two months gone, so what was he waiting for? Rachel snorted, wagged her head, and grabbed the saddle horn to steady her shivering body as she trotted her pony toward a couple of heifers who'd strayed from the body of loose-herded cattle.

Silverthorne had been watching Rachel and Rosser and he noticed when she turned her head to look at him. An uneasy feeling stabbed his vitals whenever he saw the dashing gambler making his advances, but Silverthorne suppressed his competitive urge.

When Rosser had said his motive for moving west with the Howells was similar to Silverthorne's, did he mean Rachel? Rosser seemed not the type to seek a permanent relationship, and that's what scared Silverthorne most of all. Rachel could be an easy prey for the sophisticated Southerner. By her own admission, she'd had little experience in affairs of the heart.

On the other hand, Silverthorne had known loyal love that superseded lust. He had a strong desire for Rachel, but he could not be sure of the extent of his feelings so soon after losing Marylois. That's why he was careful not to say or do anything that would appear to justify Rachel's expectation of an imminent love affair.

Aside from the uncertainty of his own emotions, Silverthorne had misgivings about Rachel's steadfastness. She'd toyed with Oliver Holloway, at the same time making overtures to a married man. Now she seemed to welcome the attentions of the gambler.

Rachel Rosser. It had a ring to it. If she took up with Chance, that would end Silverthorne's quandary. Or would it? The fire she'd ignited in his soul would not be easily quenched.

Silverthorne pondered his dilemma again as he trailed the remuda across the rugged terrain, and he always reached the same old impasse. It would take time to resolve the questions in his mind and heart, but Rachel Howell and Chance Rosser were going to force him to act hastily or not at all.

At last the long day was over. Chad Howell took over the remuda for the nighttime vigil and Silverthorne went to the fire pit for a cup of hot brew and a plate of Martha's stew. Maybe he could warm himself from the inside out. There was certainly no way to get warm from the outside; that infernal wind penetrated the heaviest of clothing. Silverthorne moved closer to the fire, but the breeze dissipated the heat before it could be felt. It had been necessary to scoop out a hole in the ground and build up a wall of rocks around it just to get a fire started.

Most of the hands had already eaten and were getting ready to crawl into their bedrolls. Ramey and Warner had ridden out to relieve Grizell and Whitecraft, who'd stayed with the herd while the others ate. Calvin was the only one at the campfire with Silverthorne.

"I wonder if we're in New Mexico yet," said Cal. "We passed the big red bluff on the Pecos today and they's another little river just ahead that runs to the Pecos from the west. It must be the Delaware."

"We were told there's some dispute about the Texas-New Mexico line, but once we cross the Delaware there's no doubt. We'll be in Lincoln County, New Mexico. Even moving slow and loose-herding, we should reach the trading post at Seven Rivers in about a week."

"*Lincoln!* They would have to name the county after him. Maybe we can start a new county someday and get rid of that name."

"It might happen sooner than you'd think, Cal. At Fort Concho they said more and more Texans are moving cattle onto the Pecos rangelands. It's a long ride to the county seat up in the Capitan Mountains. Folks will want their local government closer to hand. As 'tis, that trader the army kicked out of Stanton has started a store at Lincoln and gotten control of all the buying and sell-ing, and his henchmen control most of the county of-fices. He and his partners have secured the beef contract with Fort Stanton and the Indian agency, so you're going to have to deal with Murphy yourself, or take your steers elsewhere. There are other markets in western New Mexico, Arizona, and even Colorado.''

"You shore picked up a lot of Yankee intelligence at Fort Concho, Doc.''

"I looked in on the post surgeon. He has very few opportunities to speak with another doctor.''

"Wal, you can talk to some cows tonight, Doc. I want you to go with Scotty to relieve Ramey and Mitch in an hour or so.''

"Suits me, Cal. I'd sooner get my nighthawk early so I can sleep solid till we roll out in the morning.''

"Doc?"

Silverthorne turned his head to see Millie Warner ap-proaching from one of the wagons. He got to his feet and tugged the brim of his hat. "Ma'am.''

"Martha sent me to fetch you to the wagon. Rachel's took the ague or somethin'. She can't stop shiverin' and her teeth are chatterin' so bad she can't even talk plain.''

"I'll get another hand to take your nighthawk, Doc,'' said Cal. "Millie, fetch his bag from the other wagon, please, ma'am.''

"Rachel ain't been sick a day in her life,'' he said as he strode with Silverthorne to the wagon.

Silverthorne climbed inside, where Martha had stacked some household items aside to make a pallet for Rachel on the wagon bed. The canvas wagon cover whipped and popped in the moaning wind as Silver-thorne gently held his hand to Rachel's brow.

"She's burnin' up now, ain't she, Doc?'' asked Mar-tha, who'd squeezed aside to give Silverthorne room. "She's never been sick before and she don't know what to think of it.''

"I've noticed the dark circles under her eyes the last several days," said Silverthorne. "She's been pushing herself too hard, trying to pull as much weight as the rest of us. I should have tried to talk her into slacking up a bit."

"I keep tellin' her she don't have to work like a hired hand," said Calvin from his position at the tailgate. "But it don't do no good. She's gotta be in on ever' little thing. Always been thataway." The pride shone in Calvin's eyes.

Rachel reached up and grabbed a fistful of Silverthorne's sleeve. "I think I'm dyin', Doc."

Silverthorne chuckled in a reassuring tone. "It just feels that way because you've never been sick before, Rachel." He put his free hand on hers.

"How come I was freezing and now I'm so hot?"

"I'm afraid we don't know how fevers work, or how the body conquers them. We can do some things to help bring them down—cold compresses, juices, broth, water. I've had some success with a drop or two of foxglove extract in water."

"Millie's brought your field kit, Doc," said Calvin. He took the Gladstone bag from Millie and handed it over the tailgate. "Has Rachel got the ague, or what?"

Silverthorne opened the bag and got his stethoscope. He hooked it in his ears and pressed the sensor against her right breast just inside the collar of the nightshirt her mother had helped her change into, then the left. Then he put his fingers on the back of her jawbone just below the earlobes, turned her face to the light of the coal-oil lantern swinging from a wagon bow, and had her open her mouth and extend her tongue.

"Can't put a name on it, Cal," he said finally. "I expect she just drove herself to the point of exhaustion and her body couldn't take it any longer. All I can do at this point is keep a close eye on her and fight the fever until it's broken. Then, with rest, I think she'll be all right.''

Silverthorne and Martha tended Rachel throughout the night. Just before dawn the fever broke and she drifted into a peaceful slumber.

Calvin decided to take the stock and the other wagon on across the Delaware to set up camp and hold the cattle and horses on the grama just north of the river for the rest of the day. Silverthorne and Chad were to stay at the bed ground for several hours to give Rachel a chance to rest before catching up with the main body. Chad would graze the mule team and stand sentry. The new camp would be less than two miles away, so he could signal for help if strangers should approach. By midafternoon, or sooner if Rachel was ready, they were to hitch up the team and move on to the new camp.

Silverthorne thought Martha would stay with her daughter. But since Rachel was on the mend she decided to go on across the river with the other wagon to help Millie set up camp and cook for the crew.

Silverthorne spread a blanket in the shade of the wagon. With the dawning the wind had dwindled to a light breeze, and the new day was clear and sunny. Silverthorne slept, waking up every thirty to sixty minutes to look in on Rachel. She slept soundly until about noon. Silverthorne had eased into the wagon and knelt beside her to feel of her forehead when her eyes flashed open.

''Tal? What's goin' on? Oh, now I remember. . . . Am I gonna live?''

''You'll be all right once you've rested up,'' said Silverthorne with a smile. ''The rest of the outfit went on ahead a mile or so to get the herd across the Delaware. We'll catch up to them now that you're rested. But first, are you hungry? Your mother left a pot of gruel warming on the fire for you.''

Rachel wrinkled her nose. ''How about a big ol' slice of rare beef?''

"So you do have an appetite. That's a good sign. Now open you mouth and let me have a look-see."

After Silverthorne had checked her throat he got his stethoscope from his bag and put it on. Rachel sat up and quickly unbuttoned several buttons of her nightshirt and shrugged it off her shoulders.

Silverthorne's breath caught in his throat. He tried to be nonchalant as he listened for congestion in her lungs, but he could hardly hear anything for the pounding of his heart. She took her deep breaths without any coaching.

"All clear," he said finally, and started to take the stethoscope away. But Rachel grabbed his hand and pressed it hard against herself.

"Oh, Tal," she said breathlessly, gazing into his eyes.

"Not like this, Rachel," he replied, summoning all his fortitude and wresting his hand from her grip.

"What's the matter, Tal? Has it been so long you've forgot how? Well, I know how and I've never done it before."

"Rachel, it's got to mean more than this."

"It means everything to me, Tal."

"Right now you think it does. But . . . Rachel, have you ever read the story of Amnon and Tamar in the book of Second Samuel?"

The pleading in Rachel's eyes changed to incredulity. "Most younguns in Texas learn to read by reading in the Bible," she said with a nod. "Are you fixin' to preach to me, Tal?"

"No, it's just that the story shows how passion can turn to hate if there's not a more noble feeling behind it."

"Are you sayin' lust is all you feel for me?" Rachel's shoulders slumped and she bowed her head.

"I'm saying I don't know yet, and I'm afraid you don't either."

"*I* know," said Rachel. "But if you don't know by

now . . .'' Her voice trailed off and she sniffed, closing
her eyes to hold back the tears.

"Give it time, Rachel," said Silverthorne in a gentle
voice. "Now, how about a little something to eat before
we pull out?"

Rachel wagged her head and put her hands over her
face.

Silverthorne climbed out of the wagon and signaled
Chad to bring the mules up.

SIXTEEN

Dick Reed came to Seven Rivers in 1867, the year after Charles Goodnight and Oliver Loving staged their historic cattle drive up the Pecos River to Fort Sumner and Bosque Redondo, and the same year that John Chisum brought his first herd up from Texas. Reed built a six-room adobe house not far from the west bank of the Pecos, but closer to the north bank of the Main Seven Rivers. He ran longhorned cattle on the grassy public domain adjacent to his claim and tapped the river with a sizable ditch, diverting enough water to irrigate about a hundred acres between the house and the Pecos.

The trail herds began coming up from Texas on a regular basis once Goodnight and Loving showed the way, so the big room on the east side of the dirt-roof adobe was used for a trading post where the drovers "recruited up" on supplies. Stores were hauled by ox and wagon from Las Vegas, New Mexico, some two hundred miles to the north.

Reed realized he wouldn't be alone on Seven Rivers for long. Texas cowmen would not drive herds to market across the grass-carpeted Pecos plains without getting the notion they could raise cattle closer to the markets.

It wasn't long before the Beckwith family headquartered
their ranch about three miles to the northwest, between
North Seven Rivers and the Pecos. About the same time,
old man Tom Gardner settled on the headwater of the
north prong and started a small irrigated farm to supple-
ment his herd of cattle. In seventy-two Chisum came
back to stay, first at Bosque Grande, about thirty miles
north of the confluence of the Rio Hondo and the Pecos.
In 1875 he moved his headquarters south of the Hondo
to the South Spring River, less than fifty miles from
Seven Rivers. His eighty thousand head of cattle grazed
a hundred-mile stretch of the public domain from
Bosque Grande to the Guadalupes, and newspapers as
far afield as Denver and Phoenix began calling him the
Cattle King of the Pecos. The route to Arizona used by
his drovers became known as the Chisum trail.

Dick Reed anticipated the influx of Texas cowmen
with foreboding, for John Chisum applied his squatter's
rights to all the territory his cows had claimed. There
was already bad blood between his outfit and the Beckwith clan. Chisum was certain they were stealing his
cattle.

They were not the only ones.

Lawrence Murphy's partner, Jimmie Dolan, supplied
the military beef contract, yet the two thousand head at
his Seven Rivers cow camp seemed never to diminish.
Dolan could purchase market steers from other ranchers
for fifteen dollars a head, but stolen beeves could be
bought for five.

Closemouthed, shifty-eyed men were drifting into the
county with regularity—cowboy types who made no
pretense of legitimate ranching business. They were all
cow thieves as far as Chisum was concerned—the drift-
ers and the small ranchers alike.

The trail-hardened outfit that dragged up to Seven
Rivers with a small herd of steers and breeders in the
autumn of 1875 had ''more trouble for Uncle John''

written all over it. Not only could their big Rail H brand be superimposed on Chisum's long rail, but the steely-eyed drovers who walked into Reed's storeroom had the look of men who'd left trouble on their back trail and the tolerant side of their nature along with it. Refugees from Texas feud country, Reed guessed.

"See any Apaches on the river?" he said with a welcoming smile as the men browsed among the goods on display.

"Seen a small band just before we crossed Black River," replied the tall, sandy-haired man. He appeared to be the eldest, probably the leader of the clan.

"Most likely the same bunch the army patrol that came by here a couple of days ago was out searching for. The Injuns had permits to leave the reservation to hunt, but they overstayed their leave. They give y'all any trouble?"

"Naw, we left a couple of riders with the herd and nine of us rode out toward them with our Winchesters helt at the ready and they pulled away. We doubled the night guard for a couple of nights, but we never seen 'em agin."

"If they wasn't reservation Injuns you'd of seen more of them. Their intention was probably just to talk you out of a beef."

"I wouldn't of give 'em a jackrabbit, even if they was bronco Injuns. Let 'em starve, and the sooner the better, I say."

"I reckon most of the military agrees with you on that point."

"Then that's about the only point me and the blue bellies ever agreed on. I'm Calvin Howell and these gents with me are my brothers, Mart and Merrit, and my brother-in-law, Mitch Warner, and that's my daughter, Rachel. My wife and my sister, Mitch's wife, will be here in a few minutes, after they get freshened up a bit. My son, Chad, will be along directly and they's six other

fellers travelin' with us. They'll be comin' around soon
as they get the herd settled and some of us get back to
spell 'em.''

"Well, now, that's lots of customers," said Reed with
another smile. "I hope you all settle in the vicinity."

"We seen some good grass not far to the south where
a good-flowin' crick comes down from the hills."

"South would be better than north," said Reed with
a vigorous nod. "The farther away from Chisum's headquarters the better."

"I've been hearin' about John Chisum ever since he
was appointed beef contractor for the Confederate Army.
According to my tell he can grade and tally cows all at
the same time and do it quicker'n a tomcat scratches his
chin.''

"He is a cowman, all right, and an easygoin' feller
with a lot of sensibility, from all I've seen and heard of
him. At the same time he's always looking for the main
chance and he don't cotton to folks hornin' in on his
business. The Injuns learned that lesson the hard way.
He finally got fed up with losing stock to 'em, so last
year a bunch of his cowboys and some others went over
to the reservation and cleaned up on 'em. I don't know
how many Apaches was killed, but they've not bothered
his cow camps very much since then. But Uncle John
has sold most all of his cows."

Reed chuckled at the surprised looks that were flashed
in his direction, and proceeded to explain. "That's beside the mark for the time being. Chisum's still in
charge. He made an agreement with a big beef contractor
out of St. Louie to take ownership of his cows immediately and take delivery as they need 'em to fulfill the
government contracts they hold. It'll be years before he
gets 'em all moved out."

"Still, I can't believe he's gettin' shut of the cow
business," said Calvin.

"Oh, I 'spect he's just making way for some new

herds. I've heard him speak of starting an improved strain by crossing Longhorns and Red Durhams. He believes Durham bulls are even better than Herefords for upgrading the quality of New Mexico beeves. He thinks they'll cross better with range cows and fend for themselves in rough country.

"But I'm guessin' that's not the only reason he sold out. There's a ring of lawyers and merchants and politicians in Santa Fe who're trying to get control of everything in the territory. If they figure out some legal shenanigan to attach Chisum's property, his cattle ain't in his name and they can't touch 'em."

"Chisum's got a longheaded reputation," said Calvin. "I was told he invested all his Confederate money in land and stock when it was still worth somethin'."

"Once he got his start he never looked back."

"Well, the Rail H is startin' over. And that crick we seen looks like a good place."

"Folks in these parts call it Rocky Arroyo. The only drawback is the Apaches foller it down from the mountains when they come lookin' for something to steal."

"Good! We'll know what direction to watch for 'em."

For a moment Reed thought the daughter was about to protest her father's statement, but the startled look faded from her face when her mother opened the door and stepped inside, followed by Rachel's aunt.

Calvin Howell introduced his wife and his sister, then joined them as they perused Reed's stock of goods.

Later, after the family had finished their shopping and returned to the camp, the rest of the Rail H crew came in to browse. Four more tough-looking *Tejanos* and a couple of men who were somehow different. At first Reed thought it was just that the two had washed up and shaved before coming up to the store, but upon overhearing them speak he recognized their vernacular. It was similar to that of Pap and Ma'am Jones, who lived up on the Ruidoso near Dowlin's Mill. It was said the Joneses were from Virginia.

A few minutes later Reed learned the dark-haired Virginian was different from the *Tejano* drovers in ways other than manner of speech and grooming.

A clatter of hooves attracted everyone's attention to the front of the store.

"That there troop of black soldiers is back," said Reed, peering out the door, "and they've got them Injuns." Everyone filed outside to take a look.

"Howdy, Sergeant Roundtree," said Reed. "I see you captured your runaways."

"Yassuh, we jumps 'em down near Dark Canyon," said the sergeant. "They tries to run but we shoots a couple o' hosses down and heads 'em off befo' they gets away up the mountain."

Jimmy Grizell leered at one of the Apaches who was riding double behind another. "Looks like hosses ain't the onliest thing you shot." The Indian's face was ashen and he was clinging tightly to his companion. A thick ooze of coagulum seeped from a gunshot wound in his right thigh, and his naked torso was covered with scrapes and bruises.

"His laig was in the way when we shot the hoss," said Roundtree with a snicker.

Grizell worked up his chew and spat a wad of tobacco juice on the horse's hind leg. The skittish Indian pony jerked its head up and sprang forward, causing the wounded Apache to lose his grip and fall hard against the gravelly turf.

Grizell hee-hawed. "Well, I reckon these here Apaches cain't ride so good as them Comanches we been fightin' over in Texas!"

Silverthorne stepped over to the fallen Apache and knelt down beside him. The brave tried to sit up but Silverthorne restrained him with a gentle hand on his chest, at the same time grasping his wrist with the other hand. At first the Indian jerked his arm away, but Silverthorne looked him in the eye and said, "It's all right; I'm a doctor," in a soothing tone. Silverthorne didn't know if the Mescalero understood any English, but he relaxed and let Silverthorne take his pulse.

The pulse was not very strong. It was a wonder the man was conscious. Silverthorne looked down at the mass of coagulum on the Indian's leg, and noticed the brighter color of fresh blood still seeped through from underneath.

"This man will bleed to death in ten more miles on horseback."

"Well, now, ain't that a shame," said Whitecraft, looking around at the others. Grizell, Ramey, and Scott all nodded vigorously and joined in another round of laughter. Even the Negro soldiers were chuckling.

"He'll be rode ten times ten befo' we gits 'im back to the rez," said the sergeant, "but we be gettin' 'im there, one way or t'other."

"Go fetch my bag from the wagon, will you, Chance?" Besides Dick Reed, Rosser was the only one who'd not joined in the ridicule of the Mescalero. Rosser went to his horse.

"Mr. Reed, would you boil some water, please?" Silverthorne asked as Rosser galloped away.

"Aw, c'mon, Doc," said Scott, "you ain't gonna doctor no Injun."

"We ain' got time to be waitin' round, Mister Doc, if you is a doc. We got to git to the Peñasco befo' nightfall."

"Then you'll go without this man," said Silverthorne, "because he'll be dead before dark if you drag him cross-country on horseback. He must remain perfectly still until I can get this bleeding stopped. First of all I've got to get the bullet out. . . . Reed, how about that water?"

"I'll get your water, mister, but you're not bringing him inside the house."

"Doc," said Ramey, "you come to Texas after the Injun wars was done finished in our part of the state. I'm guessin' this here's the first Injun you ever seen. Injuns are our natural-born enemies, Doc."

"I was in a war, too, Ramey, and I treated every wounded soldier who came my way to the best of my ability, whether he was wearing gray or blue."

"But they was *white* men, Doc."

"They were human beings, the same as this man."

"*Human?*" exclaimed Whitecraft. "Why, Injuns ain't no more human than—" Whitecraft cut himself short, and Silverthorne gave the black sergeant a penetrating look, knowing he knew the comparison the white *Tejano* was about to make.

"I reckon you got yo' Injun, Doc," Roundtree acquiesced. "If he lives you'll have to bring 'im on up to the fort, and if he don't you got to send word, or bring it yo'self. Doc Carballo, the post surgeon, would sho' nuff like to chat with you a spell. Be good if you could come Thanksgivin' Day. They'll be some fine feastin' in the white officers' quarters."

"*Thanksgivin' Day?*" said Grizell. "Lincoln started that holiday during the war to celebrate Union victories over the South. No self-respectin' Southerner would hobnob with a bunch of Yankees on Thanksgivin' Day."

Silverthorne gave Roundtree a wink. "We'll see, Sergeant. Thanks."

The troop pulled out with the remainder of their captives, and the Texans drifted back into the trading post. Silverthorne used his bandanna and his pocketknife to fashion a crude tourniquet on the thigh above the bullet wound. "Seems like they could've at least done this much for you," he murmured, shifting his eyes to the Apache's face. The Indian returned his look with a steady eye. His face revealed no trace of pain or emotion. It was a longer, leaner face than the round heads of the other Mescalero captives, and the man was taller and more slender than the others, too. Silverthorne guessed he was in his middle thirties, but it was difficult to estimate the age of a member of a race he'd never seen before.

When Rosser rode back with Silverthorne's medical kit, Calvin Howell accompanied him. They tied up in front of the store just as Reed came out.

"What are you up to, Doc?" said Howell as they walked over to Silverthorne and the Apache. "Rosser says you're determined to do a patch-up on this here Apache. Now I've heard about your Hippocratic oath, but you can't bring no siwash Injun into camp."

"Then I'll have to make my own camp," replied Silverthorne. He cut his eyes to Dick Reed. "Are you gonna oblige me that hot water?"

"It's on the fire, Doctor—be ready soon. I came out to tell you that I've got a little tent set up out back near the privy where a pilgrim can stay overnight when needful. I'll help you move the Mescalero over there if you want."

"I'd be mighty obliged."

Reed and Silverthorne hoisted the wounded man up with a shoulder under each arm and carefully carried him around back of the big adobe to the tent. Rosser carried Silverthorne's bag. Howell joined the men inside the store, and so did Rosser after the Indian was situated in the tent. Reed fetched the pail of hot water along with some clean cloths and promised to return as soon as he'd waited on his customers. By the time he got back, Silverthorne had gotten the bullet out and cleaned and dressed the wound.

"Dr. Silverthorne," said Reed, "if I was to let you bring this here Mescalero in the house my wife would have a conniption. She's crazy afeared of Injuns. But I'll help you what I can."

"The tent will do just fine, Mr. Reed. A good deal of my early medical experience was had beneath military canvas, so I'll feel right at home. If you'll supply us with food and water, I'll pay you whatever you deem fair."

"Never charged nobody for grub, Doctor," said Reed with a dismissive wave of his hand, "although I hear some is doing it nowadays, seein's how so many pilgrims is passin' through the country. Doc, are you really gonna take this Injun back to the agency if he lives?"

Silverthorne glanced at the Mescalero, who was sleeping soundly under the influence of the laudanum Silverthorne had given him. "That's the agreement."

"Aw, hell, the military won't hold you to it, Doc. What's one Injun more or less to them? Most of the soldiers would like to kill 'em all off, and most of the settlers wish they would. The Indian agency wants 'em protected and educated in the white man's ways. Washington promised the Mescaleros a regular issue of beef, flour, corn, and blankets if they'd stay on the reservation, but they're still going hungry, and going pert near nekkid in cold weather. Most of what the government does contract for 'em is being stole by the traders and the agents. When they get a honest agent the powers that be either corrupt him or put so much pressure on him he resigns."

"Can't the Mescaleros get meat and skins by hunting? Should be lots of game in the mountains."

"Not in the mountains around the fort, except for wild turkeys, and the Injuns don't believe in eatin' birds. The soldiers have shot all the deer for target practice. The Injuns ain't allowed to have no firearms, although lots of them do, on the sly. They're accurate from a hunnert yards with a bow and arrow, though, and sometimes the military will give out permits for a hunting party to go off to the Guadalupes or somewhere on a expedition. The bunch this here sleepin' beauty was with had gone down the Pecos to hunt antelope, but they didn't come back to the reservation when they was supposed to. Maybe they decided to join up with them broncos up in the Guadalupes.''

''Can't say as I'd blame them, judging from the way you describe conditions on the reservation. My patient may not want to go back there when he recovers.''

''It's not a good time to be going up yonder in them mountains, anyways.''

''Why? It's still early for snow, isn't it?''

''It can snow early or late in this country, but that's not what I meant. I'm thinking about the trouble that's brewing.''

''Trouble? What kind of trouble?''

''Shootin' trouble. A power struggle. Major Murphy's the cock of the walk in Lincoln County. Him and Jimmie Dolan own the only mercantile store in La Placita— Lincoln, they're callin' it nowadays—and Murphy and Dolan and their partners control the government contracts. Everybody has to go through them to sell their cattle, sheep, hogs, hay, corn, wheat, barley, or whatever they produce. None of them have any cash money so they get paid with credit at the store. They always end up owing more than their produce was worth and sometimes Murphy and his ring of thieves end up taking their stock or their land, or both. At first it was mostly the Mexicans, the original settlers that moved down from the Rio Grande valley and the Manzanos back in the fifties, that Murphy was hornswoggling. But more and more Americans are settling in the mountain valleys and a lot of 'em are gettin' fed up with the Murphy crowd. They got organized and went to the county seat for the Democratic convention in August determined to get some honest men nominated to some of the county offices in place of Murphy's minions.

''Their most respected supporter was Robert Casey of Casey's Mill on the Rio Hondo. Casey had also started a store at the mill and was taking some of Murphy's trade. The afternoon of the convention he was ambushed and shot down by William Wilson, a man who used to work for him. Murphy preached Casey's funeral, since he's studied for the priesthood and there's not a priest or a preacher in all of Lincoln County. Later on the widder Casey finds out Murphy instigated Wilson to kill her husband. Newcomb and Rynerson from Mesilla was hired to defend Wilson but A. J. Fountain took up Miz Casey's side and won a conviction and Judge Bail sentenced Wilson to hang. There was an attempt to let Wilson escape so Captain Fechet took him to Fort Stanton to keep him locked up. All they've got for a jail at Lincoln is a pit with a wooden cage over it. Wilson's lawyers are trying to get a new trial or to get Governor Axtell to commute the sentence.''

"Sounds like a political powder keg."

Reed nodded. "Colt and Winchester will light the fuse. Some of the folks who see it comin' are loading the wagon and quittin' the country so's not to get caught in the middle of the blowup. Some of the Americans are determined to break Murphy's grip on the county and a lot of the Spanish-speaking citizens are being drawed into the fracas. About ninety percent of the Anglos that are married have Mexican wives."

"I was told there are very few white women in the county."

"You get the right tell. Mr. Calvin Howell's gonna have every galin' horse between the Hondo and the Texas line tied up at his hitch rail. That Rachel's as purty as a spotted pony in a flower patch. From her getup and the way she sets her saddle, I'm guessin' she's as useful as she is ornamental."

SEVENTEEN

RACHEL HOWELL REINED IN HER PONY ATOP A GENTLE knoll and pulled the collar of her canvas jumper up close around her neck. She hoped it wasn't windy all year round in this Pecos country.

It was good cow country. Abundant grama grass. Good water in the little stream on which they'd chosen to settle. Hard water, high in mineral content, but much cleaner and tastier than Pecos River water. The stream wasn't confined to a narrow channel like most canyon runs, but spread out wide and seeped down into the soil. There were a lot of flat stones lying about and the men had already begun to gather and stack them to form holding pens for cattle and horses. They'd also stacked rocks to form ''monuments'' at the corners of the 160 acres they claimed for the Rail H headquarters. Someday it would have to be surveyed and filed on at the Federal Land Office in Mesilla. But Mesilla was a long way from the Pecos and protection for the horses and the settlers was of immediate concern.

The Rail H stock pens would be superior to the adobe corrals at the Reed ranch because Indians and other thieves could saw through an adobe wall with a rawhide or horsehair rope unless the wall was reinforced with wooden planks, and wood was almighty scarce along the Pecos. They'd have to haul cottonwood logs from the mountains for roof beams for the house, and also poles to be laid across the beams to support the flat adobe roof. The rock walls of the house would be built up three feet above the roof with rifle niches all around.

There were only two shingle roofs in all the county. They were on the only two buildings at Roswell, a little place near the cattle rest on the Hondo the gambler Van Smith had named after his father. People rode in from miles around to marvel at the shingle roofs, it was said.

The Howell house in Texas had had a shingle roof. Rachel missed the warmth and security of that house. She was tired of living outdoors. Chance had been talking about going to the rooming house at Roswell to do some gambling. She bet he'd take her with him. He'd been after her ever since they left Horsehead Crossing, and especially since Silverthorne had disappeared.

Silverthorne! Her heart skipped a beat at the thought of him. At the same time the humiliation of his rejection smothered her heart with a blanket of shame. She'd been very cool toward him since that day in the wagon, and more responsive to Chance Rosser's attentions. If that maneuver made Silverthorne jealous, as she'd hoped it would, he hadn't let on.

Now he was gone. Gone up the Hondo and the Ruidoso to deliver that stinking Mescalero Apache to the reservation. The Indian would probably rejoin the others and come back to raid the Rail H. Rachel shuddered and looked up the canyon toward the mountains from whence they'd been told the Apaches were likely to come. The wounded Apache and his cohorts would probably come storming out of the mountains before the Howells got their house built. He might even be back before Silverthorne. Actually, Silverthorne hadn't told anyone he was coming back.

Maybe she should go to Roswell with Chance Rosser and forget about Taliaferro Silverthorne.

The Indians appeared suddenly, like they'd materialized out of the ground as a wisp of smoke behind the scrubby brush and spiraled upward to become manifest on both sides and behind. One moment Silverthorne and his companion were riding alone down the spine of a low ridge while Silverthorne looked for the landmarks Dick Reed had mentioned when he gave directions about where to cross the Peñasco and the Feliz in order to intersect the Hondo, and the next moment they were surrounded. Silverthorne and the wounded Apache drew rein simultaneously, but Silverthorne was the only one with a surprised look on his face.

"Not be afraid. We not hurt."

"So you *can* speak English. You understood everything I said to you the two weeks I was treating you and never once did me the courtesy of a reply."

"Magoosh savvy *poquito*—little bit white man lingo."

Magoosh spoke to the six warriors who'd intercepted them in low guttural tones and with much gesticulation. There was an animated discussion among the seven Indians, then Magoosh turned back to Silverthorne.

"I tell them Silverthorne got strong medicine. I tell them Silverthorne save Magoosh. I tell them Silverthorne good feller. I tell them let Silverthorne go home. They say Silverthorne tell other *Indah* about us and them chase us. They say Silverthorne go to mountain with Apache. Then Silverthorne go home."

Thus began the most fascinating journey of Silverthorne's life.

Silverthorne wondered why the Indians didn't disarm him. Perhaps Magoosh had convinced them it was unnecessary. All six of them carried Winchesters, so there

was little he could do with his six-shooter even if he
was inclined to make a break.

As it turned out, he wasn't ready to turn back when
Magoosh told him he'd ridden with them far enough, for
by then Silverthorne's curiosity was captivated by the
rugged beauty of the Guadalupes. They had made camp
where a small stream cascaded over a low bluff to gather
in clear pools of emerald-green water in the bottom of
a shallow canyon. There was a cave behind the waterfall
and willows and tall grass grew alongside the creek run,
which undercut a steep wall on one side of the narrow
canyon. When Magoosh told Silverthorne he was free to
go his own way he just gazed about the canyon and
made no move toward his red dun.

"Magoosh send *caballo trigueño* back to store of
Dick Reed."

"I wasn't thinking about my horse, Magoosh."

Magoosh looked around as if to discover what Silverthorne was looking for. Then he smiled and nodded
his head. "Silverthorne like this place?"

"Yes, I like this place very much, Magoosh. There
must be a lot of beautiful places in these mountains."

"We just little bit in mountains. Silverthorne not see
much. Mebbe Silverthorne ride more with Apache."

Silverthorne sighed and wagged his head. "I would
like to, but . . ."

"Magoosh watch Silverthorne, look at eyes. Silverthorne got strong medicine for other man, but Silverthorne sick—here." Magoosh struck a fist against his
chest.

"*Ussen* make strong medicine in mountains. Mountains heal." Again Magoosh pounded the center of his
chest.

Silverthorne gazed into the emerald depths of the pool
at the base of the waterfall bluff and let his mind run
with the sound of the pouring waters. This could be his
only opportunity to discover the mysteries of the Guadalupes. He'd always been interested in geology. And an-

thropology. He was curious about the Indians and their way of life. In a hundred lifetimes he could only begin to satisfy his curiosity about the natural world. Silverthorne raised his eyes to the infinite blue of the sky above the rim of the canyon.

"Silverthorne wants to go with Magoosh to see the mountains."

"Silverthorne not see only. Silverthorne feel."

So Silverthorne rode on into the mountains with his copper-skinned companions. They took him to their camp amongst gold-and red-hued oaks and maples alongside a clear-running stream in a deep canyon, where their families awaited the six who'd gone to rescue Magoosh. How they'd found out what had happened to him and how to find him, Silverthorne could only guess.

Magoosh took Silverthorne to the highest peaks and the steepest canyons. He showed him the great deep hole in the earth, the forbidden place, where the Evil Ones swarm forth like smoke before the setting sun during the warmer months.

Silverthorne marveled at the dizzy heights, the great limestone cliffs plunging into deep canyons that sheltered clear springs and infinite varieties of trees and bushes, and the grassy slopes studded with fir, pine, pinyon, alligator juniper, and small oaks and maples. The mountains were home to mule deer, elk, bighorn sheep, bear, and turkey, besides an abundance of smaller animals, birds, reptiles, and insects. Silverthorne knew there would be an even greater variety in the warmer months, when the bats came back to the big cave.

Silverthorne did not presume to try to dissuade the Indians of their belief about the bat cave, or any of their concepts. His mission was to observe and to learn. He watched how they built their shelters, made their clothing, tools, and weapons, formulated their herbal remedies, and how they prepared their food for the oncoming winter, including the way they baked and preserved the nutritious root crowns of the mescal agave plant for which the Mescaleros were named.

Time passed quickly and one morning when Magoosh threw back the flap of the tipi he shared with Silverthorne, the world outside was covered with a blanket of white. Silverthorne decided to pass the winter with the little band of Mescaleros and return to Seven Rivers in the spring. He waited until the grass was green and his ponies were fleshed out and strong before he departed.

"I see healing in the eyes of Silverthorne when Silverthorne comes to the mountains," said Magoosh as he handed Silverthorne Tree's lead rope. "Now Silverthorne's face turns back to the world of the *Indah* and the sad comes again to the eyes."

"Silverthorne regrets he must leave these mountains. There is strong medicine here, as Magoosh has said. But some of the things that happened to Silverthorne in the white man's world that put the sorrow in his eyes are not finished."

"Magoosh thinks Silverthorne is more sad when these things are finished. Magoosh thinks Silverthorne comes again to the mountains."

Magoosh guided Silverthorne out of the Guadalupes and pointed him in the direction of Seven Rivers. "When Silverthorne comes again for the medicine of the mountains Magoosh will be watching," said the Mescalero when they parted company.

Silverthorne followed a little stream that meandered to the northeast and gradually closed with a hilly ridge that angled to the same direction. The stream curved east through a gap in the ridge of hills. By continuing northeast along the base of the ridge, Silverthorne would soon come to the south prong of Seven Rivers, according to Magoosh. But Silverthorne guessed the little stream was the same creek on which the Howells had talked about settling. He took a chance and followed it through the

canyon. When finally he rode out on the grassy flats on
the east side of the hills he spotted some cows wearing
the Rail H brand. He'd guessed right.

Silverthorne soon spied the Rail H wagons and the
new stock pens. A rock house was under construction,
with walls that had reached about four feet in height.

Silverthorne's heart pounded in his chest. Was Rachel
among those he could see working on the house? He
had not realized he was anticipating the sight of her so
strongly. He tugged on Tree's lead and nudged Rudy
into a fast trot. As he closed on the house he began to
identify the figures moving about the construction site.
He felt his heart sink when he realized Rachel was not
there to see him ride in. Perhaps she was in one of the
wagons. Or out on the range checking on the cattle.
Sure, that's the job Rachel would choose. As soon as
he'd said his howdys to the others he'd find out where
she was riding herd and ride on out to join her. He could
hardly wait to see her! Silverthorne realized the answer
to one of his questions had been resolved during his
sojourn in the mountains. He laughed out loud as he
trotted the horses up to the homesite.

Then he saw the grave on the hillside behind the
house.

"What's the matter, Doc?" said Calvin. "One secont
you're gigglin' like a schoolgirl and the next secont
you're white as a ghost."

"Where's Rachel?" said Silverthorne, looking at the
rectangle of stones and the crude cross fashioned of
driftwood. "Damn! I should have come back before
winter set in."

"It ain't Rachel, Doc. It's Grizell, and you couldn't
of saved him if you'd been here, unless you've got a
cure for a bullet in the brain. But you should of come
back sooner if you're lookin' for Rachel."

Silverthorne turned his stare to Calvin, his eyes full
of questions.

"Light down and see to your ponies, Doc. I'll go get Martha to rustle some grub and we'll tell you all that's happened since you taken out with that damned red-hide you saved. Hell, we thought you'd lost your hair as well as your brains when you disappeared like that."

Silverthorne rode to the horse corral and unloaded his mounts as quickly as he could, his thoughts darting from one question to another like a bullbat chasing bugs. Where was Rachel? Why did Calvin say it was too late to be looking for her? Did she believe Silverthorne was dead? Who shot Grizell? Would Silverthorne ever be able to solve the mystery of Marylois's death without him? Where was Whitecraft? And Rosser? They weren't among the crew working in the house. Silverthorne turned the horses loose in the corral, stashed the bridle and halter with his saddle, picked up his saddlebags, bedroll, and medical kit, and headed for the wagon.

Martha Howell greeted him with a broad smile as he approached. "Glory hallelujah! The dead has come to life!"

Silverthorne wagged his head in dismay. "Didn't you think maybe I'd just ridden away to some other place?"

"We knew you wouldn't jump the border without making arrangements to have them books of yours sent along," said Martha.

His library! Silverthorne had almost forgotten it was stored in the spring wagon, taking up valuable space. He'd make arrangements to move the books to Reed's warehouse first chance he got. "I might've just decided to wear out the winter in one of those little villages in the mountains after I'd delivered my patient," said Silverthorne.

"We found out you never made it," explained Calvin. "After you'd been gone a month or so, Dick Reed's partner, George Hoag, went up to Lincoln for Christmas, and Reed got him to ask about you at Stanton and the agency. Everyone figgered that heathen had got the best

of you. It'd be just like one of them red devils to kill a
feller after he's done saved his life!''

"No, Cal, they're not like that. At least the ones with
whom I spent the winter aren't. You see, some Mescaleros from the Guadalupes came for the one I was taking
back to the reservation. They took me back to the mountains with them to be sure I wouldn't put the soldiers or
other whites on their trail before they had time to get
away. Then they set me free. But I decided to stay with
them and explore the mountains. The man I saved served
as my guide. I knew I would never have an opportunity
like that again.''

Calvin wagged his head. "You're curious about
everything, ain'tcha, Doc?''

"I wonder about a lot of things that I'll never have
time to investigate in one lifetime. But two things are
of immediate concern. Where's Rachel and what happened to Jimmy Grizell? Also, I don't see Whitecraft or
Rosser about.''

"Wal, in a way it all sorta ties together. Me'n Martha
was hopin' you and Rachel would hit it off after Miz
Silverthorne was killed. I thought Rachel was stuck on
you, but I know how impatient she is and I knowed
you'd need some time after your wife died. We didn't
cotton much to that Chance Rosser sparkin' her.''

"Chance seemed to be a decent sort, mannerly and
respectful,'' said Martha, "but I just never could trust a
man who made his livin' by gambling. And then he
killed poor Jimmy. . . .''

"Rosser shot Grizell? What for?''

"That happened when the Injuns come,'' said Calvin.

"You've been raided already?''

"Three weeks ago about a dozen of 'em come down
the canyon,'' said Calvin with a nod. "Rachel and
Chance had took a little ride up the crick. They was the
first to see them 'paches comin' down the arroyo and
they made a run for camp, firing their revolvers to warn

us while they rode for cover. We all left off what we
was doing and grabbed up our rifles and took cover behind the walls. We was holdin' our fire until Chance and
Rachel got clear. But Jimmy didn't see too good in the
distance and I reckon he didn't realize Chance and Rachel was out there. He just seen a bunch of riders comin'
and heard the shootin' and started shootin' back.''

"And he shot the wrong person . . . again!" interrupted Silverthorne.

Calvin gazed at Silverthorne a moment before he continued. "Grizell shot Rachel's horse out from under her.
She took a bad spill, but Rosser leaned from his saddle
and scooped her up on the gallop and rode on to safety
behind the horse corral. Chad was already at the corral
because he'd been seein' to the remuda and he run the
horses in when the shootin' commenced. So with them
two shootin' from behind the corral and the others of us
takin' rest off the walls of the house we helt them red
devils off. When they seen they wasn't about to get no
horses they rounded up about ten head of cows and run
them off up the canyon. We mounted up and took out
after 'em and when we caught up they left the cows and
kept on runnin'.''

"And Chance braced Grizell for shooting at Rachel?"
Silverthorne queried.

"On the way back to camp he commenced askin' who
it was fired that first shot from the wall," said Calvin
with a nod. "Nobody wanted to say nothin', but Jimmy
wasn't gonna let nobody take the blame for him, so he
owned up to it. I've never heard the likes of the tongue-
lashing Rosser laid on Jimmy. Kept after 'im when we'd
dismounted and even accused him of shootin' Miz Silverthorne. That done it for Jimmy. He denied the charge
and went for his six-shooter. Jimmy wasn't no match
for Rosser. Chance pulled both of them .44s slick as
greased lightnin', aimed the right-hand revolver cool and

deliberate-like, and shot poor Jimmy right between the eyes.''

Again Calvin paused to gaze at Silverthorne. ''Did you tell Rosser that Jimmy Grizell shot your wife, Silverthorne?''

''He knew I suspected Grizell. You see, when I prepared Marylois for burial I discovered she'd been shot from behind, which was the opposite direction from the Holloways. Oliver Holloway had circled the square by way of the back streets, and just before he died he admitted he'd seen one of your friends on that side of town. He died before I could get him to tell me the name.''

''I wonder why he didn't speak up right away if he really seen somebody.''

''He had to know the man was on his way to back your play, Cal, yet he didn't try to stop him.''

''So Ollie didn't want to admit he was too scared to try to stop the man from joining the fight,'' said Calvin, nodding his head. ''How come you decided it was Grizell he seen?''

''Other than the men at Scotty's, only Grizell and Whitecraft would likely take an active hand in your behalf. I figured if I rode to New Mexico with your party, sooner or later there'd be a slip of the tongue or some other clue that would lead me to the truth. When I found out Grizell was myopic I was inclined to believe he was the one and he'd shot her by mistake. I wanted to find out what really happened before I decided what should be done about it.''

''But Whitecraft claims him and Grizell was at the racetrack and didn't even know what was going on in town.''

''He could be lying to protect his friend's reputation, or to cover his own guilt. Anyway, since the cat's out of the bag I'd like to talk to him about it. Where is he?''

''I don't know where he's at, Doc. There's bad blood

between him and Rosser over the killin' of Grizell, and
he didn't want to bring no more trouble to our camp so
he dragged on out of here. All I know is he rode off in
the direction of Seven Rivers. He might go to Roswell
if he finds out Chance went up yonder to see about workin' a table at the hotel. Chance left about a week after
Whitecraft. Rachel went with him.''

EIGHTEEN

RACHEL STOOD BEFORE THE WINDOW OF THE ROOM SHE shared with Chance Rosser in the hotel at Roswell, staring across the plains that rolled away south toward Seven Rivers and the Howell homestead on Rocky Arroyo. She fingered the low-cut neck of the lacy gown Chance had had a Mexican seamstress at the nearby settlement of El Berrendo make for her. The shiny cloth was soft against her skin, yet she longed for the feel of riding togs and boot leather. She wished she was riding free on the open plain like the person she could see in the distance riding toward town. She was tired of being cooped up in the little room while Chance attended his endless games of cards and dice in the big room downstairs.

Why had she decided to leave her family and her life of horses and cattle to come here with Chance? Was it the Indian raid? She'd thought the days of constant watchfulness were over. But not in New Mexico. When the Apaches attacked, the old fear became reality all over again. Was she so desperate to escape the vexation of the Indian threat? At least in Roswell she didn't have to be wary of every speck on the horizon lest it materialize into an Apache.

The speck she watched from the window came close enough to divide into two—one horse ridden and another led.

Maybe Chance had won her over by the way he'd so gallantly ridden to her rescue when she lay helpless in the path of the horde of savages. And the outrage he'd expressed over Grizell's foolhardiness having placed her in harm's way.

She regretted Chance had shot Mr. Grizell. But Grizell had almost killed her and he deserved every word of the tongue-lashing Chance laid on him. He shouldn't have tried to throw down on Chance. No one should ever make that mistake!

Perhaps she'd finally decided to go with Chance simply because it was time for her to take a man and the one she really wanted had ridden away out of her life and disappeared.

It was hard to believe Silverthorne was dead. But he'd ridden off for the agency with that savage and he'd never reached his destination. Even if he'd decided to set the Indian free and ride away to seek his fortune elsewhere, he'd never leave without his precious library. Silverthorne was dead.

Chance Rosser was alive, handsome, dashing, and the perfect Southern gentleman. The perfect lover, too, although she had no previous experience by which to make comparison.

If it was so wonderful with Chance, what would it have been like with the one she truly loved?

Moisture welled up in Rachel's green eyes and she bowed her head. Her shoulders shuddered and she blinked to stop the tears that rolled off her cheeks upon the front of her new gown. What if Chance walked in and found her crying? She was sure he already suspected she wasn't over Silverthorne.

Finally she raised her face to the window again. The rider was close enough that the colors of his horses could be seen—a plain brown horse ridden in the lead and a red dun in tow. They reminded her of Silverthorne's *Trigueño* and Rudy. And the rider . . . Her breath caught in her throat.

No! My eyes must be playin' tricks on me! Rachel fisted the wetness away, blinked some more, and squinted to reduce the glare of the sun.

Damn you, Silverthorne! You come back now? When it's too late?

She wondered if he'd been to Rocky first, if he knew she was here, if he'd come because she was here, if he just happened to be passing through. If the latter were the case and he talked to Chance downstairs and learned about her and Chance he'd probably just ride on.

I've got to talk to him!

She scrambled to the wardrobe, threw the door open, and jerked her long duster off the hanger. She shrugged into it and headed for the door before she remembered she was barefoot. Eschewing the fancy lace-up shoes Chance had bought her, she grabbed her old riding boots from under the bed and stabbed her feet into them. With boots and duster and her Stetson hat to hide her face and hair, she could pass for a puncher and slip right out of the building with no one to wonder where the gambler Rosser's woman was running off to all by her lonesome.

Tal Silverthorne crossed the Hondo and headed toward the two shingle-roofed structures that constituted the town called Roswell. There were several horses tied up in front of the two buildings, but no one stirred save for a man afoot coming toward him down the road. The fellow must have a horse staked out somewhere along the river, Silverthorne surmised.

Martha had assured Silverthorne Rachel would never have gone away with Rosser if she'd known Silverthorne

was still alive. The family was surprised that she would
leave the ranch even so. But the winter had been hard
on Rachel. She'd experienced an occasional mild recurrence of the chills and fever she'd suffered at the Delaware, and she never seemed able to get completely
warm while living out in the open with only canvas to
block the cold winter winds of the Pecos country. Martha remembered the nightmares that had plagued her little girl's sleep all her young life while the frontier
ranching family lived under the constant threat of Indian
attack in central Texas. And now they'd brought her to
a new frontier.

Ordinarily Rachel would relish the challenge of a new
beginning, but she'd never been sick before, and she'd
never before lost someone with whom she'd wanted to
spend the rest of her life.

So she'd gone to Roswell, where she could rest in a
warm house and not have to be looking over her shoulder all the time. She'd gone with Chance Rosser, the
man she admired most of all next to Taliaferro Silverthorne.

Chance Rosser would not be pleased with the resur-
facing of Tal Silverthorne. But it was Rachel's play. She
must decide. The grinding in Silverthorne's gut was not
from anticipation of Rosser's reaction. He was worried
about Rachel's response. What would she say when she
first laid eyes on him?

Was the cowboy walking down the middle of the road
drunk, or what? Maybe he was deaf, for he walked a
straight line but kept looking at the ground immediately
in front of his feet, apparently not hearing the sound of
the horses coming toward him. Silverthorne bumped
Tree with his off leg, pushing him to the left side of the
road, and grabbed Rudy's lead to manuever him alongside.

The stranger stepped sideways over the left rut,
blocking Silverthorne's passage, and jerked his hat off,

spilling a pile of dark curls upon his shoulders. Silver-thorne's mouth fell open and his eyes flared wide, locking with the glistening green eyes of Rachel Howell.

"Surprised to see me, Tal?" she said, glaring up at him. "You been slinkin' around the country pretendin' to be dead, thinkin' you'd never have to face up to me again?"

Silverthorne realized he was sitting there looking like a dern fool so he shut his mouth and dismounted. He just had time to step away from his horse before she barreled into him, pounding him on the chest with both fists.

"*Damn you, Taliaferro Silverthorne! Damn you all to hell!*"

He locked his arms around her and crushed her against himself. She quit struggling and started crying. He relaxed his grip and she pulled her arms free and threw them around his neck. This time when her mouth sought his he did not resist, but responded in kind.

"Oh, Tal," she gasped when their lips finally parted, "I thought you was dead. How come you done me like that?"

"The Mescaleros took me into the Guadalupes with them, Rachel. I could have come back sooner, I admit, but I needed some time to myself, time to sort things out. I never thought folks would think I was dead! Soon as I found out you'd run off up here with Chance Rosser I came after you."

Rachel slid her hands to his shoulders and pushed him away. "You come too late, Silverthorne! Chance will never set me free!"

"That's your decision, Rachel; he's got no hold on you. I'll fight him for you if it comes down to it."

"He'd kill you, Tal, and I couldn't bear that on my conscience. Besides, it's not that simple. I don't have a ring yet, but I'm a married woman, Tal."

"*Married?* Dick Reed said there's neither priest nor preacher in nearly two hundred miles."

Rachel bowed her head. "You don't gotta have a man of the cloth, Tal," she said in a plaintive voice.

"A civil service?"

Rachel slowly nodded.

"Why, there's not a justice of the peace short of the county seat. It's a hundred-and-twenty-mile ride up there and back!"

"If that's what it had took to make it official I'd have insisted on it. I wanted to see it was done right." Rachel sniffed, then looked up at Silverthorne. "But El Berrendo's just a hop, skip, and a jump to the north."

"A Mexican village?"

"Yes," she sobbed, "the *alcaldes* in the settlements have been performing marriages for twenty years and everybody considers it legal. You're too late, Silverthorne. You can't fight a man for his wife. If you killed him they'd hang you. But nobody palms a shooter as quick as Chance Rosser and nobody shoots straighter. Not even you, Silverthorne."

"I'll talk to the *alcalde*," Silverthorne persisted. "Surely he'll grant an annulment, considering the circumstances."

"The Mexicans don't believe in no kind of divorce, Silverthorne. My family don't, neither. We take 'till death do us part' serious. I won't go along with anything you do. It would just get you killed."

"Suppose you let me worry about that."

"*No!* I don't want Chance gettin' hurt, neither." She bent over and picked up her hat as if to leave.

Silverthorne took a deep breath and let it out slowly. "Well, I reckon I'll just have to hang around till I outlive him, then. There's no one for me but you, girl."

"Don't hang too close," she said, her voice breaking. "I'm glad you're alive, but I couldn't bear to be seein' you all the time." She threw herself into his arms for one last kiss, then tore herself away and fled from him in a stumbling run back to the hotel. She didn't look back.

Charles Mendenhall, alias Chance Rosser, stood at the window of his hotel room and watched his wife kissing another man. When she finally pried her body from his and ran back toward the hotel, Rosser figured she was coming back to get her belongings. But the man mounted his brown horse and led his red dun away to the south. So Rachel wasn't going with him. Not this time, anyway.

Silverthorne. Rosser had always suspected he was still alive. He'd known for a certainty the memory of Silverthorne was still alive in Rachel's heart. The image would have gradually faded with the passage of time, but not now, not as long as Silverthorne lived.

Rosser repositioned his American .44s and turned to go back down to the gaming room before Rachel got back.

NINETEEN

SILVERTHORNE WAS RIDING RUDY WITH TREE ON LEAD when he came to the ghost town on the Rio Hondo southwest of Roswell. The establishment of Casey's Mill and other settlers drawing off water for irrigation upstream had dried out the Mexican farmers of Missouri Plaza, and their principal markets of Fort Sumner and the Bosque Redondo Reservation had ceased to function. The lonely atmosphere of abject hopelessness engendered by the pall of dust upon empty houses and abandoned fields was a perfect match for the lifeless feeling in Silverthorne's heart.

Yet in one field a clump of volunteer cornstalks stood green against the brown rubble of the last failed crop as a stark reminder of the tenacity of life and the eternity of hope.

Silverthorne put the horses in a picket corral and cut several armloads of the young cornstalks for them. He spared several of the hardiest-looking plants in hopes they would survive to make seed for another season. He forced himself to eat a small meal and bedded down in a lean-to next to the corral to await the dawn.

Calvin and Martha would wonder what had happened

between Silverthorne and Rachel. When the two failed to return to the Rail H forthwith they would know things had not turned out as Silverthorne had hoped. Perhaps he should have ridden back to Rocky to ease their curiosity. But a rehash of his disappointment was not something he wanted just now, and since he was already on the Hondo he'd decided to journey west to search for Allen Whitecraft. Whitecraft had bought supplies at Reed's post after leaving the Rail H, and Reed told Silverthorne he'd inquired about the ranches and settlements in the mountain valleys along the Hondo and its tributaries, the Bonito and the Ruidoso. Likely he was up there somewhere.

Although Silverthorne did not want to talk about Rachel to anyone else, he could not stop going over the quandary in his own mind. "It's my own fault," he mumbled. "I stayed away too long. If I'd just come out of those mountains one month sooner . . . I figured if she really loved me she would wait, and if she couldn't wait I would know where I really stood with her. She would have waited if they hadn't presumed me dead, and she'd still go with me except she's convinced it would get someone killed. . . . Rachel, Rachel, you should have known. No, I can't blame you. What else could you have believed? Still . . ." On and on it went throughout most of the night until finally, having long since exhausted every avenue of thought on the subject, he fell asleep.

Silverthorne awoke with a start at the sound of the horses snorting and shuffling about in the corral. He threw his blanket aside and sprang to his feet, palming his Peacemaker in the same movement. At once the *ba-a-a-ah* calls of a multitude of sheep penetrated his consciousness, as well as the sound of many little hooves upon the wagon road that ran through the abandoned village. Silverthorne snatched his hat off his saddle horn, snugged it on his head, and moved to the corral gate to speak to the horses in a calming voice as the flock spread out among the deserted buildings to nibble on the scattered blades of grass that grew along the walls and fence rows. Silverthorne stepped out into plain sight when a stodgy figure on a little Spanish mule hove into view behind the drove.

"You ain't gonna shoot my sheep, are ye, Mr. Cowman?"

"Abels?" responded Silverthorne, recognizing the voice.

"Augustus Alonzo Abels at yer service, suh! Ol' Triple A, that's me! You can call me 'Lon' or you can call me 'Gus,' or you can call me anything you's a mind to, long as you calls me fer chuck," said the man with a high-pitched laugh as he swung off his mule, dropped a rein, and patted his round belly.

Silverthorne pushed his hat to the back of his head so the bandy-legged fellow could see his face.

"Wal, I swanny! If it ain't ol' Eagle Eye Silverthorne!" Abels jammed the carbine he was carrying into the saddle boot and stepped forward to extend his hand.

Silverthorne holstered the Peacemaker and shook hands. "Looks like you quit skinning buffalo and took to herding sheep."

"Yep! Ain't no place to go a-fishin' out yonder on them plains, and I do like to fish. How 'bout yerself? I heard you'd went back to Virginny. What're you doin' in New Mexico?"

"I went back to Virginia to get my wife. She was shot and killed down in Texas. 'Twas an accident, I'm sure, but I'm bound to find out who did it, anyway. I think the man with the answer is somewhere upriver."

"So now you're totin' that there shiny Colt instead of a big .50. If you're as good with that hawg leg as you was with a buffalo rifle, the feller you're after ain't got a chance."

"It might not come to a showdown. It all depends on the facts of the matter, if he'll talk straight."

"Wal, you got a mighty flashy persuader there; it ought to git his attention."

Silverthorne rekindled his campfire and he and Abels settled down to drink coffee and talk about mutual experiences and mutual acquaintances from the time they worked together on the buffalo hunts.

"Where're you going with these sheep, Abels?" Silverthorne finally inquired. "I'm told the Mexicans have raised sheep in the mountain valleys for years before the Anglos came, but the cowmen down here in the Pecos country don't cotton to sheepherders horning in on their range. Chisum won't sit still for it, and the small ranchers take the same posture on that issue."

"Wal, I swanny, they cain't be keepin' all that government grass to theyselves," said Abels. "But I'd get me some of them long-hair goats if I had the money, cause they can make a livin' in country where a cow won't even go. Meanwhile, I'm lookin' to range my flock closer to the Pecos, where I can ketch some big ol' catfish. All they is in them mountains is leetle ol' trouts."

"I reckon Chisum would let you have all the catfish in the Pecos, Abels, but he believes he has a preemptive right to every puddle of water and every blade of grass in the valley, from what I hear."

"Yeah, 'by right of discovery,' he says, and he's got near a hunnert hands to back his play. He won't even let the small ranchers cut his herds. Claims he'll keep a tally and pay 'em for any of their cows that goes to market with his Jinglebobs. But they don't trust him 'cause they know he thinks most of their stock was stolt from him in the first place. Now that beef's got to be big bidness, even them that got their own start by markin' slicks is right ready to howdy a mavericker with a chunk o' lead or a coil o' hemp. Used to be, jackin' mavericks was hustlin', nowadays it's rustlin', just the same as burnin' brands."

"There're a lot of brand doctors in the hills, I hear."

"Gangs of 'em, both Mexicans and whites. They's a big market for stolt cattle. A rancher has got to get at least fifteen dollars a head fer steers he's raised, but stolt steers is sold fer five dollars a head. Everybody knows Jimmie Dolan's buyin' stolt cows to fill his government contracts, and Pat Coghlin over to Tularosa has got the same rep. And they's other buyers to the south and west."

"You seem to have special knowledge of the situation, Abels."

"I know 'em all, Silverthorne, on both sides of the fence. Nobody pays much attention to a stumpy, gray-headed rolling stone of a sheepman, and I got big ears. I might even know where that feller you're huntin' is at. What's his dee–scription?"

"His name's Allen Whitecraft."

"Don't ring a bell, but half the hombres in Lincoln County taken up new handles when they come out here. And they's lots o' fellers I've seed but never heared the label spoke."

"He's a Texan—"

"*Tejano*, they calls 'em out here," interrupted Abels, "and they's lots of 'em jumped the border of late. Anything particular about him?"

"Nothing that would distinguish him from a lot of others, I reckon. He's close to six feet, a little heavier than average, blue eyes, sandy hair, ruddy complexion; carries his revolver on the front of his left hip with the butt to the right. It's a converted Army .44 as I recall."

"Betcha I could find out where he's at, if you was to make it worth my time."

"How much?" said Silverthorne, cutting his eyes at Abels.

"I'd like to trade you out o' that fancy Peacemaker, but I don't reckon you'd part with it."

"No, I wouldn't. It was a gift from a friend."

"Oh, well, I ain't no good with a handgun nohow. Just thought I might be able to larn with one that purty."

"So how much, Abels?"

"Won't cost you no more than the Colt's worth, and won't cost you nothin' if I don't turn up nothin'. But I got to git my flock set down somewheres before I go on a scout."

"I'll help you with the sheep and guard them while you're gone."

"If I can find a back-country canyon with grass and water they won't need no guardin' while I'm gone."

"Then I'll go with you."

"Naw, you look too much like a stock detective, Silverthorne; wouldn't nobody tell me nothin' if they seen you with me. Where at can you go on the nest till I get back?"

"I could stay at the Rail H on Rocky Arroyo, just south of Seven Rivers, if it's not too far away. I need to tell them something anyway."

"Somebody's done settled on Rocky? Chisum's liable to kick his own dog when he hears about that!"

"I expect he already knows. The Howells have been there since fall. This fellow Whitecraft came out from central Texas with them, same as I did."

"Tell you what let's do then, Silverthorne. We'll take the flock south to the Rio Feliz, then we'll go west along the Feliz to where it comes parallel with the Peñasco, drop down to the Peñasco, work our way upstream to the Sacramentos and find us a likely canyon to pasture the flock. Thataway I can make my scout, then check on the sheep on my way to Seven Rivers to tell you what I've found out."

Silverthorne and Abels took the better part of a week to move the flock to the Sacramento Mountains and select a secluded canyon with sufficient graze and water to hold them. Two days later Silverthorne arrived at the Rail H.

There was another grave on the hill.

Silverthorne reined his horses in before the corral and gazed at the fresh mound of rocks on the hillside.

Calvin Howell slowly walked over from where he'd been mixing lime and sand for mortar for the house-building project. His eyes followed the direction of Silverthorne's gaze. "Mart," he said, and when Silverthorne shifted his eyes to look at Cal's he could see the anger. "Too damn hotheaded. Never could keep a rein on him. This time he come up agin a coolheaded man who wouldn't back down and was a little quicker on the trigger."

"Who?"

"Jim Highsaw, Chisum's range boss."

"How'd it happen? Was Chisum present?"

"Naw, Chisum lets his cowboys take care of the dirty work. They say he don't even tote a shooter—just keeps one on the pommel of his saddle for shootin' snakes and such."

"Where did it happen?" asked Silverthorne, stepping down from the saddle.

"Right here. Highsaw and about a dozen Jinglebob hands come a-gallopin' in here like a bunch of wild Apaches. We seen 'em comin' and took up our positions behind the rock walls. They pulled their ponies down when they seen we was ready for 'em. Highsaw rode forward and said they just wanted to talk. They didn't have no smoke poles to hand, so we left our rifles leanin' agin the walls and stepped out for a parley. Highsaw commenced talkin' like the Jinglebob had been usin' Rocky for a roundup camp since Methuselah was wearin' three-cornered pants and said they's gonna need the water later on this spring. I told him they can help themselves to the water, just respect our monuments and hold their cows downstream."

"Sounds reasonable. I take it he didn't think so."

"I reckon not. He asks me if we'd filed on the hunnert

and sixty and I says I'll go down to the land office in
Mesilla soon as we get the house built.''

Silverthorne grimaced. "Maybe you'd best send
someone right away. Chisum could make something out
of the fact you don't hold title to the land.''

"Hell, Silverthorne, most of the settlers in the county
are just squattin', from what Reed tells me. Been doin'
it that way for years, and long as a family stays on the
land everybody recognizes their right to it.''

"The other squatters do. Chisum's no squatter.''

"Well, he is and he ain't. He's just the same as a
squatter when it comes to holdin' his control over the
public domain.''

"You've got a point there. But what set Mart off?
Did Highsaw make an issue of the fact that you haven't
filed on the land?''

"Not right off. First he goes back to what I told him
about holdin' his cows off our patent. Says even if they
could keep their cows beyond our boundary, some of
ours are bound to get mixed in with the Jinglebob's.''

"That's so. And it's said they don't take kindly to
having their herds cut.''

Calvin nodded. "Highsaw says they'll have to put up
a herd quick to meet a delivery deadline to fill a contract
at the San Carlos reservation over in Arizona so they
just don't got time for every cow camp on the Pecos to
be a-cuttin' their herd. Says they'll keep tally when the
herd's sold and settle accounts later.''

"And you don't trust them?

"Silverthorne, I'm buildin' a herd. I'm not ready to
sell any stock yet.''

"And Highsaw wouldn't accept your explanation for
not wanting him to take any of your stock to market,''
guessed Silverthorne.

"I didn't get a chance to explain, because Mart pipes
up and tells Highsaw he'd sooner stash his roll in a
Dodge City whore's bosom.''

"And Highsaw took offense."

"I reckon he did, but he didn't go to slingin' his horns and pawin' the ground like Mart done. He just smiled real friendy and keeps lookin' at me, steps off his pony and asks me how many head of mother cows we brung out from Texas, like we was just a couple of cowmen chinnin' about the business. Before I can answer, Mart reminds him he ain't been invited to light and set. Highsaw keeps on ignorin' him, which makes Mart even madder, and tells me them must be good cows we brung, 'cause he's noticed they either been droppin' two or three calves at a time or they got real short gestation cycles."

"So he's accusing you of branding Chisum calves. And Mart doesn't smile back at him and make a denial or level a countercharge; Mart pulls his shooter."

"You know Mart. Highsaw was just watchin' Mart out of the corner of his eye, but he got focused quick as a snake when Mart's hand moved. Highsaw might even be quicker'n Rosser. Shoots just as straight, too, although he shot Mart through the heart instead of the head."

"It's a surer shot and just as deadly. Then what happened?"

"The Jinglebob hands must've knowed what Highsaw was about, 'cause they threw down on us as soon as he drawed his shooter. Wasn't nothin' we could do. Highsaw mounts up, says he regrets what happened, but we'd best take his advice and go back where we come from since we got no legal claim. They keep us covered while they back their ponies off a ways, then they spin 'em around and leave out even faster then they come in. We run to our rifles but they was too far away by the time we got any shots off."

"What are you going to do now, Calvin?"

"I'm gonna get a survey and go to Mesilla soon as I get a chance."

"And what will you do when the Chisum crew comes back? There's no law at all in this part of the county and very little elsewhere."

"I know. The saying is, there's no law west of the Pecos and no God in Lincoln County."

"The Chisum crew will outnumber you two to one. There's no way you can cut your stock out of their herd."

"Maybe not, but they's ways of makin' up for any of our stock they get off with. We'll keep workin' on the house with our rifles to hand. If they don't bother us we won't bother them. I'll settle with that Jim Highsaw someday, though, same as I will with Percy Holloway."

Silverthorne rolled his eyes. "Dammit, Cal, can't you just forget Percy Holloway? I know he slandered your reputation and burned your barn, but he didn't kill anyone."

When Silverthorne looked at Calvin and saw the openmouthed stare he realized what he'd said.

"*He* burned my barn?"

Silverthorne heaved a sigh and slumped his shoulders. "Yeah, he tried to make it look like the mob had done it, but he hung around too long and I saw him. I didn't tell you because I was afraid you'd delay our departure and someone else would get killed."

"*My stallion was in that barn.*"

"I know," said Silverthorne, looking at the ground.

Calvin's face turned red and his eyes gleamed. "*Damn!* Holloway's the one killed my Red Streak." He clenched his fists, and stared at the sky for a moment.

"Well, I reckon you done what you thought was right at the time, Silverthorne," he said finally. "Turn your ponies in the trap and come on down to the wagon. Martha will be glad to see you, and you can tell us what you done wrong when you went to fetch Rachel home."

TWENTY

*Damn you, Taliaferro Silverthorne, you should
have stayed dead.*

Rachel Rosser stood gazing out her window, thinking
how Silverthorne's riding back into her life had complicated her marriage. He was always on her mind, *always.* And Chance knew it. She tried not to show it, but
somehow he knew. And it was coming between them.

Now Chance had gone off to Santa Fe with Jerry Scott
to see about getting a line of credit at Spiegelberg Brothers Wholesale in order to outfit a saloon they proposed
to build at Seven Rivers, and all she felt by his absence
was relief. Relief from pretending; relief from closing
her eyes at intimate moments to imagine it was Silverthorne who possessed her body as he possessed her soul.

But there was no relief for her compulsion of gazing
out her window and hoping every speck that moved
upon the horizon would come close and take the form
of the familiar lean figure of the man she longed for.

Chance had not seemed disappointed that she wasn't
feeling well enough to accompany them to Santa Fe.
Perhaps he needed some relief himself. Rachel could
well imagine the opportunities for consolation a man

would find in the saloons and dance halls of the old Spanish town. But she didn't care. Wasn't she unfaithful to him with nearly every thought? Maybe he would become so disgusted with the situation that he would set her free.

No, Chance Rosser would never give up anything he'd won unless he could get something more in return.

Then there was another speck moving on the horizon, and Rachel's heartbeat quickened. *Silverthorne, if you're coming back, come now, when we'll have time to ourselves.* But the speck was followed by a cloud of dust, and Rachel knew it was just another trail herd following their wagon to the cattle rest on the Hondo. She turned away and flung herself facedown upon the bed and pulled one end of the bolster over her head to muffle the sound of her sobs.

Finally she turned over, clasped her hands behind her head, and closed her eyes, calling to mind the impassioned grip of Silverthorne's arms on her body and the hungry press of his lips upon her own.

Silverthorne, Silverthorne, I've just got to see you again! I know you feel the same way I do, so how can you stay away so long? Where are you now, Silverthorne?

Rachel opened her eyes and stared at the ceiling. *Silverthorne probably went back to Rocky. He might be there yet. . . . I'll go to him. I can be gone for a week or more and still get back to Roswell before Chance comes home. If he finds out I've been away from the hotel I'll tell him I got to feeling better and decided to visit my family. I'll leave tomorrow morning.*

Rachel squinted her eyes against the horizontal rays of the bright sun that rose beyond the caprock east of the Pecos, and tried to pick her horse out from the dozen or so that milled about the hotel's horse trap. For the third time she attempted to haze them into the closer confines of the corral, but again they balked at the gate and turned aside to make another circle of the trap. But when they pulled up at the gate, a familiar yellow head popped up, and Rachel's hoolihan loop spun around her shoulder and streaked out to snag the buckskin by the neck. She put her hip against the rope and set her feet to hold him out of the plunging remuda. Then she led him through the corral to the harness shed to saddle up. Soon she was on her way.

Rachel had not been stretching the truth by much when she told Chance she didn't feel up to making the trip to Santa Fe. The exaggeration would come when she told him she'd felt improved enough to make the long ride south to the Rail H, for in fact she didn't feel much better than before. She hadn't felt really good since she'd come to New Mexico. It was exhilarating to be back in the saddle and back in trousers and boots, but she knew the wearisome travel would soon take the zest out of her pleasure.

Maybe she was just lovesick. Maybe the only medicine she needed was Taliaferro Silverthorne. *Oh, God, please let him be there!*

If he wasn't, at least for a while she could enjoy the tender comfort that only a mother can give when caring for her own. And if she didn't feel like coming back to Roswell before Chance got back, he should be able to figure out where she'd gone. On the other hand, if Silverthorne *was* at the Rail H, she'd have to return before Chance did, for she didn't want a confrontation between the two. She'd just as soon Chance remained ignorant of the fact of Silverthorne's survival.

Rachel had just ridden past the corrals and outbuildings of Roswell when a pair of riders approached on the road from the south. Probably a couple of hands from the herd that had gone on the cattle rest pasture yesterday. Rachel was glad she'd pinned her hair up to be hidden under her Stetson so that her gender was not apparent. She didn't want anybody at the hotel to know she'd left right away, in case they should try to head her off, thinking a lone woman shouldn't be allowed to attempt the journey she intended. Rachel would keep her hat brim low, grunt a short greeting to the two cowhands, and ride on by.

"Goot morning, sir," said one of the riders.

"Is a goot day dawning, yah?" said the other.

Dutchmen. The herd probably came up from the Texas hill country. Rachel grunted her agreement and ventured a peek at their faces. Quickly she ducked her head and squeezed her pony into a trot.

Alec Pabst and C. F. Andres!

TWENTY-ONE

TAL SILVERTHORNE PICKED UP A SMALL STONE AND tapped it against a dry mortar joint. The mortar was soft and crumbled away. It was the best mortar that could be made with the sand they had. Silverthorne reckoned the roof beams would stabilize the walls. They'd have to raise the walls a couple more feet before they'd be ready to go to the mountains to cut a wagonload of beams. The construction work had progressed slowly since the Rail H crew had been depleted by the deaths of Jimmy Grizell and Mart Howell and the departure of Chance Rosser, Jerry Scott, and Allen Whitecraft. The loss of Rachel was also a factor, for she was as good as any cowboy at handling the horses and cattle.

"Rock!" shouted Calvin, and Silverthorne dropped the little stone and got ready to receive the large one that would be handed off the bump wagon to him by Ramey to be handed up to Calvin, who sat astraddle the wall. Cal would set the flat rock on the fresh bed of mortar that Merrit had spread.

All the men of the rock-stacking crew would rather be with Chad Howell and Mitch Warner. They were riding a circle out toward the Pecos to throw as much Rail H

stock as possible back to the west and out of the way of
the impending return of John Chisum's roundup crew.

"Don't tell me Chisum's done started his gather."
Calvin had straightened up from his rock-setting chore
and was gazing at a cloud of dust approaching from the
east.

Merrit set aside his mortarboard and trowel and
squinted his eyes against the glare of the sun. "I 'spect
that's the only reason them boys would be a-foggin' it
back to camp like a couple of turpentined cats."

Silverthorne found a place to climb up on top of the
wall. He shaded his eyes with a hand and peered into
the oncoming dust cloud. "*Three* turpentined cats," he
announced. "Looks like Chad's white horse and the sor-
rel Mitch was riding. The third horse is a buckskin. And
the rider's got long hair."

"*Rachel!*" said Calvin. "I bet it's Rachel. She's
changed her mind, Silverthorne."

"Changed her mind about what?" said Silverthorne
with a chuckle. "Getting me shot down by her jealous,
quick-trigger husband?"

Silverthorne maintained his position atop the wall
when the rest of the men abandoned their stations and
lined up out front of the house with hands on hips to
see what the mad dash was all about. Chad and Warner
pulled their horses down as they approached, but Rachel
ran the buckskin right up to the onlookers, pulled him
to a sliding stop, and kicked out of the stirrups for a
catty dismount. When her feet hit the ground her knees
buckled and she had to grab the horse's mane to keep
from falling. The lathered buckskin stood spraddle-
legged with its head down, blowing hard.

Calvin stepped forward and grabbed Rachel by the
arm. "Ramey, take her pony and walk him out, will you
please? It's a wonder if he ain't wind-broke. Looks like
you run him all the way from Roswell, Rachel." Calvin's tone was mildly scolding.

"She's got news, Pa. Big news," said Chad, as he and Warner rode up.

"Did you have to bring it all by yourself, Rachel?" said Calvin, still irritated. "I can't believe Rosser would allow you to travel alone."

"He went to Santa Fe with Mr. Scott, Pa," said Rachel. The perturbation in her eyes softened when she glanced at Silverthorne, and for the moment she took to smile at her mother, who was walking up from the spring wagon with her Aunt Millie. The fierce gleam returned when she looked back to her father.

"Holloway's at Roswell, Pa."

"*What?* What's he doin' out here?"

"Brought a herd up. Must have got a contract up to Colorado or somethin'."

"Now's our chance to settle the score for him runnin' us out of Texas, Pa," said Chad.

"We can take him by surprise," urged Warner. "Holloway don't know where we went when we left Texas, so he won't be lookin' out for us."

"They must have drove right past here about a week ago," said Calvin, wagging his head. "They's so many herds comin' up the Pecos that we don't pay much attention to 'em anymore."

"He came through here more like four or five days ago, I 'spect," said Rachel. "His cows was as ganted as my pony is now. Looked like they'd been pushin' 'em hard and fast. I rode close by the cattle rest to get a good look at them after I run into Pabst and Andres on their way to town. I wanted to be sure they was H3 cows and the big augur was with the drive. Hunziker's with 'em, too, along with some colored hands. Nobody recognized me."

"You done good, Rachel," said Calvin. "If Holloway's cows is drawed down he'll likely hold 'em on the Hondo for several days."

"If we don't catch up to him there, we'll just keep after him till we do," declared Merrit.

"Just hold up a minute!" shouted Silverthorne from atop the wall. He waited until everyone was looking at him.

"Calvin, your brother Mart's run-in with the law is the real reason you were forced to leave Texas. Sure Holloway was trying to push you off your range, but you'd already been thinking about New Mexico for some time. You've got a good start here. The country's bigger, the grass is better, and there's a better market for your beeves. Coming here was a good thing. The events that precipitated the move were a blessing in disguise. Can't you count your blessings and let bygones be bygones?"

"I've got one more blessing to count, Silverthorne—the fact that Holloway's been delivered to my doorstep, so's to speak. And thanks to you I know that he burned my barn and killed my stallion and Rachel's colt. Horse thieves deserve to be hanged or shot, so what about a man who burns horses alive?"

"He didn't intend for the stock to be trapped."

"But they was, and it's his fault. Now, we're riding for Roswell first thing in the morning. You can go with us or you can stay here with the womenfolk."

"I reckon I'll be riding by the light of the moon, Cal. If I can't talk sense with you, perhaps I can persuade Holloway to stay out of your way."

"He'll tell 'em we're coming", said Warner. "We'd best not let Silverthorne ride out ahead of us."

Calvin looked hard at Silverthorne for a moment, and Silverthorne thought they might try to seize him and strap him to a wagon wheel. He eased his hand close to the mother-of-pearl grip of the pistol Holloway had given him.

"No, let him go," said Calvin. "I reckon Silverthorne ain't knowin' Percival Holloway as good as he thinks

he does. Holloway won't run. In fact, if he was aimin'
to move his herd out, he'll stay put and wait for us when
he knows we're comin'. That way nobody can say we
didn't give 'em a even break.

"Silverthorne, you tell him there will be four of us—
me, Merrit, Chad, and Mitch Warner, all men of the
clan. I'll leave Ramey to watch over the womenfolk
while we're gone. Them three Dutchmen will stand with
Holloway. That's even odds, four against four, if you
stay out of it."

"I'll just be there to treat the survivors, if any."

The Howells discontinued the wall-building and set
about getting things in order to depart the next day. They
would select their mounts and tend to the animals'
hooves, and clean and oil their rifles and revolvers. The
women would prepare food and drink for the journey.

Silverthorne packed his possibles, saddled Rudy, and
put *Trigueño* on lead. He planned to change from one
mount to the other throughout the night and part of the
next day, riding nonstop to his destination on the Hondo.
Holloway deserved to be warned, and Silverthorne felt
especially obligated to warn him since his slip of the
tongue had revealed Holloway's guilt in the death of
Calvin's stallion, thereby intensifying Calvin's resolve
to have his day of vengeance. Silverthorne thought there
might be a chance of talking Calvin out of it if not for
that. Silverthorne untracked Rudy and led both horses
behind the stacked-rock wall of the corral before he
stopped to double-check his cinch.

"Mama doesn't want you to go hungry on the trail,
Dr. Silverthorne."

Silverthorne turned a surprised look upon Rachel,
who'd stepped around the corner of the corral and was
holding out a bundle of food to him. Her eyes were
bloodshot and her cheeks were stained with tears. Evidently she'd been told about her uncle Mart. Silver-

thorne accepted the package and stowed it in a saddlebag.

"Please convey my gratitude to your mother, Miz Rosser."

He finished adjusting his latigo, thinking Rachel would turn her back on him and walk away. She was bound to be disappointed that he'd chosen to take the warning to Holloway instead of siding with the Howells. He pulled his stirrup leather down and toed the stirrup with a glance over his shoulder. Rachel was still standing there, glaring at him. Silverthorne heaved a sigh, withdrew his foot, and turned to face her.

"Rachel, I know you don't understand—"

"No, I don't, Dr. Silverthorne. Chance Rosser would stand with his friends if he was here. He's a *real* Southern gentleman. It's a good thing I married him instead of you, or you'd be turning against your own kin, including me!"

"I'm not turning against anyone, Rachel. The old Southern code of honor by way of vengeance has been carried too far too many times. I've been trained to save lives, and I've seen too much killing. I'm not going to Holloway so much to warn him as I am to try to talk him into avoiding the confrontation."

"Holloway lives by the code, same as us. And *his* friends will stand by him. Maybe even some of them darkies that ride for the H3. And if they do, we'll be in a jackpot, just because you've taken the advantage of a surprise attack away from us."

"Sounds like you're planning to go with the menfolk."

"Even though I've been feelin' poorly, I'd go if Pa would let me. I wish Chance and Mr. Scott were back from Santa Fe, and we could find Mr. Whitecraft. Then it wouldn't matter if Holloway's black drovers should fight."

Whitecraft. What if Abels came with word of Allen Whitecraft while Silverthorne was gone?

"Rachel, I know y'all don't think too highly of me just now, but I've got to ask a favor of you."

"Mama's not mad at you. She wishes you could talk them out of going. Says she's got a premonition."

"I've got one, too. That's why I'm trying to stop the feuding before it goes too far.

"Tell Martha I'm expecting a Mr. Augustus Alonzo Abels to come to the Rail H looking for me. If y'all will let him wait here for me, I'll be much obliged. I should be back in about four days, unless someone needs on-going medical care. Will you do that for me, Rachel?"

Rachel nodded. "I'd do almost anything for you, Taliaferro Silverthorne. But I'll not turn against my own family."

Silverthorne breathed another sigh and mounted up. "I've got to do what I think is right, Rachel. But remember: I love you. Even though you belong to another man, I'll always love you." He clucked the horses into a trot and rode away.

Rachel watched him out of sight, then buried her face in her hands and walked slowly back to the wagon.

TWENTY-TWO

"I SEE YOU'VE STILL GOT THAT BROWN HORSE LUPE gave you," was the first thing Percival Holloway said to Silverthorne when he rode up to the H3 wagon.

"Yeah, he's special. Lupe trained him to do things an ordinary cowpony never gets the opportunity to learn."

"Or needs to know."

"He's got a lotta cow, too."

"Have you been cowboyin', then? Or doctorin'? I hear the military's got the only doctor between the Rio Grande and the Brazos, so you haven't much competition."

"I haven't settled down to anything in particular yet, Major."

"I see. Well, I surely didn't expect to cross trails with you out here in this godforsaken country. Light down and set a spell, Silverthorne. Enofrio will have dinner ready directly."

"Got you a Mexican cook on this drive, eh?" said Silverthorne as he dismounted.

"And a good one, as you shall see." Holloway stepped forward to shake hands. "You appear not surprised to find us here, so you must have come on purpose and with prior knowledge of our whereabouts. How'd you find out? Are the Howells in this part of the country, too?''

"Yes, I'm afraid so. Rachel Howell—Rosser, that is—saw Alex and C. F. riding into town the other day. She's been living up yonder in the hotel with the gambler.''

Holloway raised an eyebrow. "Married Rosser, did she? Well, I'm glad you had sense enough not to get tangled up in her petticoat, Silverthorne. Not that she ever wears one." Holloway laughed at his own wise-crack.

Silverthorne chuckled, too, but more at the irony of Holloway's assumption. "Yeah, well, anyway, she scouted your herd and dern near wind-broke her pony riding down past Seven Rivers to where the Howells are filing on some water.''

Holloway blew a deep breath through his nose and bowed his head. "I be damned." He raised his brows and cut his eyes at Silverthorne. "How far behind you are they?''

"I rode all last night. They were gonna leave this morning. I expect they'll stop to rest tonight. They'll want to be sharp-eyed when they get here.''

"That would put 'em here about this time tomorrow?''

"I expect.''

"How many?''

"Just four. Calvin, Merrit, Mitch, and Chad. They figure Alec, Fred, and C. F. will stand with you. Four against four.''

"How about Mart?''

"Mart was killed in a shoot-out with Jim Highsaw, Chisum's range boss.''

"I've heard Jim Highsaw's a salty hombre. Now I believe it. What about the others?''

"Rosser had a disagreement with Grizell and killed him. Whitecraft dragged out after that happened. Ramey's staying home to guard the womenfolk. Rosser and Scott are in Santa Fe, but they'll be back soon.''

''Well, you got here just in time. We were planning to move 'em out in the morning.''

''Do it! I'll go with your crew. Make yourself scarce for a while. You can join us later, after Calvin gives up trying to find you. He can't stay away from his claim very long, because he's got a difficulty with Chisum's outfit.''

''No, Silverthorne, I won't run from him. I guess I always knew I'd not seen the last of Calvin Howell. I don't want to be looking over my shoulder for him any longer. It's time for a showdown. Does he know you're with us?''

''I didn't come here to join your forces, Major. I came to warn you, and to see if I could talk you into avoiding the conflict, since I couldn't talk any sense into Calvin. I was hoping you'd be more reasonable.''

''Still in the middle, eh, Silverthorne? Well, I'm more reasonable than you are, Silverthorne. You see, now I know for certain that Calvin will never give it up. I know there's only one way to end it.''

''Then why don't you and Calvin Howell settle it between just the two of you and leave the others out of it?''

''That would only settle it if I'm the loser, Silverthorne, because if I win it's a blood feud for sure.''

''But what if they agreed—''

''If I killed Calvin they could never let it rest, no matter what they'd promised. Eventually I'd have to kill them all. So it might as well be now.''

Silverthorne leveled a probing gaze at Holloway.

''Even Chad,'' said Holloway, reading his thought. ''We saw a lot of young boys in gray uniforms toward the end of the war, didn't we, Silverthorne? If they're old enough to fight they're old enough to die. As far as

I'm concerned Chad took an active hand in the fray the day he tried to kill my Galahad.''

"That's absurd," said Silverthorne, remembering how unreasonable the major had been about the incident, and realizing the futility of further argument about the issue at hand. There would be a showdown and nobody could stop it.

Even when the Howells failed to show up at the expected time the next day, Silverthorne did not doubt that the battle was imminent.

"Are you sure they were leaving yesterday morning?" Holloway wondered. He and Silverthorne were sitting their horses on a low rise that commanded a view of the big flat that lay between the Rio Hondo and the South Spring River, south of Roswell. The three ex-Union soldiers from Burnet County were waiting at the base of the hillock for Holloway to join them with the news that the Howells were coming. Earlier Holloway had ridden out upon the flat and along the Hondo where its generally eastern flow made a bend to the north along the western side of the plain. Silverthorne dreaded the aftermath when the two little armies would ride forth to face each other on the broad battleground.

"The Howells will be here," said Silverthorne. "If not this afternoon, in the morning. They're probably taking their time in order to spare their horses, knowing it could be a running battle. Their mounts aren't going to be as fresh as yours, even so. Calvin said he wanted it to be an even fight. That's why he didn't try to prevent me from riding ahead to give you fair warning."

"They'd be smart to rest their horses another night," said Holloway, nodding his head. "But Calvin's been waiting a long time for this. He might be too impatient to put it off another day. Sure is gettin' late, though."

"I see dust!" said Silverthorne, putting his right hand to his temple to block the slanting rays of the sun.

Holloway shaded his eyes and studied the approaching riders for a moment. He took a deep breath and let it out slowly. "Well, this shouldn't take long. I'd best get down yonder and brief the troops." He reined his horse away to join his men.

Silverthorne watched him huddle with his charges, using a stick to map out a battle plan in the soil and gesturing this way and that as he described the tactics they should employ. Once again he was *Major* Holloway, military commander.

Silverthorne shifted his gaze to the four riders coming up from the south. A queasy feeling crept into his gut. What chance did the Howells have? They had no strategy. They could only ride headlong into whatever stratagem Holloway presented, with each man acting independently on the spur of the moment.

Silverthorne realized his warning had given Holloway an unfair advantage. A feeling of guilt infused the dread in his gut. He tried to assuage the guilty feeling by reminding himself that it was the Howells who'd instigated the confrontation. And it wasn't the first time Calvin Howell or Mitch Warner had ridden to an uncertain rencounter to be confronted with maneuvers that were devised by a Union officer. No doubt Merrit had faced similar situations during his years of duty with the Home Guard.

Silverthorne wished Calvin had left Chad at home instead of Ramey.

Major Holloway and his men mounted up and rode forth with their rifles at the ready. As the two factions approached each other the Howells began to spread out. Silverthorne wondered why Holloway held his men in closer rank. Suddenly the answer became evident when, at Holloway's signal, they all reined right and spurred their mounts into a desperate run toward the setting sun. Holloway was trying to flank the Howells on the west to put the sun in their eyes! The oldest trick in the book! The men from the Rail H reacted immediately and in

unison, turning their ponies west and racing across the
flat to cut the maneuver short, firing their repeaters as
they rode. The H3 horses were fresher and faster, but
they would not be able to come around the flank in time
to force the Howells into facing the direct rays of the
sun.

But Holloway didn't even try to outflank them. He
rode straight for the river. He just wanted the Howells
to think he was trying to get between them and the sunset. Now he had them strung out and burning ammuni-
tion. He and his men rode over the riverbank in a group,
dismounted, and flung themselves against the slope of
the bank at a spot Holloway had selected during his
scout of the battleground. They were obscure targets,
had the protection of the embankment and a good rest
for their rifles, which were fully loaded.

Calvin Howell was leading the charge of the clan and
he was the first to go down. Major Holloway knew the
most steady part of a running horse is the saddle, so
that's where he aimed, and his .44 slug slammed into
Calvin below the navel, bursting his innards and shat-
tering his pelvis.

The gound came up fast and Calvin hit the turf hard
and lost his grip on his Winchester. Instinctively he
pulled his Colt and cocked the hammer. Hearing hoofbeats, he turned his head to see who was riding up on
him. It was his own horse, who'd circled and come back
to stand near its fallen master. "Good boy," said Calvin,
but he knew he'd never mount a horse again. He craned
his neck to see what was going on around him.

Mitch Warner's mount was down and he was firing
at Holloway's position from behind its carcass. Evidently Chad's white gelding had been burned by a bullet, for it was pitching viciously and Chad was hard put
to stay in the saddle. Calvin was thankful it was bucking
off to the south, away from the range of those deadly
rifles on the riverbank. Where was Merrit?

Calvin heard a whoop from the riverbank south of Holloway's entrenchment and saw Merrit running four horses out onto the plain. He'd been next behind Calvin in the pursuit and had obviously overrun Holloway's position and driven the H3 mounts ahead of him up the river so Holloway and his Germans couldn't ride out to follow up on breaking the Howell's charge. From the way Merrit was swaying in the saddle, Calvin knew his sally had not been without mishap. The H3 horses spread out and started grazing and Merrit dismounted to pull his neckerchief off and bind it around his left arm. He used his teeth to help hold it in position while he tied the knot with his right hand. Then he knelt down behind a clump of bushes and reloaded his carbine to start firing at the place he'd last seen Holloway and his men.

Calvin knew Mitch and Merrit were trying to cover him, hoping he'd be able to crawl away out of rifle range. They didn't know he couldn't move his legs. If he could turn over maybe he could drag himself along on his belly with his hands and arms. The pain in his abdomen was so bad he doubted he could even turn over. It would be better to play dead, if he could keep from moaning out loud. It would be dark before long and Mitch and Merrit would come to get him. But he would not be able to stand the pain of being moved. They'd just have to leave him where he was until the fight was finished and they could fetch Doc Silverthorne.

"They've got us pinned down," said Holloway, "but we've got a defensible position. And we've improved the odds. Calvin Howell's dead. One down and three to go."

"I think I hit Merrit when he was running away with the horses," said Alec Pabst.

Andres nodded. "I watch him drive the horses out on the flat and by the way he was riding I am sure he is wounded."

"I should've plugged him when he jumped his horse over the bank," said Holloway. "That took me by surprise."

Holloway cautiously raised up to get a better view of the plain. "It's getting so dark I can't see where our horses wandered."

"They scattered when Merrit runs them out of the bottom," said Andres.

"If I could catch one I might be able to round up the others," said Holloway, "even in the dark."

"Yah, there is half a moon tonight," Hunziker agreed.

"That's also good for us in case the Howells try to creep up on our position," said Holloway. "You boys move back down the embankment a little way so they'll be skylighted if they come, and listen for unusual noises. I'm going to work my way upriver and ease out onto the flat to see if I can locate any of our horses. If I can capture as many as two we'll ride double back to the remuda and remount. I'll signal you when I come back, whether I be afoot or ahorse."

The light of the half-moon was sufficient for a man to have a general idea of the lay of the land. By the time Major Holloway emerged on the plain, the wind had risen and the sky was filled with floating clouds that effected short spells of alternating darkness and light. Holloway slowly worked his way farther and farther out upon the broad flat. Where had those horses wandered off to? He stopped to gaze at the sky and watched a dark cloud drift toward the moon. The moon seemed to struggle with the leading edge of the cloud, pushing light through the thinner portions here and there, finally to be overcome by the thickening gloom. Holloway strode forth in the darkness, straining his eyes lest he brush against a thorny bush or a spiny cholla.

What was that? He was sure he'd heard the low whicker of a horse! It was close enough that it had smelled him. Suddenly the cloud mass slipped past the moon. There was the horse, not fifty feet away! Which one was it? He couldn't tell.

"Whoa, boy," said Holloway, advancing slowly, his eyes searching for the trailing reins. "Just take it easy. It's all right. I've got some barley back at the wagon that you're gonna like just fine. Remember how good it tastes?"

"*This pony's never tasted your barley, Major.*"

Holloway froze in his tracks and flashed his eyes to the shadow on the ground from whence the voice had come.

"What's the matter, Major, did you think you'd come upon Balaam's ass?" There was a chuckle, but it was cut short by a ragged cough.

"I recognize the voice, Calvin Howell."

Holloway eased forward, trying to get a clean image of the obscure form in the grass. He reached his hand to his revolver, thinking the shadow of his body would hide his cross draw from the grounded man even though his silhouette was plain against the moonlit sky. But Calvin didn't wait for further palaver. Just as Holloway's hand closed on the grip he saw a slab of flame, heard the roar of Calvin's .44, and felt the ball drive deep into his chest. He staggered, gasped at the fire in his heart, and crumpled to the ground. For a moment he gazed at the sky. Then the darkest cloud of all slid across the moon and there was no light.

TWENTY-THREE

DICK REED LOUNGED AGAINST THE DOORJAMB OF HIS trading post at Seven Rivers and watched the solemn procession passing by on its way down the Pecos. "Looks like Doc Silverthorne riding his brown and leading his dun with a body tied acrost it. That's Merrit Howell coming along next, hunched over like he don't feel so good. And Mitch Warner and the boy Chad are bringin' up the rear."

Allen Whitecraft stepped up behind Reed to take a look. "The dead man must be Calvin Howell."

"Yep, I reckon so. And I reckon you'll be ridin' out to join them, seein's how Mr. Howell was a friend of your'n."

"Not just yet. We've got to bury another *friend* first." Whitecraft cut his eyes at the short, bandy-legged man who joined them at the door.

"Well, I swanny, I believe we do," agreed the little man with the round belly.

The somber troop rode past Seven Rivers. They'd be home soon. Another grave to dig in the rocky hillside. Bad news for Martha and Rachel.

It would be a while before Alice Holloway found out she was a widow. The three Dutchmen had decided they would deliver the herd before they went back to Texas. At least they'd have the money to take back along with the news of the showdown with the Howells. They'd been afraid their friend and employer had found something more than a horse when they heard the single shot in the night. With the dawning their fears were confirmed. They could see his body lying out on the flat, about six paces from Calvin Howell's.

Silverthorne had had a view of the same scene from his vantage point on the knoll. He could also see Merrit, Mitch, and Chad huddled together just out of the Dutchmen's rifle range, planning their attack. They already knew Holloway was dead, for Mitch had left the shelter of his dead horse and crawled over to Calvin after he heard the shot. He'd stayed with Calvin until he died, then he'd taken Calvin's horse and begun searching for Merrit and Chad. Silverthorne rode off the hillock and out to where the bodies lay, trusting that neither side would fire upon a neutral. He loaded Holloway's body across his saddle, mounted up behind it, and took it over to the Dutchmen. They readily agreed that further hostilities would be senseless; the wise course would be to deliver the herd to the buyer and see that Alice Holloway got the proceeds and the hands got their wages. Then Silverthorne rode across the flat to talk peace with the Howells. At first they were reluctant to pull in their horns, but finally, considering the fact that the two principals in the confrontation had killed each other, they consented to allow the Dutchmen to go on about their business unmolested. The fact that the Howells could field only one competent warrior, what with Merrit wounded and Chad so young and inexperienced, was no doubt a factor in the decision. Silverthorne rounded up the H3 cow ponies on his way back to inform the Holloway hands they were free to go, and the men mounted up and went back to the herd. Silverthorne went with them so as to get his spare horse to carry Calvin Howell's body home to Rocky.

But there wasn't much of a home left when he got there.

Silverthorne led the sad procession across the slope of the hilly ridge south of Seven Rivers and began to scan the valley for sight of the Rail H camp. Soon he could see the bright canvas of the spring wagon. He squinted his eyes against the glare, trying to make out the corrals and the walls of the house. There was the bump wagon—but it was turned over on its side and its load of rocks was spilled on the ground! The walls of the house and the corrals had been turned into piles of rubble, too! Silverthorne reined in and called the others forward.

"What do you make of it, Merrit?"

The glint in Merrit's eyes and the clench of his teeth were not entirely from the pain in his arm. "Highsaw's been back. They must have brought some grappling irons to pull the walls down. Somebody told Chisum we were gone. He has his spies, I hear, mostly farmers he's befriended, like Bob Gilbert on the Peñasco and Felix McKittrick up at South Spring. Either one could have seen us riding north."

"Chisum probably thought y'all were riding off to steal some cows."

"He's got his way of justifying everything they do, I hear."

"There ain't no justification for shootin' women," said Mitch.

"Highsaw's boys probably got the drop on them before they could resist," said Silverthorne, "if Chisum knew there was only the three women and one man in camp."

"I bet that damned Bob Gilbert told Chisum we'd

rode out,'' said Chad. ''We orter ride over there and—''

''Let's get your daddy buried first,'' said Mitch.

''At least we'll have plenty of rocks for the grave,'' said Merrit with a sigh. He urged his pony forward and took the lead the rest of the way to the wagons. He dreaded the look on Martha's face when she took inventory of the ones riding upright and realized who was coming home facedown.

But Rachel was the one who fell apart. She sank to her knees and buried her face in her hands and gave way to gut-wrenching hysteria. Martha just stood there stone-faced. It was what she'd expected.

Martha remained stolid during the burial, but late in the night as Silverthorne prowled about the camp in the moonlight he overheard the woeful sounds of her anguish coming from the spring wagon where she'd spread her lonely bed.

Silverthorne wagged his head and stalked away from camp. He went down to the arroyo and stood on a grassy plane at the edge of the stream, pondering the aftermath of all that had happened. He was soon mesmerized by the sparkles of reflected moonlight dancing on the ripple of the water flowing across the rocky streambed.

The soothing spell of the gurgling stream was shattered by the sound of a footstep close behind, and Silverthorne whirled about, slipping the thong from his Peacemaker and snatching it from the holster. When he saw that it was Rachel he relaxed and let the iron slide back into the leather socket.

''You shouldn't creep up on a man like that, Rachel.''

''I wasn't trying to be sneaky, Tal. I couldn't sleep and I saw you walking about. I thought you'd hear me coming before I got so close.''

''I reckon I was lost in my thoughts, Rachel.''

''Thinkin' about what to do next? That's what we

were talking about after you left the campfire so early this evening.''

''I thought you and your family should have some time to yourselves. Too bad Ramey didn't take the hint.''

''It's just as well he stayed. He's goin' back to Texas, too.''

''Y'all are going back?''

''The rest of them are. I suppose I'll have to stay at Roswell. Or Seven Rivers, if Chance and Mr. Scott get their saloon started. The others can take our cows back to the old range at Lampkin Springs and live in peace now that Major Holloway's gone. Merrit and Mitch might have to face charges because of the jailbreak, but nobody saw their faces, so they'll probably be acquitted.''

''The men are going to leave without avenging Mart?''

''The odds are stacked against them right now, Tal. They'll always be thinking about coming back to settle accounts with Highsaw. That's the only thing that would ever bring any of them back to New Mexico.'' Rachel bowed her head. ''I'll probably never see my family again.''

''Now, Rachel, someday you'll be taking Martha's grandchildren home to show them off.''

''Won't be no children, I reckon. Chance claims he's got reason to believe he's sterile. Are you gonna stay out here, Tal? The country could use a good doctor.'' Two steps moved her against him. She put her arms around his waist and pressed her cheek against his chest. ''Please say you're gonna stay, Tal.''

Silverthorne put his arms around her. ''I thought you were mad at me.''

''You just done what you thought was right. Merrit said it would have been even worse if you hadn't risked your neck to ride down and negotiate a truce. That's all

you was tryin' to do all along, wasn't it? Now I wish
we'd had sense enough to listen to you.''

Rachel tightened her grip on him. ''I don't want to
be left in this godforsaken country without you, Tal.''
She turned her face to his, but he had no answer for her.
She moved her hands to his shoulders, gently pulling
him to his knees and on down as she lay back on the
grassy turf.

''But, Rachel, you're a married woman!''

''I don't care!''

''Well, I do!''

''This may be our last chance forever, Tal. Make the
hurt go away for a little while. Leave me with a com-
plete memory of you.''

Rachel's hungry lips found his and suddenly he didn't
care either.

TWENTY-FOUR

SILVERTHORNE SADDLED UP IN THE FIRST GRAY LIGHT. He was disgusted with himself. One thing he'd sworn he'd never do was to have another man's woman. The fact that Rachel's heart had belonged to him all along was of little consolation. If he'd had any idea that he'd ever be able to forget her before, there was certainly no possibility of it now. His first impulse was to ride to Roswell, face Rosser with the facts when he got back from Santa Fe, and let the chips fall where they may. If Rosser wanted a duel, then let there be a duel. But Silverthorne would never kill a man to get his wife. Besides, Rachel would feel responsible if harm came to Chance because of her liaison with Silverthorne, and her guilt would be a constraint to their relationship.

If Rosser ever found out about last night he'd probably come looking for Silverthorne. And what would he do to Rachel? It would be better for her if Silverthorne drifted on out of New Mexico and Rosser never found out he was still alive.

But first he would talk to Augustus Alonzo Abels to see if he'd located Allen Whitecraft. Just before she'd gone back to camp last night, Rachel had remembered

to tell him that Abels had ridden by shortly after Highsaw and his men left. He'd promised to wait for Silverthorne at Seven Rivers.

Silverthorne knew something was amiss as soon as he
walked in the front door of Dick Reed's trading post.
The sociable trader acknowledged Silverthorne's entry
with only a curt nod and a grunt from his station at the
counter, yet his eyes bored into Silverthorne's as though
he were trying to establish a silent communication.

Abels, on the other hand, was his usual effusive self.
He swung his stubby feet off the table at which he was
seated and jumped up from his chair to shake hands vigorously and slap Silverthorne on the shoulder, saying that
he was proud to see him hale and hearty, especially since
he'd seen Silverthorne pass by with a dead man in tow.

Silverthorne sat down at the table with Abels and
briefly recounted the chain of events that resulted in Calvin Howell's demise, for the benefit of Dick Reed as
well as Abels. He concluded by telling Reed he would
be losing some business as the surviving Howells, except Rachel, were intent on rounding up their cows and
going back to Texas. Reed just leaned on his counter
and looked serious. He gave a slight wag of the head
when Abels produced a bottle from his vest pocket, took
a swig, and offered to share it with Silverthorne. Silverthorne imbibed a snort to be social but refused any more,
commenting that Abels should remember from their buffalo hunting days that he was not fond of hard liquor.
When further persuasion could not induce Silverthorne
to share the bottle, Abels said he hated to drink by himself, corked it and put it away. Silverthorne took it to
be a good time to ask him if he'd uncovered any information about the whereabouts of Allen Whitecraft.
Abels glanced at Reed and suggested they remove to
outside of the store to discuss the subject. As Silverthorne followed Abels out the door, Reed gritted his

teeth and cut his eyes in a manner that made Silverthorne think perhaps the little potbellied man's constant chatter during the days he'd waited at the store for Silverthorne had gotten on Reed's nerves. Even so, Silverthorne wouldn't have thought Reed would be so uncommunicative. And what was it with the subtle facial expressions? Was he trying to convey a silent warning?

"Let's go round back of the 'dobe so's we can palaver private-like," said Abels.

Silverthorne slipped the thong from the hammer of his Peacemaker as he followed Abels around the building. He kept a sharp eye as they rounded the back corner and quickly surveyed the shadow of the rear wall of the big adobe. There was no one lurking there, just some discarded packing crates that Reed intended on breaking up for kindling. But one long crate caught his eye. It was standing upright, angled slightly toward the corner of the building with the open side toward the wall. There was enough space between the slats for a pistol barrel.

Abels glanced over his shoulder at Silverthorne and saw that he'd stopped and was eyeing the crate. Abels took off running as fast as his stubby legs would carry him, shouting, "It's now or never!"

Silverthorne jumped back toward the corner, palming the Peacemaker in the same movement, but the man in the box already had his revolver to hand and Silverthorne saw the flame, heard the blast, felt the slug slam into his right thigh, and lost his balance. As he was falling the shiny Peacemaker roared a reply, and when he hit the turf he rolled over twice with slugs kicking up dust where he'd been, then fired his four remaining shots into the box, splintering wood and burning holes right, left, top, and bottom. Suddenly all was quiet, save for a gasping sound that came from behind the box.

Abels had stopped about fifty yards away to see what had happened. He was bent over with his hands on his knees, breathing hard. When he saw Silverthorne punch the empty shells out of the Peacemaker, look his way and start digging fresh rounds out of his belt, thumbing them into the cylinder, he threw his hands up and started wagging his head. "I had to do it, Silverthorne," he shouted, "or that there gambler man would of kilt me! 'Twasn't my idee, I swear it!"

Silverthorne stopped loading the Colt and stared at Abels. *Gambler? Chance Rosser?* But Silverthorne never got to voice the question, for Abels caught his breath enough to take off running again, heading for his mule.

Silverthorne let him go.

The back door of Reed's store creaked and slowly opened a couple of inches.

"It's all over, Dick. Come on out and help me to my feet, will you? Just keep an eye on the hombre in the box. I can hear him breathing, but he sounds like he's out of action."

Reed emerged and tiptoed over to peer at the man in the box. "He's played his last card in this hand, all right. It'll likely be the last card he'll ever draw, if you don't help him."

"Shoot a man who's trying to kill you and then nurse him back to health? That'll be the paragon of irony. Do you know who he is?"

"Allen Whitecraft, the ex-Rail H hand you was askin' about a while back. He's been waiting for you with that talkin' toad frog who calls hisself Augustus Alonzo Abels."

Reed came on over and helped Silverthorne to stand up. Silverthorne pulled his neckerchief off and bound up the hole in his thigh.

"Ain't bleedin' too bad," said Reed. "Must not of hit a major blood vessel. You'll be all right. . . . Aw, hell, you know all that," he added with a sheepish look. "You're the doctor."

"It would be a lot worse if you hadn't warned me by acting so peculiar."

"Silverthorne, they's lots of hard cases come by Seven Rivers runnin' from somebody or lookin' for somebody. I got my business and my family to think about, not to mention my own hide, so I've made it a rule to stay shut of other folk's difficulties. But in your case I just had to do *something*. 'Sides, what would I do with all them books o' your'n?''

"Well, I'm beholdin' to you,'' said Silverthorne with a chuckle.

"Are you gonna be able to walk?''

"I think so,'' said Silverthorne, taking a tentative step. "Now if you'll fetch my medical kit from my packhorse, I'll see what I can do for Mr. Whitecraft.''

"You orter dress your own wound first.''

"It'll wait. Expedition may be the essence in Mr. Whitecraft's case.''

Reed went to get the Gladstone bag.

Silverthorne limped over to the box, keeping the Peacemaker at the ready. Whitecraft was lying on his side in the space between the box and the adobe wall, doubled up with pain and bleeding badly. His revolver was lying in the dust next to his face. Silverthorne kicked it out of his reach and knelt down beside him.

"Let's see if we can get you turned over on your back so I can see where you're hit.''

Whitecraft peered at Silverthorne, his teary blue eyes full of misgiving. "What're you aimin' to do to me now? Rosser only said you was aimin' to kill me, and I think you done that, if you'll just give me a little more time.''

So the gambler Abels mentioned was Rosser.

"Rosser lied, Whitecraft. It was never my intention to kill you—not unless you killed my wife on purpose, and I never thought you did.''

"I don't know nothin' about how your wife was shot! That's the God's truth of the matter.''

"Better not lie to the man who's going to try to save your life, Whitecraft. Do you stand by your claim that you and Jimmy Grizell were at the racetrack during the shoot-out at Scott's Saloon?''

Whitecraft's eyes wavered and he looked away from Silverthorne's gaze, clenching his teeth against the pain.

"Truth is, Silverthorne, I don't know where Jimmy was," he managed to say between grunts. "He'd *been* with me at the track, but we wasn't together all the time. . . . He never said or done nothin' that would make me suspect he was anywheres else. . . . Rosser said you'd done made up your mind it was me and him shot Miz Silverthorne and you was out to get me, since he'd already done for poor ol' Jimmy.''

"When did he tell you that? How'd he know I was alive?''

"I don't know; maybe Abels told him. . . . Abels had went to Rosser to ask him about me. . . . Rosser was expectin' me when I showed up in Roswell to get even with him for Jimmy and he seen me first, in the hotel, and said he wanted to talk. . . . Said you sicced him on Jimmy before you disappeared. . . . Said you claimed you had proof we killed Miz Silverthorne.'' With that Whitecraft threw his head back and let out a squall.

"Let's see if we can get you on your back, Allen. I'll give you something for the pain soon as Reed gets back with my valise. Here he comes now.''

Silverthorne cleaned Whitecraft's wounds while the anodyne took effect. One slug had grazed his hipbone, glanced off, and passed on through the flesh of the buttock. The chest wound would be life-threatening if not properly treated. Silverthorne got Reed to help him remove Whitecraft to Reed's ''pilgrim tent'' before he dug the bullet out. It appeared that it had not struck anything vital, but the flow of blood would have to be stemmed and the wound would need frequent attention in order to avoid infection.

"I successfully treated one patient in this tent,'' said Silverthorne. "I reckon I'll tend this one out here, too.''

"They stayed the nights out here while they was waitin' to kill you," said Reed, "so he orter feel at home. When are you gonna see to yerself?"

"Soon as I get this last bandage tied off."

"I'm probably gonna need to fetch some more cloths for your bullet hole."

"No, I believe there are enough. Think you can get the bullet out for me? Feels like it's lodged against the femur. Shouldn't be difficult to reach with my instruments. I won't be able to take any painkiller if I'm going to doctor it myself when you get through."

"I've dug slugs out of a couple of hombres when whiskey was the only painkiller we had. But you better let me break a stick offa one of them crates so's you'll have somethin' to clamp yer teeth on."

Reed found the lead ball in Silverthorne's thigh on the first probe and quickly extracted it. While Silverthorne disinfected, medicated, and bandaged the wound, Reed fetched his bedroll and his packs from the horses. Then Reed repaired to his store with a promise that he'd check on the wounded men from time to time and supply them with food and drink. He also assured Silverthorne he would see to his horses.

Whitecraft was sleeping soundly, so Silverthorne unrolled his blankets alongside the opposite wall of the tent and stretched out on his back with his hands clasped behind his head. Sleep would serve the healing process, but his mind was too busy sorting out the bits and pieces of information his discussion with Whitecraft had revealed.

Whitecraft had gone to Roswell to avenge the death of his friend Jimmy Grizell. No doubt he would have waylaid Rosser much the same way he'd set Silverthorne up. Silverthorne knew of several dry-gulching cases in Texas in which the jury acquitted the killer on the grounds of self-defense because they felt he'd had good reason to be in fear of his own life and was consequently forced into a "shoot first or die" situation. No doubt

Whitecraft felt an ambuscade was justified on that basis.
Since Rosser knew he and Jimmy were pards, the dead-
shot gambler would expect a chance meeting with
Whitecraft to be a shoot-on-sight situation.

Evidently Abels had discovered that Whitecraft was
on his way to Roswell to kill Rosser and decided to sell
the information to Rosser. Perhaps he also mentioned
Silverthorne, or Rosser may have already known Silverthorne was still alive. Rosser saw in Whitecraft an opportunity to put Silverthorne out of the way without
Rachel knowing he was involved. Rosser would be far
away in Santa Fe when the killing took place.

Rosser intercepted Whitecraft and convinced him that
Silverthorne had talked Rosser into believing Grizell had
shot Silverthorne's wife. That accusation had provoked
Jimmy into reaching for his six-shooter, so Rosser shifted
the blame to Silverthorne and warned Whitecraft that Silverthorne was still alive and intent on tracking him down
and killing him. Abels probably backed Rosser up by ad-
mitting that Silverthorne had hired him to search for
Whitecraft. Whitecraft had every reason to believe the
tale, for Rosser, being forewarned of his arrival, could
have simply faced up to him and shot him down.

Rosser must have hired Abels to help Whitecraft in
order to assure the success of the deed and to report the
outcome. Abels said Rosser threatened to kill him if he
didn't assist in the bushwhacking, but Silverthorne expected Abels was motivated by pure greed. Anyway,
Rosser would soon know the ambuscade had failed and
Silverthorne was alive yet. But he couldn't know that
Whitecraft had survived and talked. Rosser couldn't
know that Silverthorne knew he was behind the attempted murder, unless Abels told him what he'd said
just before he ran for his mule, and that wasn't likely.

That Rosser would try again *was* likely.

TWENTY-FIVE

THE GRASSHOPPER PLAGUE THAT STRUCK SOUTHEAST-
ern New Mexico in 1876 would be overshadowed by the
black smallpox epidemic of seventy-seven and both
would be eclipsed by the all-out shooting war that would
erupt in seventy-eight from the political and commercial
power struggle in Lincoln County. But the popping canvas and moaning wind of the three-day blow that subdued the swarm of voracious insects before they could
wreak havoc on the Pecos grasslands was as unnerving
to Silverthorne as the blasts of gunfire and wails of be-
reavement would be to the citizens of the mountain valleys two years hence. The savage gusts threatened to rip
the tent from its moorings and sweep it across the prai-
rie, taking Silverthorne and his patient along with it.

When the raging windstorm finally abated, Silverthorne felt a compulsion to spend a day outside the tent
and away from Seven Rivers. Whitecraft had recovered
to the point that Silverthorne could leave him to be
looked in on occasionally by the Reeds. Silverthorne's
own wound had healed sufficiently that he was willing
to attempt a short ride, so he saddled Rudy and headed
south for Rocky Arroyo.

Silverthorne walked Rudy for a mile or so, then
clucked him into a jog. Finally he squeezed the gelding
into an easy lope to relieve the stress on his gun-shot
leg. As the sun rose higher in the sky, the reddish brown
hide of Rudy's neck, chest, and shoulders turned dark
with sweat. Silverthorne reined him down to a walk for
the last half mile to the abandoned Rail H camp.

Silverthorne dismounted and eased his cinch. He
walked Rudy out, at the same time working the stiffness
out of his wounded leg and gazing about at the rubble
of Calvin Howell's dream of a new beginning. He could
see evidence that the Chisum crew had camped on the
site when they'd put up the herd for San Carlos. Silverthorne hoped Merrit, Mitch, Chad, and Ramey had found
a lot of Chisum's unmarked weaners to gather in with
the Rail H herd when they rounded up and headed back
to Lampkin Springs. At the same time he had to admit
he might feel the same way Chisum did about the vast
grasslands if he'd been the one to brave the dangers and
uncertainties of unsettled territory in order to bring in
the first cattle to put the land to use.

But Chisum was bound to lose. No matter how many
settlers his cowboys scared off their claims and no matter how much water his hands filed on for him, he
couldn't keep it all. Already permanent cow camps were
spreading north from Pope's Crossing along the east side
of the Pecos—Pearce and Paxton, Ramer and Nash,
Powell and Yopp working for Bob Wiley out of Fort
Worth, and Dick Smith. The Beckwith family had established ranches on both sides of the Pecos near Seven
Rivers. L. G. Murphy and Company had a camp near
Seven Rivers, too, and a man named Blake had claimed
a spring farther north, beyond the Peñasco. Others would
soon arrive, and many of the newly arrived cowmen
would not be intimidated by John S. Chisum's high-
riding cowboys. Calvin Howell could have been one of
those to subsist if only he could have foregone the op-

portunity for a day of reckoning over the things he'd left behind.

Silverthorne paused to gaze at the three lonely graves on the hillside. A chill, hollow feeling crept through his vitals when he thought of the lives that were lost and the dreams that had turned to dust in the little valley. Silverthorne led Rudy down to the rushing stream, slipped the bridle, let him drink, and staked him out on the grassy bank where he and Rachel had finally consummated their forbidden love. He gazed into the clear, swirling water and conjured up memories of that fateful night. The emptiness turned to loneliness, and he thought about how lonely Rachel must feel now that the remnants of her family had forsaken the country where she must remain. He remembered how she'd pleaded that he should not also leave her. But what else could he do? She wouldn't go with him. She'd already broken her marriage vow, but she knew Rosser would try to kill him if he took her. She didn't know Rosser had already tried.

And what was Silverthorne to do about that? If a confrontation resulted in Rosser's death, Rachel would surely blame herself, and her love for Silverthorne would be plagued with guilt. He might win Rachel, but it would forever cast a pall on their relationship. So even if he won, he'd lose, and so would Rachel.

As soon as Whitecraft was well enough to take care of himself, Silverthorne had better drift. In the meantime, he reminded himself to keep a sharp eye on the strangers drifting through Seven Rivers. Rosser might send someone else before Silverthorne could make himself scarce.

When he got back to Seven Rivers late that afternoon, Silverthorne found out Rosser had already sent someone. When he ducked into the tent he discovered Jerry Scott seated next to Whitecraft's pallet.

"Hell of a thing to shoot a man just so's you can practice up on your doctorin'," said Scott, as he grinned and offered his hand.

"Like I said, it was just a misunderstandin'," said Allen, giving Silverthorne a direct look that told him Whitecraft had not divulged the real story behind his shoot-out with Silverthorne. Obviously Scott did not know about Rosser's part in the "misunderstanding." Or else he was a very good actor.

"How'd you know Allen was here?" asked Silverthorne, shaking hands with Scott.

"I didn't know he was here until the storekeep told me."

"Well, if you came down to help the Howells drive their cows back to Lampkin Springs, you're too late. I went down to Rocky today, and it looks like they pulled out over a month ago."

"I knew from what Rachel said when she come back from the homestead that they'd already be gone by now. But if me'n Chance's plans to build a saloon here at Seven Rivers don't pan out, me'n Allen might go back together when he gets well enough to travel. Chance won't never go back, no matter how much Rachel begs him."

Scotts demeanor turned real serious. "Rachel needs a doctor, Silverthorne; that's what I come for. It's too far to fetch the doc from Fort Stanton, even if he could come, but Chance said you was in Seven Rivers last he heard. So I come down to see if I could find you and fetch you back to Roswell."

"What's wrong with her?" said Silverthorne, at the same time flashing a troubled look at Allen Whitecraft.

"Go ahead, Doc," said Whitecraft. "Scotty said he'd stay with me while you're gone. You can show him what to do. About all I need from now on is rest, anyway."

"Rachel's took a fever, Doc," said Scott. "At first we thought it was like the one she had on the trail last fall, but it's worse. Lots worse."

Silverthorne rode across the Peñasco as the last gleams of sunset reflected red upon the water. He clenched his teeth against the pain in his thigh and pushed *Trigueño* hard in order to reach the Feliz by midnight, knowing he'd have to rest the tough little gelding when he got there. After he'd hobbled Tree and turned him loose on the grass north of the rio he spread a blanket and stretched out on his back to stare at the stars and contemplate.

Did Rosser have any idea that Silverthorne knew he was behind Whitecraft's attempt to bushwhack him? Probably not, for he would have no doubt that Silverthorne had killed Whitecraft. Whitecraft was down and disabled, perhaps dead, and Silverthorne was reloading and trying to get up when Abels fled the scene. Most anyone in Silverthorne's position would counterattack until his assailant was surely dead.

Even if it hadn't occurred to Rosser that Silverthorne might know he was after his scalp, he must be pretty desperate to condescend to calling on Silverthorne for help. Rachel must really be seriously ill. Silverthorne could hardly stand to wait for Tree to recuperate. But he knew he must, and he even managed to get a few snatches of fitful sleep during the several hours he tarried at the Feliz.

By the time the lathered brown gelding stumbled up to the hotel at Roswell in the early light of a new day Silverthorne was exhausted, and the searing pain in his leg was the only thing that kept him from falling asleep in the saddle. It had occurred to him that Scott and Rosser could be setting him up with the story about Rachel's illness, and he had the presence of mind to slip the thong from his .45 before he dismounted, just in case. Rosser popped out of the door immediately. He'd been watching. But there was nothing but worry on his face as he strode forth to greet Silverthorne. Rosser gripped Silverthorne's left arm to steady him as he piled off the horse, untied his medical kit, and limped inside.

"See that my horse is cared for. He's in bad shape," said Silverthorne as Rosser guided him to the stairwell.

"I'll see to it," said a man who was standing by the foot of the staircase.

"Let me carry your bag," said Rosser. "Grab hold of the banister. Looks like you're favoring that right leg. What's the matter?"

Silverthorne felt like asking him if Abels hadn't told him how close his dupe had come to getting the job done. But it would be best to keep the peace, at least until after Rachel was out of danger.

"It's just stiff from the long ride," said Silverthorne. "It'll be all right once I get the kinks out. What are Rachel's symptoms, other than the high fever?"

"Sick to her stomach, vomiting. But she'd been like that every morning for several weeks before she came down with the fever."

Silverthorne paused on a narrow step and looked Rosser in the eye. "You know what morning sickness means, Rosser. Congratulations."

"Congratulations to whom, Dr. Silverthorne? I know you were at Rocky when she went to tell her father about Holloway. I know to whom the child belongs."

"I know what you're thinking Rosser, but you can't be certain."

"I'm sterile, Doctor."

"You can't be certain of that, either, unless you've been emasculated, which certainly you have not."

"She told me, Doctor. . . . You needn't look so surprised. She tried to keep your little secret. I had to beat it out of her."

Silverthorne shrugged his arm away from Rosser's grasp and went ahead of him up the stairs.

"We shall settle that score later, you and I," said Rosser to Silverthorne's back.

Silverthorne waited at the head of the stairs for Rosser to come abreast and show him into the room where Rachel was. The coverlet was thrown back on the bed where she lay and there were beads of sweat on her forehead. Her eyes were closed and her breathing was rapid. Silverthorne hooked a toe in a straight-backed chair and pulled it up to the bed, motioning for Rosser to put the valise on it. Then he hitched up his gunbelt and sat down on the bed beside her.

"Damn!" he said, seeing that her eyes were blackened. "Rosser, I swear . . ." Rachel's nose was swollen and no longer perfectly aligned with the middle of her features. Silverthorne flashed a menacing glance at Rosser. "How could you do such a thing?"

"*Me?* How could she do what *she* did? And what about *you?*"

"I cannot abide a man who will strike a woman, no matter what the circumstances, Rosser. If you feel that strongly about what she did, it's a wonder you didn't just let her die instead of sending for me."

"I've still got a craving for her, Silverthorne. And I want her to live to see you dead. I want her to understand what it means to belong to Chance Rosser."

"Her heart never belonged to you, Rosser, and it never will." Silverthorne bent over Rachel and gently pried her mouth open, noting the paleness of the skin around her lips. He looked at her tongue. It was bright red. He unbuttoned her nightshirt.

"Just can't keep your hands off my wife, can you, Silverthorne?"

Silverthorne ignored the jibe and pushed Rachel's gown back to expose the bright red spots on her chest.

"Scarlatina."

"What?"

"Scarlet fever."

"That's a children's disease. I don't believe it!"

"She's got all the symptoms. Adults are occasionally infected. Besides, Rachel's not far beyond her childhood." Silverthorne probed along Rachel's neck below the jawbone, then reached inside her gown to examine an armpit. "Glands are swollen. It's a bad case. The rash will soon cover the whole body except for the head. Or at least her torso.'' He put his right hand on her forehead. ''I've got to get that fever down.''

Suddenly Rachel gasped, flung her right arm out and grasped Silverthorne's other wrist. ''Tal? Oh, Tal. Don't leave me out here all alone, Tal.''

Silverthorne glanced at the deep scowl on Rosser's face. ''She really doesn't even know I'm here, you know. She's just talking out of her head with the fever.''

''I know,'' said Rosser, releasing a pent-up breath. ''She's been babbling about you ever since she took the fever.''

Silverthorne gently removed her hand from his wrist to hold it between both of his own. He leaned close and spoke gently in her ear. ''I'm here, Rachel. I'm going to take care of you.''

Rachel's eyes flashed open. They were bright with fever. ''Stay with me, Tal. Don't leave me. I'd do anything for you. I set you free from her, Tal. You belong to me now.''

Silverthorne's mouth fell open and he jerked his head around to see if Rosser had gotten the import of what she had said. Rosser's stunned expression said that he had.

''*She* shot Marylois! She killed Marylois before I could explain to her . . .'' Rosser blinked his eyes and shifted his stare from Rachel to Silverthorne.

''Before you could explain what to my wife, Rosser?'' Silverthorne's eyes narrowed. He'd seen a daguerreotype of Marylois's brother. A younger, clean-shaven Chance Rosser without the shoulder-length hair? Yes, it could be. ''Or should I say Mendenhall? Charles Mendenhall, Confederate deserter.'' Rosser just kept staring at him.

Silverthorne nodded. ''So that's why you came to Lampkin Springs. You found out your sister was there. And before you could muster up the courage to try to explain to her why her beloved brave brother turned his back on his country and his family, she was killed. She'd have probably died of natural causes before you ever got the guts to reveal yourself.''

"No! I was going to..." Rosser shifted his gaze back to Rachel. "Let her *die*, Silverthorne. She's a murderer. She deserves to die."

"That's not for me to decide; nor you, *Charles*. I'm as shocked as you are over what she did." Silverthorne looked at Rachel, squeezed her hand, and wagged his head. "Right now I don't know what should be done about it. But I do know I can't stop loving her, and I'm going to save her if I possibly can. I would do the same for anyone. Even you, Charles, and I know you set me up to be murdered by Allen Whitecraft."

"You'll both die!" Rosser's right hand flashed across his body to the butt-forward American on his left hip. Before he could bring it up, Silverthorne had dropped Rachel's hand, grabbed his .45, thumbed the hammer, and aimed it, all in one swift motion. Rosser stared in disbelief at the black hole of the Peacemaker's muzzle and slowly eased his .44 back into the holster.

"Now get ahold of yourself, Rosser," said Silverthorne. "You and I shall work together to save this woman's life, if it can be done. I shall need cool compresses to lower the fever, and you can tell the hotel cook to make ready a supply of broth. And fresh milk, if she's got any."

"The hotel's got a milch cow," mumbled Rosser, turning toward the door.

"Bring cloths and cool water just as quickly as you possibly can!" said Silverthorne as Rosser trudged out of the room.

For the next six days Rosser dutifully fetched the things Silverthorne needed to treat Rachel, and brought meals and other personal necessities for Silverthorne. When he wasn't needed he spent the time in the gaming room. Around Silverthorne his demeanor was subdued, in a surly sort of way. He'd clearly been shaken by the fact that Silverthorne had so cleanly outdrawn him, and it seemed to have instilled a grudging respect for Silverthorne in the egoistic gambler.

By working day and night Silverthorne managed to keep Rachel's fever under control, and on the sixth day it finally broke. On day seven he could see a definite diminishing of the red flush that covered her body. The skin would soon start peeling off in tiny pieces.

Rachel had not said much since her fever broke, but her eyes followed Silverthorne's every move when she was awake. In those eyes he saw fear whenever Rosser was in the room. When she and Silverthorne were all alone on the eighth day she finally told him what was on her mind.

"You don't think I'm pretty anymore, do you?" she began, putting a finger to her broken nose.

Silverthorne smiled at her. "Rachel, hardly anyone's nose is perfectly centered. Now you're just a little more like the rest of us imperfect mortals."

Rachel gave him an unbelieving look.

"Look at me, Rachel, straight on," he said, sitting on the bed next to her and facing her squarely. "My nose is just a tad off center to the right, see?"

Rachel nodded.

"And you never even noticed it before, did you?"

Rachel smiled, and when Silverthorne smiled back, she giggled.

"But I'm not going to take a chance on your getting hurt by Mr. Rosser anymore. As soon as you're able to travel, I'm getting you out of here."

Fear flashed up and drove the amusement from Rachel's eyes. "He'll kill you, Tal. Nobody's quicker on the draw than Chance Rosser."

"He's already tried it, Rachel."

"You beat him?" Rachel's eyes filled with wonder.

"It wasn't even close. I could have killed him."

"You should have killed him when you had the chance. He won't give up."

Silverthorne turned his face away from Rachel and put a hand to his forehead. The coldness in her voice when she spoke about killing her husband reminded him of how ready she'd been for "Colt and Winchester" to settle the Holloway-Howell feud back at Lampkin Springs. But most of all it made him acutely aware that this woman had shot his wife down in cold blood. She was the person Oliver Holloway had seen in the alley. That's why he didn't want to tell.

"What's the matter, Tal? You got a headache all of a sudden?"

Silverthorne couldn't bring himself to tell her he knew. Not yet. He still loved her in spite of it. He'd caught himself rationalizing, telling himself Marylois didn't have much time left anyway, that the killing had just saved her a lot of pain and suffering, just like the dying mare Rachel had shot. "Did her a favor and sent her on up yonder," Lupe Proffit would say. But no excuse could justify what she had done. Silverthorne could never live with the knowledge of it and live with Rachel at the same time.

"Rachel, I know why Rosser beat you. I know you're pregnant."

"I tried to keep from tellin' him, Tal," she said, "because I knew he'd try to kill you. But he'd found out you're still alive, and that you were at Rocky when I went down there. He knows I love you more than him, so it wasn't hard to figure out. He just wanted to make me admit it."

Rachel's expression brightened. "I'm gonna have a son, Tal, I just know it. Your son, Tal, yours and mine. We'll—"

"Son or daughter, you'll never see it, Silverthorne." Rosser had been eavesdropping just outside the door and he stepped into the room with a revolver in his fist, pointed at Silverthorne. "And neither will you, my pretty little black-eyed, crooked-nosed wife. I've located an old Mexican hag in El Berrendo who'll take care of the little brat before anyone even knows you're carrying it. If we're fortunate, the procedure will also render you incapable of conception. My plans for you do not include pregnancy."

"You'll likely get Rachel killed, you fool!" Silverthorne started to get up from the bed, but Rosser made a menacing gesture with his .44.

"Just sit tight and keep your hands where I can see them! I just caught you trying to take advantage of my beloved wife's weakened condition, Dr. Silverthorne. I've already told the boys downstairs I suspected you'd taken liberties with her. No one can fault me for killing you."

Rachel frowned and turned to lie on her right side, propping herself up on an elbow. "If you're so sure you can't make babies, why do you want me sterile?" She laid her left hand on the mattress next to Silverthorne's right side, which was turned toward her and away from Rosser.

Rosser laughed. "Since you're so fond of extramarital activity, I'm going to see you get all of it you can stand. Cowboys from near and far will be riding to Seven Rivers to patronize Rosser and Scott's Saloon when the news gets out about the pretty little strumpet we've got on duty."

Silverthorne started to rise again, but Rachel grabbed the back of his shirt and tugged it, signaling him to sit still.

"You can't force me to be your whore," she said, sliding her hand down Silverthorne's back to his waist.

"You'll do whatever I say, my dear, or I shall reveal your little secret."

"What are you talkin' about?"

"Well, I declare. You mean you haven't told her, Silverthorne?"

"Told me what?"

Silverthorne turned his head to speak directly to Rachel over his shoulder. His body moved also, bringing the grip of his .45 close to her hand. "You did some crazy talking when you were out of your head with the fever, Rachel. It doesn't mean a thing."

"I daresay, Silverthorne, a confession to murder is hardly insignificant, no matter what the circumstances."

Silverthorne heard Rachel's breath catch in her throat, and out of the corner of his eye he saw a look of panic flash in her eyes. The gleam of terror was quickly replaced by a burning determination he'd seen there so many times before, and he felt the tug on his gunbelt as the long-barreled Peacemaker was jerked out of the holster.

Rosser heard the whisper of metal on leather. But Silverthorne's hands were in plain sight! He swung the Smith and Wesson toward Rachel. Silverthorne sprang to his feet and Rosser veered his barrel back to the right and pulled the trigger. His bullet slammed into Silverthorne's abdomen below the rib box on the right side, knocking him back on the bed. The Colt erupted in unison with the .44 and Rosser's left knee exploded in a splatter of blood and bone, spinning him around and dropping him to the floor. Before he could turn back to face her, Rachel sat up and steadied the Peacemaker with her right hand and pulled the trigger as fast as she could. Four scarlet dots popped out on the back of Rosser's white shirt and he slumped forward and hung his head as if he were staring at the floor between his knees.

Despite the bedlam from the six shots that had been fired, the sound of the hammer being cocked and the firing pin falling on empty cartridges seemed to fill the room as Rachel kept thumbing the hammer and pulling the trigger. Silverthorne gripped his side and sat up on the bed next to Rachel. He put his free hand over the revolver and gently wrested it from her grip.

"No!" said Rachel. "Leave me have the shooter or they'll think you did it."

"They'll think I did it anyway."

"I'll tell them what happened. I don't care what they do to me as long as you're safe. Are you shot bad?"

Silverthorne wagged his head. "They wouldn't believe you, Rachel. Besides, we have to do what's best for the child."

"But they'll hang you, Tal. They'll come up to see what happened soon as they're sure the shootin's all done."

Silverthorne got up off the bed, holstered his pistol, and stepped over to the window to rip a curtain down and tie it tightly around his waist. The blood did not immediately soak through. Perhaps the wound wasn't too bad. The window was open and the roof of the front porch of the hotel was immediately below it. Silverthorne put a leg over the sill.

"Wait, Tal, I'm comin' with you!"

"You can't, Rachel. It's too dangerous, you're too weak, and there isn't time."

"What am I gonna do, Tal? I'm all alone out here."

"Go home, Rachel. Jerry Scott and Allen Whitecraft will be going back to Lampkin Springs in a couple of weeks. They'll take you home to your mother. If I make it as far as Seven Rivers I'll tell them to come for you. In case I don't get away, you must ride to Seven Rivers as soon as you're able."

Rachel nodded. "When will I see you again, Tal?"

Silverthorne smiled at her. "Take good care of our baby."

Rachel lowered her eyes and put a hand on her abdomen. When she looked back to the window he was gone.

TWENTY-SIX

SILVERTHORNE LAY ON HIS BELLY ON THE COLD, ROCKY *ground of a New Mexico mountainside somewhere south of the canyon that secluded the waterfall where he'd camped when he was with Magoosh the Apache. He'd gone to the waterfall because he knew the way. He didn't know exactly where he was now. Somewhere among the lesser ridges of the massive Guadalupe reef. He hadn't been able to go any further. Rudy needed rest and Silverthorne had gotten too weak to stay in the saddle.*

He hadn't thought the bullet wound in his side was very serious when he'd jumped off the porch of the hotel and stolen the best-looking horse at the hitch rail. He'd nearly killed that horse racing it to Seven Rivers, and the curtain he'd tied around his waist was soaked with blood by the time he got there. He'd exchanged the stolen horse for his own red dun before he went to the tent to tell Scotty and Allen to fetch Rachel home to Lampkin Springs with them. He told Scott why Rosser would not be building a saloon at Seven Rivers, that it wasn't a fair fight but he'd won it anyway, that Rosser's friends at the hotel would not see it that way and would be coming along after him very soon. Then he'd ridden out of Seven Rivers for the last time and kept on running. And bleeding.

There was no way he could have hidden his trail. The blood had soaked his trousers and seeped down the outside of his thigh and calf to drip off the heel of his boot and mark his passage. They should overtake him very soon now. He listened for the hoofbeats of the posse.

All he heard was the clip-clop of one animal. It sounded like a small animal. Then he saw it. A mule! The little potbellied man on the mule carried a carbine across his saddle bows. He was concentrating on Rudy's hoofprints and the drops of blood, so he'd not yet seen Silverthorne lying facedown amongst the rocks and brush in front of him. And he didn't hear the slow click-click of the cocking hammer as Silverthorne raised the fancy Peacemaker and tried to take careful aim. Silverthorne couldn't hold the revolver steady and the image of Augustus Alonzo Abels riding his mule up the slope wavered before his eyes. He steadied the Colt with both hands and pulled the trigger. But there was no blast of gunpowder, only a snap when the hammer hit the groove. In his haste to escape the hotel he'd forgotten to reload!

Abels heard the sound of the empty pistol and saw his quarry at the same time. He raised the carbine and took aim, but Silverthorne dropped his weapon and slumped flat-out against the turf just as Abels was about to pull the trigger. He lowered the carbine and carefully dismounted. He crept over to Silverthorne and, pointing the carbine at Silverthorne's head with one hand, bent over and picked up the Peacemaker and stuck it in his waistband. He cautiously extended a foot and toed Silverthorne over on his back.

"Well, I swanny! Don't believe I've ever seed that much blood on the outside of a livin' man." He bent over for a closer look. "Either you done run out or there

just ain't enough left to dreen, 'cause you's about stopped bleedin' now. Danged if you ain't still breathin', though. Don't see how. I orter put you out of yer misery, but them rannies from Roswell would hear the shot and come a-runnin' over here and I wouldn't get to keep this here flashy shooter I been cravin' ever since I fust laid eyes on it. I best make it hard on them boys to find you so's I can get a good head start on 'em when I ride off with it.''

Silverthorne's eyes opened just wide enough to see a bleary image of Abels's stubbled face and rotten-toothed grin. He felt the silver-studded gunbelt being unbuckled and jerked away. Then his boots were slammed together as the loop of Abels's lariat rope was pulled tight around his ankles. He heard the little mule grunt and dig his hooves into the gravelly soil and Silverthorne's head bounced against rocks and roots as he was dragged across the slope and into a ravine. He managed to crack one eye open and saw nothing but sky. Then the blue was gradually obliterated by the shadows of brushy branches as Abels gave him a makeshift burial.

The sounds of Abels's slow departure gradually diminished and faded out.

Silverthorne thought he heard the sounds of distant shouts and the scraping of horseshoes on stone, but no one disturbed his coffin of limbs and leaves and thorns and twigs. Abels must have hidden him well and done a good job of obliterating the signs of his crude funeral procession.

Silverthorne felt like he was floating on air and he could tell he was about to lose consciousness. So dying wasn't so difficult after all. Just like going to sleep. "Be a good mother, *Rachel*," *he whispered just before he lost touch with all his senses.*

Silverthorne opened his eyes. At first he didn't know where he was, then he remembered. He could scarcely

*believe he was still alive. He wondered how long he'd
slept. He could tell it was still daylight. Or was it another day? The foliage on top of his body swayed in a
cool wind that moaned through the brush. The breeze
felt good on his feverish brow.* Got to get out of here.
Silverthorne pushed against the limbs on top of his chest.
No use. Too weak. Maybe he could turn over and crawl
out underneath the branches. *He struggled to twist his
body around, trying to ignore the searing pain in his
side. He just hoped the wound didn't start bleeding
again. Finally he was on his belly. He heard some of
the brush tumble from the top of the pile, dislodged by
his frantic twisting and turning. Then he heard hooves
up on the bank of the ravine.* Someone hadn't given up
the search and he'd given himself away. Probably
wouldn't have gotten out of these hills alive anyway.
*Silverthorne breathed a sigh and rested his hot forehead
on a cold rock as the brush was pulled away. He expected to be grabbed by a shoulder and yanked over on
his back. But a pair of gentle brown hands grasped both
shoulders at the same time and carefully lifted him up
and turned him around to a sitting position. One sinewy
arm supported his back while the other reached a hand
to untie the bloody curtain and ease the shirttail aside
to expose the bullet hole.*

*"Magoosh say Silverthorne will come back someday
to the mountains. Magoosh watches for Silverthorne. Silverthorne almost waits too long. But Magoosh has med-
icines that will heal the hole in the body, and the
medicine of the mountains will heal the hole in the soul
of Silverthorne."*

EPILOGUE

NOT LONG AFTER THE LAST OF THE FOLKS FROM LAMP-kin Springs, Texas, had gone home, Dick Reed died of the dropsy while at Casey's Mill on the Hondo, and his partner moved to Colorado. The Jones family, who'd been living at Dowlin's Mill on the Ruidoso, took over the six-room adobe at Seven Rivers and turned it into a hotel and restaurant. Mrs. Jones was the nearest thing to a doctor to be had in the Pecos Valley. She made good use of the medical library Silverthorne had left behind.

Several of the Jones boys established ranches on Rocky Arroyo, and the author is acquainted with a number of their descendants. Some of them run cows on Rocky to this day.

Other settlers moved to Seven Rivers to start ranches, stores, saloons, and other businesses, so that Seven Rivers quickly became the largest town between Del Rio, Texas, and Fort Sumner, New Mexico. It was notorious for its drunken brawls and shoot-outs. The Seven Rivers graveyard soon filled with men who died with their boots on.

Seven Rivers's notoriety led to its early demise, for Charles B. Eddy of the Eddy-Bissel Livestock Company and the Pecos Valley Land and Ditch Company determined he'd build a "respectable" town a few miles down the Pecos. Eddy, New Mexico, flourished and became known as "the Pearl of the Pecos," modern-day Carlsbad. For many years some meager ruins and weathered tombstones marked the site of the old Seven Rivers, but today those ghosts of one of the most violent epochs in the history of the Old West have been drowned by the waters of Brantley Lake.

Rachel Howell Rosser started calling herself Rachel Silverthorne when she got back to Lampkin Springs. She named her son Calvin Taliaferro Silverthorne. She raised him on the Howell ranch and sent him to the University of Pennsylvania and its new school of veterinary medicine. She never remarried. And she never quit scanning the horizon.

When the government finally relocated the last stray Apaches from the Guadalupes in 1912 they missed Silverthorne.

The Shattuck brothers used to tell about the time they were exploring Cottonwood Cave and their light discovered a ghostly figure with a rifle in hand sitting on top of a formation watching them. He didn't say anything. They didn't either. It's difficult to talk when your heart's pounding and the hair's standing up on the back of your neck and you're scrambling as fast as you can to get out of a hole in the mountain.

Then there was the "old mountain man" who used to show up from time to time at the store and filling station at Pine Springs in Guadalupe Pass to trade arrowheads and spear points for items of personal use. The last time anyone recalled seeing him was in the late forties or early fifties.

It appears Taliaferro Silverthorne lived a long life in the rugged mountains he loved so dearly.

•. • •

Silverthorne's day of reckoning with Augustus Alonzo Abels and the later history of his silver-plated, pearl-handled Peacemaker are included in the novel *John Stone and The Choctaw Kid,* published in paperback by The Berkley Publishing Group.

Wayne Davis was born in Richmond Virginia, and grew up in southeastern New Mexico, where he lived on the Castle Springs Ranch on the Black River, owned quarter horses (he still does), and hired out for day work on area ranches. He and his wife, Joan, and their daughter, Sheri, currently reside in Nacogdoches County, Texas.